Dervishes

Also by BETH HELMS

American Wives

Dervishes

A Novel

BETH HELMS

Picador | New York

www.picadorusa.com

Picador® is a U.S. registered trademark and is used by St. Martin's Press under license from Pan Books Limited.

Book design by Jonathan Bennett

For information on Picador Reading Group Guides, please contact Picador.
E-mail: readinggroupguides@picadorusa.com

ISBN-13: 978-0-312-42619-4
ISBN-10: 0-312-42619-4

First Edition: March 2008
10 9 8 7 6 5 4 3 2 1

For Mary Frances and Charles, but most of all, for Gary: friend, great love, D.D.E.

Ankara, Turkey

THE TELEPHONE CHIMED AS IT ALWAYS DID, IN THE DEEP, DEAD middle of the night. The jangling noise reached the farthest corners of the apartment, calling out to us from the table in the hallway—the table with the pencil and the notepaper, beside the coatrack, the wood-edged mirror, the prayer rug. Drugged with sleep, we climbed up to the sound in our separate, darkened rooms, each of us hoping someone else would make it stop.

I heard the phone replaced and then his footsteps; a narrow angle of light woke beneath my door. My father moved heavily down the hall, collecting his necessities. He passed my room, and then he was in the closet, taking out his suitcase. At the time, I thought all fathers kept a small, heavy suitcase packed in the hall closet, with another pair of shoes, perpetually shined, and several changes of clothes. From time to time, he checked it, inventorying the contents, replacing one thing, removing another. It was not uncommon to see him crouched in front of the closet, his knees splayed and his face in worried profile, his hair thinning at the temples. Each time he opened the suitcase he buffed those shoes, fitting them onto his hands like ungainly gloves, studying them up against the light.

For a while—in other apartments, other houses, other countries—I'd checked the suitcase closet every morning as a matter of habit, even if I'd seen my father only moments before over breakfast. The sight of it, safe amid boots and the finishes of coats, was more reassuring to me somehow than his smell of hair tonic and drugstore aftershave, the sound of the ancient coins he jingled in his pockets, or the Russian folk music he liked to play on the hi-fi. (My mother, stopping in the doorway, would say: Will you please, I beg of you, turn that racket off?)

The wind that morning was already busy—I heard it through the open window of my room—fretting leaves in the street, harassing tendrils of vine in the vineyard across the road. The air was full of the smell of changing seasons, stained faintly with smoke and dying leaves, the odor of tar from the construction site next door. Autumn was quickly turning to winter.

In those days my father traveled often and we rarely saw him go, dispatched as he was in secret by the government agency he worked for. Anytime he walked out the front door he might as well have been vanishing off the face of the earth.

I was lying in my brass bed—*French,* my mother liked to remind me—and the apartment was still thick and smoky from a party the night before. There was the lingering smell of liquor and fried foods, the echoes of pleasant, politic chatter. Our maid Firdis was gone, having left bags by the front door, filled with bottles and the detritus of cooking and cocktails: the emptied-out ashtrays, the lipstick-smeared napkins. I closed my eyes and opened them, over and over, faster and faster, keeping myself awake, trying to make the spots come. Would he remember to say goodbye? Would she remind him?

My father had left many times, and since we never knew where he went, we certainly couldn't predict when he'd be back. We must have trusted the government to return him to us when they were finished with him. To us, his leaving reinforced how indispensable he was, how direly needed elsewhere, and in that way we were taught, tricked, into making a prize of our sacrifice.

I heard my mother get up from the couch in the den, where she had been sleeping—I pretended not to know about these arrangements—and pad down the hall. I heard whispering, the familiar edge to their voices. I couldn't make out the words.

He did not come to my room. The front door closed and he was gone. His footsteps sounded on the marble stairs, three flights down to the lobby. The sun was not yet up, and his steps were all I heard: clear, measured, strong.

Moments later my mother moved down the hallway past my room, headed for the master bedroom, the warm, rumpled sheets he'd just abandoned. In his absence she reclaimed many territories: chairs and beds, the best coffee cup, the moral high ground. She spread out like a great moth, laying dusty, ashy wings across everything in sight.

How does a woman hear her husband leave the house one morning—listen, as I did, to the sound of his steps receding, his ring hand scraping the railing, the hushing our lobby door made, closing softly, as if the air itself were being squeezed—and think so little of it? Didn't she feel, as I did, the sudden loneliness of the rooms, the sighing of the bedclothes as we readjusted in the dark, the changes, when he had gone, in the very texture of the atmosphere around us, in the molecules and the spaces between them, in even the temperature of the air?

My father's driver would be waiting downstairs; he often stood on the sidewalk holding open the door of the blue station wagon, his peaked hat in his hand at his side. His name was Kadir: a big, kind man with a million children, a great black mustache, fraying cuffs, a stiff, endearing pride in his job. Sometimes, especially when my father was gone, Kadir drove me to school—the Ankara streets slid by, curving down the hill into the city's teeming center and then up again, into affluent Çankaya, where the apartment buildings were taller and clean faced, where windows gleamed and the oasis of the city's botanical garden stretched west, a glittering emerald in an otherwise unbroken line of concrete-colored streets and buildings.

The apartment grew quiet; I felt the hallways and corners fill up with our breathing, my mother's and mine—we were alone together again—and I imagined my father's other life, his life away from us, beginning.

It was a December morning; I was nearly thirteen years old. Later that day it snowed, the first of the season, and that night shadows flickered on the snow and the hill below our apartment became a mass of dark and milling bodies, bundled in coats and scarves and balaclavas. Screaming children hurtled down the darkened slope, riding the metal lids of trash cans, scraps of plastic and even garden chairs, affixed somehow to makeshift runners.

That was the last time I heard or smelled or saw my father: his heavy steps and the drifting breath of his aftershave, the gray suitcase thudding on the stairs, the hushed strains of an argument, loving or bitter—how was I to say?—between them. What did I know then? I knew everything; I knew nothing.

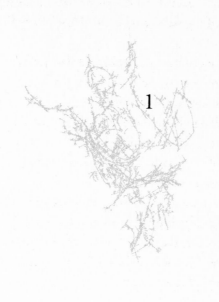

1

JUNE 1975

1

MY FRIEND CATHERINE AND I WERE PLAYING A GAME OF can't-touch-the-ground in the alleys behind my apartment at the crest of the hill. The buildings were set against the hillside in terraces, a descending series of walls, separated by concrete ledges, iron railings and great spiked fences. Sometimes I would stand on our own balcony, look down and map the walls we had climbed so far; the ledges we had traversed, teetering, our arms spread wide, breath held—the entire perilous terrain of our makeshift playground. Catherine stood on the ground with her pale hands stretched up, waiting for me to pull her onto the ledge. Her face was flushed, her eyes bright as a bird's. I grabbed her wrist and hauled her up beside me. Her shoes scrabbled against the stones; bits of cement kicked away under her feet. We stood at the top and looked around. Below us was the garden of another apartment building; in the middle, an enormous woman was hanging enormous sheets. All around, the neighboring gardens were bare brown rectangles littered with cheap plastic toys, abandoned kites, their stillness occasionally interrupted by the darting motion of a stringy cat, moving hungrily, slinking up a wall in a gravity-defying way, pausing, then leaping into another garden, to begin again. Crisscrossed above these walled spaces was a web of clotheslines that on predetermined days streamed and billowed with washing: vast white sheets, enormous underthings, men's shirtsleeves and pant legs that animated with

Ankara's polluted air; all day they bobbed and flapped, ducked and waved.

Catherine and I clung with our toes scrunched in our shoes to the edge of the cement wall. Laundry moved in the hot wind; our arms strained against the iron rail for balance. I pointed up, at the ledge several feet above us—we'd need to be cats almost, to get to that one.

"But it's too narrow," Catherine said. "Too high." The woman in the garden looked up at us, shook out her sheets, spat onto the dirt. She made the kind of hissing noise people use to shoo cats, waved her arms and stepped a little nearer. She spoke angrily in Turkish; I ignored her.

"It's not," I said. "Martin and I did it all the time. Besides, you say you're a ballerina. Act like one."

I inched away from Catherine, away from the woman's voice, her miserable garden and depressing laundry, along the edge, and scrambled up onto the next wall. Catherine followed, her face unhappy, her steps reluctant (she had wanted to go to the pool today, but no one would drive us).

At her back now was my apartment building: my window, our balcony, and on it, watching us, our huge white cat. I had found him under a car on our street only three months earlier, just days after we'd arrived in Ankara; he'd not been even half his current size then, bedraggled, filthy, spitting with fury.

ALREADY, IT seemed like we'd followed my father halfway around the world. The Middle East, and Germany, and just before Turkey we'd waited Stateside, on a baking street on a military base, while my father went off to work as other fathers did, in a business suit and polished shoes, carrying his briefcase. Six months passed there and my mother and I grew docile and stupefied, as blunted as pack animals. We were killing time on a street called Olson Loop, drained almost entirely of hope and sick to death of each other's company. We waited side by side with other families just like ours, in temporary quarters, with derelict furniture and hand-me-down decor and the accumulated scents of other people and their own waiting, and all of it made my mother quite pale with unhappiness. She'd always liked the traveling better than the waiting, the knowing rather than the wondering—and she liked almost anything better than being stuck all day alone with me, obligated to provide regular meals and her own lackadaisical brand of maternal interest. When they came, the papers said Turkey, and my mother faced it with regulation stoicism, with the relief of having something—anything—to do. She set about packing and organizing, filling out shipping forms, rolling up her sleeves for inoculations.

Here in Ankara, my parents had been in a rush—school was in session, we were living in a hotel—and they'd taken this apartment across from an abandoned vineyard and a mountainous coal heap, next to a new building under construction (perpetually, it would turn out) in a section of the city called Gasi Osman Paşa. The apartment building, ten squat stories, sat at the top of a perfectly arcing hill, with a long, wide flight of steps leading down one side onto a boulevard lined with hotels and ice cream vendors, corner groceries and bakeries. Catherine lived with her parents on the other side of the hill, where it flattened out again, on a street more residential than ours—there were no construction sites, no desolate vineyards—a road lined prettily with shade trees and tiny, fenced gardens, where even the apartment buildings seemed friendlier, smaller and more congenially arranged, their balconies painted in creamy pastels.

In the alleys, our rules were simple. The staggered walls were the highways of the game, the tall black fences obstacles to be skirted post by post, feet clinging to the lower rail, hands curling around iron spikes. Once we were up, once we had hoisted ourselves onto the first wall, the ground was off-limits. The walls ran mazelike between the colorless apartment houses, past dirty windows and gardens—we could, if we wanted, make it all the way down to the broad, busy street at the bottom of the hill without ever touching a foot to the earth.

Martin, the English boy I'd invented the game with, had once impaled his knee on one of the ugly rusted spikes that intersected the railings. My mother still told the story as a caution, in grisly, manufactured detail. But Martin and his family were gone, their tour of duty in Ankara finished. They'd returned to England with their scarred son and numerous, wriggling pet ferrets, which the mother had cooed to as though they were kittens. Personally, I'd been glad to see Martin go; I had grown to hate his mother, her doughy face, her smell of black-currant syrup, her coy references to a romance between us. They had taken Martin to the hospital with a piece of spike still through his knee—absolutely *skewered*, my mother said, like a shish kebab.

But Martin's mishap in no way discouraged me. Ankara was hellish in the summer; in the morning the heat came on like a sudden fever, and when it did, the electricity snapped off almost immediately. Energy rationing began in June; the power was cut at midday and the city simmered until evening, when lights finally splashed onto the darkness from the windows and appliances started up again. The cycle was utterly reliable, marked by the strange, expansive silence of the daylight hours and the sudden, audible sound of electricity coursing again, whirring, speeding across the city, buzzing toward outlets and the spoiling contents of iceboxes, neon advertisements over kebab restaurants, baking ovens, bedside lamps. Cooking chores, left off in the morning, were resumed; televisions snapped on (*Starsky and Hutch* dubbed in Turkish; incomprehensible, but oddly riveting); lights reached for and clicked on, satisfyingly, at last.

It was hotter, my mother liked to say, than the very sizzling hinges of hell. Letters she wrote to her friend Edie often contained clever lines like: *What do Turkish women do when it's 110 in the shade? Go to the hamam, of course!* So, left to our own devices—our mothers were usually busy playing cards and shopping, socializing or planning to—Catherine and I waited, entertaining ourselves as best we could, hoping for a ride to the pool, for school to start, for a spike through a soft, tender place. Really, we welcomed almost any distraction. Catherine and I had met in school at the British Embassy. I had been drawn to her quiet, her pretty clothes and manners and her dancer's grace. I'd talked to her and bothered her and followed her down the street from the bus stop until she finally relented and became my friend. By summer, we were inseparable.

We went to the alleys to escape the noisy silences of our own rooms and the suffocating heat that seemed to consume all the breathable air inside by noon. We avoided Catherine's, where even when her mother was gone the apartment was dominated by John, the houseboy. He was a young man with skin like toffee and beautiful hands, but his eyes, behind thick, girlish lashes, were hostile and cold. John both fascinated and repelled us—his effete mannerisms, his slender waist, his disregard: for people, for animals, and most of all, it seemed, for us. Also, he seemed to belong, in every way imaginable, to Simone, Catherine's icy mother. Simone had been a minor kind of ballerina herself once, at home in Montreal, and now she directed those dreams and a coiled, manic energy into socializing and endless games of one-upmanship.

AT THE end of the alley, the finish of our game, were a house and garden we always assumed to be abandoned. If we got there without touching the ground, we'd won—the prize was nothing, of course, but the satisfaction of having arrived in the chosen manner, shunning the earth, leaping wall to wall, jumping down the stepped cement. That it was a real house—not a massive concrete cube housing hundreds—made the place valuable. That it had an actual garden, with a stone bench, fruiting trees, dark cool spaces and an iron gate with a catch, thrilled us almost as much.

On summer afternoons like this one, when we were not taken to the pool, Catherine and I picked our way along the walls to the end of the alley, clambered down, and sat on the stone bench in the relative cool of the garden. Our pockets bulged with sweets, our hands were sticky with sugar and dirt, the toes of our shoes scuffed in the dry earth. The house was shuttered and quiet. Early on, we lost the need to creep around it like thieves, having grown quite certain that no one lived there, that no one had for years. We felt proprietary. We would have been offended had a face appeared in the window, or a hand unlatched the gate. A grimy, blackened trellis climbed one corner of the house, and the stone walls were greening with moss. From the street front, where we walked during the school year to meet the bus, this house was invisible, obscured by another square-faced apartment building with stacked balconies and an etched-glass door. So the house was a doubly secret place, likely belonging at one time to the vineyard across the street, but finally abandoned in the same thoughtless way.

It never occurred to us to enter the house itself. We were happy enough with the small garden, the overgrown bushes, fruit trees that dropped their rotting yields—overripe apricots, bitter little oranges, bursting figs—onto the ground for us to find. Before leaving, we carefully gathered up our wrappings and discarded cellophanes; we latched the gate behind us and strolled back up the alley with our feet firmly on the ground, the day's game concluded.

That day we were eating candy and comparing wounds. I had a tear in my shirt; a cat scratch on my arm like a line of red stitching, a raw knee from the rough wall we had just scrambled down. Catherine sat on the listing iron bench, white terry shorts hiked up around her thighs, elbows on her knees, staring down at a spider making erratic progress across the crumbling flagstone. The spider scuttled back and forth as if confused, into the cracks and out again, its tiny shadow round and blurred. The sunlight through the trees made a filigree on the brown earth of the garden, a duotone, and there was almost no grass at all; pitiful tufts of it grew here and there in the dirt.

Against the red ribbing of Catherine's shorts, between her legs, was a spatter of round bruises, plummy and soft-looking, no bigger than the small lira coins we used to buy individual scoops of ice cream or pieces of gum. She hadn't accounted for them and I reached out to touch one: a question. She stood swiftly and moved away from me, and in that abrupt movement was the faint implication that I'd overstepped. I fell back, looked around, put fingers to my hot face. Catherine turned away and bent to examine the spider more closely, at eye level, squatting down to the ground.

I watched her back: the gathered-together, winged jut of her shoulder blades as she hunched over, the wispy tendrils of hair at her neck, clinging there in the heat, pasted down. I drew in an airless breath; the garden was still and primitive, the noise of traffic seemed faraway.

"Where did those come from?"

"What?"

I could barely hear her. Her back was to me and her voice sounded blurry, muffled by her posture, distorted by her downward gaze. Standing again, she lifted one sneaker and let it hover, the elongated shadow of her foot dwarfing the spider, erasing its silhouette; it was just a dark pinprick under her sole. She brought her foot down slowly, grinding it on the ground—there was no noise, just the shift of dirt, the horseshoe of her heel mark.

When she walked away I put my hand down on her shoulder to make her stop.

"The bruises on your legs. What are they from?"

"The barre," she said. She looked me straight in the eye and my hand fell away. Catherine's eyes were hazel, shot through with yellow and green, the irises wide. Her eyebrows were thin and looked cultivated, though I don't believe they were. They were a fine architectural detail, a surprised peak in each one. My own brows were mismatched, arcing in an irregular way. I had tried to correct this with my mother's tweezers but had only made matters worse.

The bruises made me think of John, Simone's houseboy, and the way his fingers looked in the kitchen pressing tissue-thin dough out on a wide marble board. The shallow indentations left when he lifted his hands away; the delicate swirls of his fingerprints etched in pastry. When we ate the things he'd made I always felt a shivery sense of something like cannibalism, as if I were taking him inside me—his smell of lemons and starch, his crisp shirts and dark eyebrows, his pretty, insolent manners.

"Any more questions?" said Catherine and raised one of those perfect brows; her forehead wrinkled.

We watched each other. Her skin was pale; her lips sucked in at the corners, as though she were biting hard at the insides of her cheeks.

So I brushed my hand on my backside, ostentatiously, as if I had dirtied it on Catherine's hot, round shoulder. Beneath my hand her shoulder had felt like a rock warmed in the sun, perfectly hard, smooth as an egg.

Catherine let the air out of her mouth, whistling; it resolved into a short little tune she'd learned from my mother.

"Stop," I said and hit her on the leg. No matter how hard I tried, I couldn't master whistling, could not get the components of my mouth to cooperate. My mother's whistling was an accompaniment to the sound of her bangles, which she'd acquired in the gold district on Tunali Hilmi. She moved through the apartment completely without stealth, the notes of music and bracelets fading and approaching, pausing, resuming. The sound made my teeth hurt.

Catherine moved toward the gate, still whistling, and hurried her steps to avoid my hands, which hustled the air, lightly smacking at her as she unhitched the gate, slid out. Then she took off down the alley at full speed, her shoes making rubbery noises on the cement, the whistling coming in sharp, jagged bursts as she ran.

And then there was a roar of wind in my ears and that tune of my mother's was caught up in it like the eye, the vortex: I heard a woman screaming in Turkish at a neighbor high above, many floors up, the two of them shouting from balcony to balcony. The laundry flapped like great white wings above us. The noise of the traffic grew louder, we were running toward it—it was a wall of sound we were approaching, headlong, as solid and impenetrable as steel.

THE LOBBY of Catherine's apartment building looked like this: dim, gritty floored, a dirty-orange railing running tubelike along open concrete stairs. The smell of something floral mixed with dirt. Our school shoes scuffed on grime, sliding through swooping wet tracks left by the kapıcı's wife. Three or four times a day she squatted beside a leaking bucket, dunked a rag and made crablike progress across the lobby, from one side back to the other, cleaning. The kapıcı—whose name we were told over and over but never retained—hunched outside in a box of shade thrown by a balcony and clenched squat cigarettes between his lips. His mustache was thick, dripping over his mouth at the corners, and his uniform—a frayed pinstriped shirt and sagging workpants—never changed. His duties were almost as mysterious as our own fathers'. For one thing, he dug his finger in his ear like a man who'd lost something valuable, digging and digging before withdrawing his filthy nail, examining it and then returning to business. He could, and did, do this for hours. At the top of the first flight of stairs, a quick turn around the railing—fingers trailing on the orange cylinder—and then two doors opened into Catherine's apartment: one to the entry hall, the other to her parents' bedroom suite, which was strictly off-limits.

Inside, quiet: our footsteps made a brief clatter on parquet and then nothing; our feet sank into the muted patterns of carpet after carpet. We made a game of leaping from one to another. Through the swinging door at the end of the hall was the kitchen. Inside we could hear John working—the clatter of china, the ping of crystal, the heavy, muffled whoosh of the refrigerator door. Even when he was not audibly busy, we could sense him in there—leafing through a comic, patting his winged black hair, scrutinizing his impeccable white shirttails for stains.

In Catherine's room down the narrow hall—one, two, three doors on the right—were two twin beds with matching ruffles, a dresser, framed prints of ballerinas. All was neatness, order, girlishness. Shoes off on the white carpet, quiet games only when Catherine's mother was home—but when she was gone, as she was today, we mounted furtive expeditions into her perfumed bedroom.

We moved cautiously down the hallway, Catherine behind me, her hand hovering just above my shoulder. Inside: the oversweet smell of gardenia, the nose-clogging dust of talcum rising in motes, captured in the freckled light that filtered through the bunched damask draperies. The dressing table was a world unto itself: crystal atomizers, a drape of beads, a lone earring, the little stool upholstered in velvet tucked into the crotch of the mahogany table. The room whirled with damp, secret scents; our hands reached for things and drew back; we glanced over our shoulders, edged open drawers for a glimpse of lace and lilac silk, brushed them with our fingers and then pulled back as if burned.

I reached for one of Simone's atomizers—a delicate, crystal thing, designed to hold scent or genies—and it slipped from my hand and fell with a muffled thud to the floor. As it rolled under the bed we scrambled, our hands touching and grabbing beneath the bed skirts, feeling desperately for its shape, its weight, its diamond-cut facets. We heard footsteps outside the door and froze. The noise moved away; it was only John, on some unrelated errand.

We left the room breathless, gardenia in invisible blankets around our bodies; we used our hands to beat it from our clothes and ran silently, on tiptoe, back to Catherine's room. Noiseless laughter, amazement at our boldness, our narrow escape—we fell on the twin beds and pulled our knees to our mouths, bit the soft flesh like fruit and rocked ourselves back to calm, until our breathing was smooth and even and our trapped hearts arrived again at a bearable pace.

Catherine said, "Are you my best friend, Canada? Absolutely and forever?"

"I am," I chanted, giddy. "I am, I am, I am."

"Feel my heart." She pressed my hand to her chest, flush against its hammering cadence. I felt her thin collarbone, the starch of her school shirt, the frantic drumbeat of her center.

After school, as afternoon wore slowly away to evening, sounds would awake in the dining room beyond Catherine's closed door: John, moving through the hallway holding a stack of laundry—tiny ironed panties and undershirts, knotted pairs of anklets—would straighten a perfectly straight carpet with his sock feet (the hushed noise like leaves moving restlessly on a forest floor) and suddenly, Catherine's mother would be moving through the apartment like an angry little wind, checking up on the evening's preparations. Then I would get up, locate my book bag and my shoes, let myself out onto the landing and clatter down the concrete steps into the evening air—which would not have changed appreciably, or cooled, but quieted somewhat, the traffic noises having given way to those of insects whirring in the trees, the shadows throwing leafy semaphores across uneven sidewalks, the waning light against the long hill that led up to my apartment glowing a deep, burned red, and the slopes and hillocks of the empty field between our homes taking on human

forms. I saw hips and haunches curling in sleep, breasts pressed together in flirtation, the profile of a woman in a sulk, her lips a mogul
we had once flown bumpily, dangerously over while sledding alongside the Turkish children, children who did not speak to us or ac-
knowledge us except to spit in our direction, or shoulder us aside at
the top of the hill. This didn't disturb us particularly; we didn't want
to be included or liked by them, and their hostility was no more or
less than we expected.

What kind of girls were we? We were similar in many respects,
easy in the company of adults, well read through necessity, adept at
amusing ourselves, and mostly secure in our secret lives, aware that
our parents—those adults we shared rooms with, under whose loose,
sporadic authority we lived—were generally disinterested in us, and
could be counted on, for the most part, to be otherwise occupied.

We were not children who believed their parents' lives revolved
around them—we would never have entertained such a conceit. We
were adaptable, malleable, we went along: reading books under the
table at restaurants, fading into the scenery at cocktail parties when
babysitters could not be found, trailing our parents through
churches and ruins and, though bored stiff, maintaining pleasant
expressions, rarely whining, and able to sleep in the most unaccom-
modating circumstances.

Of course, we had the normal talents—listening at doors, piecing
together through fragments the substance of our parents' discord—
but we had others as well. We could muddle whiskey sours and set a
reasonably elegant table, count to twenty in at least three languages,
competently hail taxis and make simple transactions in foreign cur-
rencies. It didn't occur to us that these were uncommon dexterities;
they were nothing more or less to us than knowing how to play hop-
scotch, jump rope or hold our breath under water.

But we were different from each other. Catherine's biddable exterior disguised a certain immovability; I was impulsive and suggestible,

given to quick passions and imaginings of every stripe: romantic, vengeful, fantastical. Catherine was steadier and more disciplined, a cautious, watchful girl. At least that's what people thought of us, and we believed it ourselves, falling into our roles comfortably. And perhaps we just liked to be thought of at all, to be categorized or noted, by anyone.

During the school year Catherine and I sat in her room and played games of our own devising and long, dull matches of concentration with packs of dog-eared cards. We didn't speak as adults will of interests and activities—we never discussed Catherine's ballet, for example; and later on, the subject of my horses never arose between us. Our points of intersection were those of children—immediate, discrete and confined to the small places and rooms of our friendship. When I left her house I often did not think of her until the next day, when she appeared at the bus stop, or met me in front of my apartment building's iron gate to make the walk together. We were busy after all, having our own tricky domestic landscapes to negotiate. We sometimes traded books back and forth—boarding-school series, thick anthologies of poetry, gothic paperbacks and enormous sagas of Welsh families beset by tragedy, volume after excruciating volume. We stole some of these books from our parents, hid them beneath our pillows and mattresses, though really, I can't imagine anyone would have cared what we were reading. That kind of censorship wouldn't really have occurred to our mothers, and if they'd found us with these books their response would likely have been a vague, amused disapproval, or the flick of an overplucked eyebrow. It might have been something they'd mention to their friends at a cocktail party—they might even have liked, within certain strict parameters, to believe us precocious.

But in truth, or this version of it, I can really only speak for my own mother.

2

FOR GRACE, THE DIM AND SWELTERING AFTERNOONS BRING
endless games of whist, small plates of olives and cheese and honeyed pastries scattered on lace tablecloths. She's joined a group put
together by the embassy, advertised as a meeting of Turkish and
English-speaking ladies for the purpose of exchanging culture and
language. She assumes, of course, that it's intended to keep them all
out of trouble.

She sits with these new friends, playing the unfamiliar game—
where hands are swiftly dealt, bids made and quips and affectionate insults fly by in both languages. The afternoons in the dark put her in
mind of hours spent with Edie, her friend from Olson Loop in the
States, where they'd bided their time before the orders for Turkey had
arrived. But here the noise of the city is heard through the windows, its
raucous tenor softened by the height at which the days are idled away,
high above the city among Mediterranean furnishings. The walls are
swagged here and there with velvet draperies, and painted in hues that
make Grace think not of the color but rather of the taste of cinnamon. All day handsome young houseboys move quietly through, replacing plates, refreshing tea served in voluptuous gold-rimmed
glasses, set on tiny saucers.

All these women speak exquisite English when they need to, and
under their gentle tutelage, during the sleepy afternoons, Grace's Turkish progresses nicely. Flicking cards, their slender wrists sing with

stacks of scored gold bangles; Grace has recently affected ones just like them. Beside them, the foreign women—American, British, Canadian—seem drab and stiff; their glasses of tea balanced carefully, their faces arranged in attentive expressions. Powder, pinkish and overapplied, cakes in the lines of their polite faces; their limbs, set rigidly on the antimacassared arms of divans, remind her of old-fashioned china dolls. Grace stirs the cloudy tempest of sugar at the bottom of her glass and daydreams of Victorian women dropped into a sheik's harem: she loves the Turkish ladies and their hazy, nodding, pouting hours, their languid postures across pillows sewn from exquisite remnants of carpet.

Her hostesses, dark and diffident, hold children with one drowsy arm as the other hand takes tricks, ringed fingers clicking on the sharp edges of cards. Grace hears that odd Turkish noise of disgust when a hand is lost, a sharp cluck of contempt or dismissal that she herself has picked up—it is strangely satisfying, and perfectly articulate.

Everyone rises in unison when the muezzin calls for the fourth time; even Grace tells time by him now. Soon the electricity will hum to life again and chores will be resumed, husbands will arrive expecting dinner and consolation, children will be roused by the noises, by the cooling air, and demand attention. At home, in a nearby section of the city, Canada will return wrung out from her day with Catherine.

Always, these afternoons must be shaken off like overlong naps, or hours lost in an opium den, deep and disorienting. Grace wanders home, half drugged, through the newly familiar streets, past the shops and rug merchants, stopping along the way to buy pastries or dates, to finger an evil eye, a silver puzzle ring. The faces of the merchants no longer seem sinister, but friendly, eager to enter into a haggling session over some trinket. In this way Grace acquired the Maşallah pendant around her neck, and the string of rough blue beads she has hung over the kitchen doorway for luck. Maşallah,

İnşallah, Avallah, as they say in Turkey. God bless, God willing, praise be to God.

Often Grace walks home with wealthy, beautiful Bahar, who lives close-by, in her own concrete aerie. Today, they pause in the tiny park that lies at one end of Tunali Hilmi. A sign shaped like a swan hangs at the gate and inside is a round coin of water surrounded by benches. Here a few women carry babies or let them totter around on the grass. The swans on the lake—a gift from Beijing—are huddled together and the women stand near the edge and watch them. The park is buffered from the traffic by a ring of ancient poplars, though the main street of the market is still visible through a leafy arch, and apartment buildings encircle the skyline.

Bahar has become one of Grace's closest friends in Ankara, a frighteningly chic woman with a wicked tongue and an expensive European education. She befriended Grace quickly, with the irresistible force of her personality, her seductive way of inclusion, her confiding, intimate manner.

Bahar kicks with her heel at a loose stone on the cobbled walkway. In the background, small children run past, screaming, and a few women give halfhearted pursuit.

"How is Ali?" Grace asks her. "The boys?" Bahar has two little ones, miniatures of her bearish doctor husband, dark fire hydrants of boys, always hitting each other, racing around Bahar's feet in one war game or another, which she serenely ignores.

Bahar lights a cigarette with a mosaic lighter, blows curling streams from her wide nostrils. She shrugs, and moves her mouth in that uniquely Turkish way, that disdainful gesture of "so what?"

"Husbands," she says. "Children."

Grace looks at the water: the swans move their feathers in a motion like a shiver. The grass is browning: there has been no rain for weeks, just the soupy heat, the swelter, the broiling, rancid smell of the city. Not far away she hears the faint cacophony of traffic, the honking and screeching of tires that has become background music to virtually everything.

This city, Grace has written to her friend Edie, is an utter contradiction: in places it is the worst of bedlam, ugly, concrete and charmless, but turn a corner and ivy grows on the walls of brick houses, at night the Ankara castle glows from a hilltop, minarets reach up through the smog and flowers explode from window boxes. Men spit on the street like animals, then offer an arm to help you through traffic. The streets are filthy, but trees bloom and there is always color and music. Everything is in opposition. *But, it is magical, in its way,* she has written, *and I think I will love it.*

"What about you?" Bahar says. "How do you like our roasting pan of a city?"

Grace smiles. "I do like it, very much."

"And Rand? Is he happy too?"

Grace lifts her hands, palms up. "Who knows," she says. "He doesn't say. Locked in the embassy all day playing at his secret job, he doesn't tell me a thing. Can't or won't, who knows which."

Bahar puts her hand on Grace's arm. Her nails are tapered, perfect, the color of dark plums. "Well," she says, "this is why we have our own lives, our days, our card games. Do you think I pay attention to what Ali says, when he comes home from the clinic? Or do I nod, like this, and hand him a plate of something? I do not think to confide in him my troubles. That would be foolish. I do not ask where he is when he is late or when he travels. And I do not care particularly, because my life is quite nice."

Grace, lost for a moment in thought, does not respond.

"What will worry accomplish?" Bahar says. Her open hand strikes Grace's shoulder in a playful gesture. "We'll go to the baths, or to that rug merchant on Tunali. Forget it, you will only make yourself unhappy." She grinds her cigarette out with the fragile heel of her sandal and continues. "I am not unsympathetic, but what you describe is the manner of all marriages I know. I went to Switzerland, you remember, a few weeks ago? Was this for jewelry shopping, as I said? No. It was for a plastic surgery and to get rid of a baby. Did Ali notice? And he is a doctor."

"You did what?"

Bahar smiles her mysterious smile. "I am like a movie star now, yes?"

"But wouldn't Ali have wanted another baby?"

Bahar tucks her arm inside Grace's as they cross the street. She has the enviable, imperious quality of all women who are wealthy and beautiful: she does not wait for traffic to pause, rather she halts it with her eyes, or steps carelessly into the middle of it. When horns blare and drivers curse, she stares them down or offers an obscene gesture, which from her is a strangely elegant motion.

Grace says, "If I did that, I'd be squashed."

"Certainly Ali would want a baby; if it were his."

Crossing the street into the gold district, they are surrounded by street merchants and shopkeepers, caught up and swept along, suddenly part of the city's frantic daily business. Always here, Grace feels her senses rushed, overwhelmed. She smells lamb roasting, the char of bread in a wood fire, a sharp scent of dried apricots, the heavy animal damp of wool. Gold glitters in window cases and everywhere men sit high on piles of rugs, drinking tea from slender glasses. They throw dice, smoke pipes and stunted cigarettes, laugh raucously.

Bahar, calm as an island, smiles, fingers the gold chains and bangles held out to her and shakes her head no. From the corner of her eye, as they walk along, Grace catches Bahar looking at her. Some expression, some interior decision-making process, works swiftly across her features.

"Otherwise it would not be worth the screaming," she says, "the— how do you call them? Interrogatories. My friends and I always go to Europe, in such a predicament."

Grace is silent for a moment. Long enough that Bahar nudges her arm and laughs. "Are you so naïve?" she says. "If so, then I apologize for being indiscreet."

"No," Grace says. "Not at all."

She is thinking of Bahar's husband, his charm and practiced hands. She remembers a recent cocktail party she and Rand gave and how Ali's laughter had echoed around the small space, how he had helped Rand to bed when he'd staggered and then afterward, in their bedroom, how his hands had strayed down the back of her dress, suggestively but without commitment, a touch that might have been a friendly accident.

Standing on the street corner in the shimmering heat, with Bahar's silk cuff against her wrist and the smell of sesame from the simits stacked on the heads of the vendors, Grace feels a faint shiver of hope, an odd and unexpected lightness. It might be the glint of Bahar's jewelry, or the merchant winking at her as he holds up a cheap cotton dress, but it might be something else—some promise of intrigue, perhaps, or adventure. Maybe it's just the allure of these new cosmopolitan women—women who seem to inhabit airy and secret places, in which they are free to live out their private, fantastical lives.

Despite the bad publicity, and all her initial misgivings, Grace does love Turkey. On the mad streets, with crowds streaming by, and this new foreign friend, Olson Loop and America seem a million miles away. It's almost hard to remember now—the numbing sameness of those days, the churchy darkness of Edie's house across the street, the raging irritability brought on by the heat and the waiting.

WHEN THEY arrived on Olson Loop it was summertime, bright and humid; all day bicycles whirred in increasingly reckless orbits, gathering speed for the steep hill down the far side near the school. Children shouted and mothers called out cautions in ever-louder tones, rarely leaving the stoops where they gathered in clutches, drinking coffee or iced things, collectively smoking or quitting, painting their faces or nails, tanning their shoulders and thighs, gossiping from sunup to nightfall.

Grace quickly learned the facts: Olson Loop was a tight circle of asphalt and rumor. Stunted driveways bore numbers painted in acid yellow, and the semidetached brick structures—two families sharing a common wall, a front lawn, a porch—were separated only by a low brick divider, easily stepped over.

Noisy, she'd complained to Rand. It's so goddamn loud here. (She could not say why this bothered her so. They had just come from a post in Frankfurt, Germany, a city far louder than this place. Perhaps it was merely the nearness to the ground that irked her.) Rand just turned on the television and ticked the volume up, up, up.

But before long she had befriended Edie, or perhaps it was the other way around. Edie lived directly across the street with her own uniformed husband, in her identical little house. She was small framed, of Spanish descent, and she ate tapioca pudding all day, spooning it from an earthenware bowl in the refrigerator, hunkered down inside her dark brick house.

"Those women," she said to Grace early on, speaking of the stoop-women. "They make me tired."

Edie was perpetually tan, lion-shaded—tawny skin, chestnut haired, golden eyed—though she seemed never to leave the house, never ventured much beyond the stoop or the two short steps below it. Instead she paced barefoot, like an edgy housecat, through the shag carpeting. She set the table for dinner, using her good service and silver, every day at ten in the morning. These gestures and protocols, without meaning in the shared purgatory of Olson Loop, were things Grace easily understood. Edie set the table for the same reasons Grace herself had unwrapped her few boxes of knickknacks and breakables and photographs and arranged them on the scarred furniture they'd found when they'd moved in. The same reason she'd moved an end table to cover a virulent, juice-colored stain on the carpet and scrubbed the walls until they lightened almost imperceptibly, by half a dingy beige shade.

Edie kept her house shuttered and dim, a manufactured darkness enhanced by heavy, carved furniture and low, flickering votive candles. Unlike Grace and Rand, Edie had all her own things—she and Greg had been on Olson Loop nearly two years. Most of Grace and Rand's household goods remained in storage in some distant warehouse, ready to be shipped as soon as their new orders arrived. "Your house makes me want to genuflect," Grace once said to her, when they were friendly enough. And that had happened in the sped-up way Grace had come to expect—there was no wasteful dawdling over preliminaries on Olson Loop, no auditions.

Usually they sat just inside the screen door of Edie's house, on the cool tiled floor beside a potted hibiscus and the ornate carved legs of a hallway table, watching the street through the wire netting. They played simple card games, and once in a while the hearts and spades and queens and jacks, loosed from their fingers, would catch a rare breath of wind and slide or scuttle across the grooved entryway. They would scramble after them in a halfhearted way, laughing. When they rose for a drink or to visit the bathroom, they found that the diamond-shaped tiles of the floor had embossed the backs of their bare legs. They carried those grooves, etched by the long idle days, around with them, through dinners and television and marital arguments, until sleep smoothed them away.

While they played and mixed pitchers of iced tea, Edie relayed information, details Grace thought she couldn't have learned just by watching the street in her patient, flickery-eyed way.

"That one," Edie said once, pointing sideways into the street, toward an overweight woman in blue shorts standing on her scrap of lawn. The woman was mysteriously lifting up first one leg and then another, like a shorebird. "That one and her daughter, they kiss with tongues. I've seen it."

Edie had no children of her own and the subject was one she mostly veered from. Inside her friend's house, Grace kept one ear tuned for Canada's voice; the screen door was all that separated her from the street, but the difference in light was so great that even when she stepped to the door to check—infrequently, with a sudden jolt of guilt—it took a few long moments for her eyes to adjust, to roam the small circle, to identify Canada in the bunch, to classify her as alive, kicking.

The children were still swarming when the sun went down, as Grace picked her way across the hot, rocky street in bare feet and began to think about getting her husband's dinner. By then they were playing statues and red rover, swinging one another wildly by the arms or barreling toward a line of clasped wrists. The grass was green and prickly, the insects gathered, and Grace stood for a moment shading her eyes. The children moved from one lawn to another as though in a public park—no fences, no boundary lines. A mutt dog chased up and down behind them, a bicycle bell rang endlessly, the sound of hot wind whipping spokes, a smell of hamburgers somewhere close. She shivered. The heat on her body, after the long hours indoors, chilled her.

During the days, while Grace was closeted inside with Edie, Canada became briefly close with the girl across the street, the mother-kissing girl, a little doll with dimpled legs and long blond ringlets. Grace was relieved: the appearance of a playmate, someone with whom her daughter engaged from time to time in some inexplicable, painstakingly ruled game, made her feel a little less neglectful.

Then one afternoon near the middle of the summer, for no apparent reason, Canada gave this little girl a fairly brutal shove, knocking her down hard in the driveway. The screams brought Grace and Edie to the screen door, then outside it, and finally across the street to where Canada was standing over her friend without any trace of remorse. Her face was blank as the street itself; she looked up as Grace came running, blinking as though she'd just been woken from a dream. The girl came up screaming, spitting blood—she'd struck her chin hard on the driveway—dark specks of gravel embedded in her knees and palms. Briefly, there was some emotion—chilly and triumphant—on Canada's face, which Grace caught as she crouched barefoot on the hot tar and examined the victim's fat, raw knees. But still, even later, shaking her, she could not get out of Canada why she'd done it—what on earth had possessed her. She called Rand at the office, then sent Canada to the willow tree to break off a switch. That she'd even thought of this amazed her, but she was terribly angry and it had made her inventive.

Rand laughed when he came home and saw the switch on the hall table. He'd accused her of hysteria. Then, standing at the screen door, his back to the street, he turned angry. Didn't she know, he said coldly and slowly, that he was busy? Did she have any idea what he did for a living? Did she think he'd nothing better to do than solve the problems of little girls? He'd meant—she understood him clearly—all of them: her and Edie and Canada and the girl with the torn-up knees—all you little girls, your petty squabbles. Then he left, banging the screen door hard behind him.

When he'd gone, everything was terribly quiet. She heard nothing from Canada's room, where she had been sent to think about it, and even the street outside, normally so caught up in itself, so bursting with noise and activity, seemed now to be hung up in a long, airless lull.

Afterward, Grace began taking Canada with her across the

street. They let her watch television in the darkened living room for hours while they baked and played cards and kept their eyes on the street. One day in the middle of July, she and Edie stood staring out the narrow kitchen window, watching a car pass at a snail's pace.

Edie said, "It's strangling here, don't you think? I feel that way, like there's always something around my neck." She put her hands there. "Never mind. Let's play cards: I need to do something with my hands. I'm trying not to smoke."

The summer wore on. In other brick two-families, up and down Olson Loop, orders were received. Boxes were packed and sealed, vans stole up to doors in the dawn hours, families peeled off and drove away, waving. Write, people called to each other, and the departing families called back, We will. But nobody really did. Certainly not for longer than a month or two.

One night in the fall, Rand came home even later than usual. It was early October by then. The trees were creeping with color, the air brisk. Canada had started school. Grace heard the sound of a car pulling away and looked up to see him standing on the sidewalk. He'd worn his uniform that morning and for a moment he looked quite handsome to her: he might almost have been someone else. The papers in his hand fluttered. He came to the screen door and called for her. In the kitchen, washing her hands, Grace took her time. There was salmon loaf in the oven, something on the radio—she had the fanciful thought that it might float out to him on the sidewalk. She moved quietly, not answering him, drying her hands, refolding the dishtowel. The moment had, just then, the feel of a Christmas morning: the knowledge Rand held out on the walkway seemed at once as enormous and as trivial, an item to be eagerly torn into, exclaimed or despaired over, but in the end, it would be what it was. She wanted to know; she didn't. She raised her eyes and looked out the window, over Rand's shoulder, toward Edie's house. Their orders had finally come in last week—Saudi Arabia—and Edie seemed happy enough.

Grace ran her hands along the countertop; she used her fingernail to pry up a sticky little stain. She studied her husband's expression for some sign. He had a slight smile and he swayed a little, side to side. The street beyond him was unsettlingly hushed.

He called her name again, louder this time.

She went to the screen and looked at him through the torn wire—the cat had clawed herself a little exit on the left, by the frame. Clever cat, she'd thought, but then the small hole she'd torn kept ripping, tearing away from the flimsy wood, and the flies came in, the mosquitoes and the no-see-ums. Grace pushed the door open and stepped onto the porch.

"Tell me," she said. "Just tell me. Don't make me guess."

"Guess," he said.

She went back inside. Clearly he'd found out earlier, gone to celebrate with the boys. He'd known for hours and kept it. She sat down at the dining room table, feeling murderous. She sat there until he came inside and put the paper on the table in front of her, back in its envelope—official-looking, with a big blue seal. Grace picked up the envelope and held it square in her hands, then turned it. She lifted the flap with her thumb, smelled its gumminess, tested it with her finger. Dry.

"It's Turkey," he said. He was in the kitchen then, rummaging in the fridge for a beer.

She put the envelope down. "Turkey?"

The kitchen door pushed back open and he came in. "Ankara. There's a book coming, and a dictionary. Briefings. Shots. Not gamma globulin though, thank Christ. Better start soon. Tell the school."

He surveyed the room, mentally packing. He looked exasperated at the prospect, though most of their things were still in storage.

"I'll take the cat to the pound some morning this week," he said.

He flicked on the television and sat down in his chair. The news was on; they were moving to Turkey. Grace went across the street to tell Edie. The frame of the screen banged behind her in a suddenly resonant way—once, twice, a diminutive little third, then the bare brush of a fourth note. She rubbed her dry hands on her hips and let them open at her sides to push the cooling air in front of her.

She spent the next week packing, attending briefings, learning about a country she'd barely even heard of. She was suddenly busy, and it lit a little blaze inside her. The night before they shipped out, she and Edie carried sweet sherry in thimble glasses out onto the stoop and sat down. Canada was hugging a dog a patch of grass away; her pigtails were ragged, her knees raw.

"We'll write, won't we? We'll make the effort."

Grace leaned back, her hands flat on the rough concrete of the stoop. Directly opposite, only a few hot steps away, were her own temporary twinned steps, her door, the empty, peeling window boxes. She sipped the warm, viscous liquid from her glass, then set it down. "We will," she said, with more certainty than she felt. "We absolutely will."

"Hey," said Edie. "Is that dog humping Canada?"

Grace leaned forward. "Absolutely yes," she said. "Yes, he is."

They sipped their drinks and watched the sun go down; they made some promises, exchanged their new temporary addresses on carefully folded slips of paper.

GRACE LEAVES a letter addressed to Edie on the telephone table in the hallway and slips out the door to meet Bahar for lunch. She rushes down the steps, crosses the marbled lobby and pulls the front door shut behind her. She wants to miss Hidayet, the kapıcı. *Who ever heard of such a thing?* she'd written Edie early on. *Here the apartment super does your grocery shopping. Fresh bread twice a day, milk, fruit. Will wonders never cease?* But now she wants to avoid him: his eyes, his cringing brand of insolence, the way he holds pieces of fruit up for her to admire, apricot by apricot, peach by peach.

After lunch in the gold district, they walk through the crowded streets to the park. Bahar deftly eludes the merchants and beggars, towing Grace behind her. "You need a maid," Bahar says. "She'll keep the kapıcı in line. That's how it's done."

They've only been in the apartment a month but Grace already hates being cornered by this smelly little man on the landing, forced to admire what he's brought, to fumble in her coin purse for small lira.

"Fine," she tells Bahar. "A maid. How do I get one?"

Soon, they're standing in the park near the swans. "Or a house-boy," Bahar says, passing her a cigarette. "Either one."

Grace considers it. Maids and houseboys, she's discovered here, are not quite the same animal. Houseboys lend an undercurrent of voltage to a household, a quiet, subterranean pulse that makes her think, unwillingly, of sex. Furtive, illicit sex: in pantries and closets, against household appliances, the kind of acts committed in daylight with one's eyes closed and never spoken of again. Standing there with Bahar's eyes fastened on her, Grace thinks that the choice between the two alternatives, maids and houseboys, probably speaks some essential truth about the chooser.

She thinks of Canada's friend Catherine and her dreadful mother, Simone. Grace doesn't much care for their houseboy. He materializes as if conjured when a glass is empty, holding a champagne bottle, his arrogant, beautiful head cocked in question. All the reservations Grace has about houseboys are distilled in Simone's: his air of scorn, a faint expression of derision—vanishing as if imagined when one looks again—his serene, appraising manner. With merely a glance in the doorway as he relieves her of a wrap, he manages to make her feel old and small.

Grace knows she is not alone in the opinion that something unusual is afoot in that household. If Simone is absent from a card game with the Turkish ladies and talk turns to servants, someone will mention Simone and then, almost always, a conspiratorial, gossipy hush will hang for a few moments above the table and the women's eyes will slide from one to another, twinkling. A houseboy, passing through the room on some innocuous errand, might be subject to a long, evaluating glance. And Bahar, to put an end to it, will slap her fan of cards against the table's edge, and with wicked eyes make a crack about how hard it is to find good help in this city.

Grace glances at Bahar, who is watching her carefully. A boy in ragged clothes passes, simits are piled high on his head and he's calling out his quavering sales pitch: *simit, simit, simiiiiiiit.*

"Houseboys make me nervous," she says. It's true. Grace does not think she can abide that cool arrogance in her own home: lately, living with Canada brings all the domestic disdain a person can be reasonably expected to tolerate. "A maid," she says to Bahar. "Definitely."

And Bahar raises her eyebrows and laughs in a way that might mean anything.

Not long after, Rand gets a tip from someone at the embassy and they drive over to Çankaya together one evening. Not to meet the maid, but to be interviewed by her current employers. They hope to inherit this woman—this being the way domestic help commonly changes hands in Ankara—from a Mormon family leaving for another post. The maid is called Firdis.

Grace stands with the wife, completing the transaction, in a pantry they've custom built for the apocalypse. A staggering sight:

stacked boxes of powdered milk, sacks of flour, towers of cans and rolls of toilet tissue and candles and batteries. The woman seems to think all this is perfectly normal.

"Have you begun stocking up?" she asks. "Remember, one never knows."

Grace shakes her head. She feels cramped, skeptical and awed; but she's also a little on edge. She herself is lapsed, devoid of any recognizable brand of faith. She loves Ankara's mosques and minarets, the men bent on prayer rugs, the idea of a whole city facing one direction in unison, responding to an ancient, nearly tuneless call. Ezan, it's called here. In contrast, the antiseptic church gatherings on the British compound—which at first they'd all attended regularly, at her insistence—now seem tiresome and terribly staged. She'd skipped the previous Sunday, let Rand and Canada sleep, and when they woke up and wandered out, confused and relieved, she pretended to have forgotten what day it was. While Grace speaks with the woman about the maid, Rand drifts out onto the balcony with the husband, probably tamping tobacco into his pipe, admiring tomato plants and homegrown peppers, or something just as useless. Since they've arrived in Ankara, Rand has been supremely unhelpful, leaving, as usual, all the pedestrian details of life to her. She'd chosen the apartment. He had stood in the bare, dusty living room, swiveled once around, said "fine," and decamped immediately for the embassy. She'd fought with the shippers over water damage, filed the reimbursement claims and trotted Canada to her cursory interview at the British school. She'd even waited, for nearly seven freezing hours one day at a depot, for his beloved red car to arrive on a trailer from Istanbul. ("It smells of rot," he'd said accusingly, when she presented it to him at the embassy.)

Near the end of the interview about the maid—*a one-way interrogation,* Grace wrote to Edie later, *in entirely the wrong direction*—the woman says, "Now she's wonderful, don't get me wrong. She's miraculous. There is just the one thing."

Grace is standing pressed against a shelf of canned beans, desperately wanting out. The space is suffocating; the shelves loom precariously. Hand built, she assumes. This Rand will later confirm, shaking his head and muttering about fanatics.

"What thing?" Grace asks.

Not that it matters. Lately she's been weeping over the wringer-washer, pulling torn, mangled clothing from its pernicious jaws. She can't communicate at all with the kapıcı, who just grins at her and nods every time she speaks to him from her phrase book. Grins and nods and vanishes.

"Well," says the woman as she lowers her voice and leans too close. "Things move."

Grace shakes her head a little. She runs a hand through her sticky hair. "Move? She steals?"

The woman draws back and puffs herself up. "Certainly not," she says. "I'm just saying that items change places. When I haven't touched them."

Grace assumes, comfortably, that the woman is certifiable. She confirms it with a glance around her—the teetering canned goods, the bedrolls and flashlights and first-aid paraphernalia.

Rand and the husband come in off the balcony together a moment later, looking satisfied and male and jolly. As she and Rand leave, he offers to sell the contents of the pantry to them—lock, stock and barrel, he says, including shelving.

"Can't take it with you?" Rand says heartily. The two men are shoulder clapping each other, saying goodbye.

Grace stands nearby, her hand on the doorknob. She squeezes it hard. Miniature plastic rain boots are lined up under the coat hook in military formation. Orange, red, blue, green.

The woman reaches around Grace for the door. "It's all specific for the climate, for Ankara," she says seriously. "We'll have to start again in Paris."

In the car, Grace says, "Paris? They're going to Paris?"

Rand says, "I pity Paris."

Grace sighs and leans back in her seat; Rand steers around a clump of dirty sheep congregating on a residential roadway. Canada is playing at her friend Catherine's—Grace hopes she will stay for dinner. At home, there is nothing in the refrigerator or the cupboards; Grace cannot seem to accomplish even the minor everyday haggling that constitutes commerce in Turkey. The price of nearly everything, it seems—flour, fruit, bread, floor polish—is infinitely negotiable.

"Who suggested this woman?" she asks him. "Who gave you the tip?"

"Paige Trotter," he says. "You like her. The one who reads cards."

"He's CIA, isn't he? That's what everyone says."

Rand doesn't answer—she isn't surprised. No one discusses what the men do for a living here, or whom they work for. It isn't polite; not even appropriate, it seems, between husbands and wives. But Grace does like Paige Trotter. Many of the other wives here remind her of the insipid women from Olson Loop; at parties, they gather and chatter in little parliaments around the room, giggling and making eyes—but not Paige. She drifts around in caftans and turbans, drinking scotch neat and laughing just as loudly as the men. Late at night, in her own messy house, she lays out fortune-telling cards, rolls back the carpets and initiates dancing and games of charades.

Grace watches her husband's big hands gripping the steering wheel; it seems like a child's toy under them, a circus car. "I had a letter from Edie yesterday," she says. "She says Saudi reminds her a little of Paris. The shopping, I suppose."

Rand ignores her through Çankaya's winding hills. They pass the American Residence and Ankara University; the electricity returns as they drive and she watches it punch bright holes through the darkness. As they enter Gasi Osman Paşa, Rand says, "I wouldn't advise either of them to get too comfortable there. They can't possibly last out a full tour."

"She sounds quite happy."

"Goldfish are happy," he says. "Greg hasn't got mettle enough for Saudi . . . and she's not exactly made of the ideal stuff either. In fact, he should probably be filing papers somewhere right now, not in a sensitive field post."

"I'm sure you're wrong."

Rand shakes his head wonderingly. "I'd have bet money they'd be sent to Guam or something. But Saudi Arabia, for God's sake. Saudi."

"You don't sound very happy for them."

He keeps his eyes on the road and doesn't respond. She lets it go. Rand has always disapproved—in his maddeningly oblique way—of Grace's friendship with Edie. *Of all things,* he'd said, when he'd learned where they were going. *Of all the goddamn things.* And when she'd asked, *What goddamn things?* he had merely looked at her as if she were shockingly dim. *Never mind,* he'd said, popping a beer and sucking foam from the lip. *Forget it.*

He glances at her now in just the same way and eases the car into a space across from their apartment building.

SMALL THINGS move first. Almost imperceptibly. A picture that has been propped against a wall seems to hang itself, directly above its original resting spot. At first Grace wonders if she's done it herself. Then a carpet shifts, from one side of the bed to the other. Silver serving dishes go from inside the china cabinet to the outer shelf; a chair from the right side of the fireplace to the left. A heavy crystal ashtray sweeps around a room—on a coffee table one day, a side table the next, then the mantel, then the sideboard, before finally landing on the desk in the corner by the window.

On the fifth day Grace comes home and finds her dressing table moved—mere inches, from east to west. The contents are untouched, but the table itself has definitely moved.

She says to Rand, "Do you notice this?"

"What?"

"The *moving,* is what. Do you not notice it?"

And like a line in a radio skit, he says, "Who's moving?"

"Never mind," Grace says and concludes, not for the first time, that she's married a handsome, brilliant idiot.

She gets used to it. When an entire seating section of the living room gets up and rearranges itself in a different corner, she sits down there and smokes a cigarette. When the contents of the kitchen cabinets change entirely, up going down and down going up, she asks Canada where the powdered milk has gone and proceeds accordingly. Because Canada always seems to know. If Grace comes home and finds her nose-down in a book, oblivious, and asks her where such and such is, Canada knows. "She put it there," she'll say. At times, Grace suspects collusion. Others, she chalks it up to Canada's observant nature—very little gets by her. Even when she has a pulpy paperback tucked inside the pages of a huge, battered poetry anthology, she'll have managed to memorize some terrible, boring poem, in case she is asked.

A few weeks into Firdis's tenure, Grace is at lunch with Bahar and brings the subject around to her new maid. "The woman is miraculous," she says. "But I do feel as though she's taking over my house."

Firdis scours and cooks and cleans from morning until night; she hunches on her knees, polishing the wood floors one meticulous inch at a time, swaddled in her many layers of multicolored fabric. The woman is a walking, scrubbing coatrack. She also leaves in her wake a pungent combination of sweat and lemon oil, which Grace has become almost completely accustomed to.

Bahar lifts an eyebrow and plays with her salad. "This is something wrong? A bad thing?"

"No. I suppose not."

They pay the bill and walk over to the park. Grace has with her a thick military-issued binder on cultural matters, on protocol, on navigating the city and tipping: *Dependents' Guide to the Customs and Culture of Turkey*. "Turkey" is typed in on a separate line below the other words, indicating that an entire library of such books exists somewhere, with the names of other lands filled in by some anonymous clerk.

She shows it to Bahar. "Military efficiency," she says.

Bahar takes it from her, flips it open and skims the pages. She laughs out loud. "No," she says. "Not correct. Nor this. This is not true either. Who writes this merde?"

Grace leans over to follow Bahar's finger. She has read the book several times but is still drawn to its peculiar information: how much leg is appropriate, how one must avoid stray dogs, respect Islam and Kemal Atatürk. A strange collection of topics, a glossary of phrases, bits of trivia compiled, she imagines, in the same choppy, haphazard way it's presented: religion leading into history, government flowing into the role of women, economics and foreign exchange devolving into matters of courtesy.

Bahar is absorbed in the binder when Grace notices a woman standing nearby at the marshy end of the lake, holding the hand of a dark toddler who gnaws busily at its fist. The woman is wrapped in clothing and headscarves and wears heavy socks under pink plastic sandals. The layers of fabric beneath her coat are wild and mismatched and she seems perilously overdressed for the weather. Grace cannot tell where one article of clothing ends and another begins. The child is similarly bundled; no determining if it is a boy or a girl.

When the woman smiles back at her, Grace sees gold teeth and wide, dark gaps between them.

The binder and the briefings Grace attended before shipping out have taken pains to point out the chasm here between East and West, Christianity and Islam, between the poor and the privileged. Driving to the city from the airport on the night of their arrival, their host had pointed out the shantytowns—geçekondus—cobbled together from bits of tin and cardboard, where families lived in huddles, barely sheltered from the elements, cooking over smoky coal fires. These were squatters' camps, erected at night and torn down quickly in the morning. Bleary-eyed from travel, Grace saw ragged children running alongside the car or stepping brazenly into its path, holding out their hands. Don't give them a thing, the binder warns (and their uniformed host had echoed sternly from the front seat that evening), or you'll never get away. On the other hand, with no hint of irony, it suggests that one always carry American cigarettes and booze, if possible. Charity is frowned upon, she gathers, bribery openly sanctioned. Rand's nondescript government car already holds a stash of bottles and red and white cartons stacked in the trunk.

Grace feels around in her pockets and finds some peppermints. They are quite old, left over from the airplane, in fact. For a moment she examines them—the wrappers are slightly soiled, the pink stripes running together from heat and moisture—then looks up to find the child's eyes watching her above a grubby fist. She decides it's a boy, for no particular reason. But when she offers him the candies, the woman's face changes swiftly. She shakes her head and begins to back away. The little boy bursts instantly into tears and pulls at her hand; they tug at each other like that for a few moments until the woman, with her brute strength and harsh tone, prevails. She sweeps the child into her arms and carries him away. Embarrassed, Grace tucks the candies back in her pocket.

When she turns back, Bahar is watching her.

"You think we let our children take candy from strangers?" she says. "I wonder: would I do this in your country, with your children?" She closes the book, sets it down on the bench and stands up. Grace feels her face burn as she hurries across the grass behind Bahar, apologizing. Bahar slows, finally, before she crosses the street and lets Grace tuck her arm into hers.

"Not everyone here wants your American charity," she says, more kindly. "You cannot learn everything from that silly book."

But as time passes and summer comes on in earnest, the early missteps she'd made seem humorous, just beginner's mistakes. Grace grows comfortable with the Turkish ladies and their afternoons, with the crazed bustle of the streets, the barking of vendors and the constant presence of Firdis, who continues to effect her own arbitrary changes within her household.

Soon, summer weekends bring driving trips to the scalloped coastline, to the ruins and treasures at Ephesus, Pamukkale, Pergamum, Bodrum. Nights are spent in cheap beachside hotels where snails cluster above the beds like textured wallpaper. She is folded into the clique of English-speaking women with the same ease with which Canada had joined the children on Olson Loop. There are long days at the pool; card games and shopping in the Old City with Bahar. Under her expert instruction, Grace learns to study the intricate knotwork to tell a good rug from a cheap one, to weigh gold appraisingly in her palm, to click with her mouth when she is outraged by a price. She becomes close with Paige Trotter as well. The Trotters live in a real house, not an apartment, and in the pretty garden out back, tattered Japanese lanterns are strung from fraying clothesline, weighing down the stunted trees that grow up through the patio. The furniture is rickety and weather stained and Grace ruins countless dresses with rust marks from leaning up against the tables and chairs. But she spends some of her loveliest hours there, in Paige's garden and the untidy living room, with its low windows and sprung couches, among the dusty spill of books and artifacts and papers and general material confusion.

Some days it feels as if she's been swept up in a great, ongoing party, without consequences or repercussions, where drinks flow and food appears, where the women are lovely, the men bright and interested, and the children out of sight and productively occupied.

JULY 1975

3

SIMONE. SIMONE OF THE FRENCH-BLUE BEDROOM SUITE, THE gardenia and vetiver, the atomizers and glass pots of face cream, the jewel-hued bath beads and lace-trimmed bed jackets. Simone Tremblay, Catherine's mother: climbing, bloodless, her heart as frosty as her perfectly coiffed hair. Simone and her houseboy, John: her minion, her underling, her co-conspirator, and something else we couldn't yet define.

On Tuesdays, in the heat of the day, John folded laundry in the small, matching blue room off Simone's bedroom suite. Tuesday was Simone's day at the salon. Of course, it didn't occur to Catherine to ask her mother to go along, and Simone would never think to offer.

Sometimes, passing the doorway, bored and ill at ease, Catherine and I would linger, watching John fastidiously fold Simone's panties and delicates, his hands moving quietly among the lace and silks, his mouth slightly curled. The iron hissed on the table and we heard the bright tinkling of oud strings from the small black radio, its antenna pointed toward the tiny square of window that looked over the alley and, we'd been told, toward Mecca. This was also the room in which John prayed in the afternoons, on a rug he kept rolled behind the washing machine.

In a pile on the floor were Simone's clothes—lavender silks and demi bras, camisoles, madras shirts and long, pleated skirts requiring meticulous ironing. As John aimed the iron into the darts and cuffs and creases, wet heat gathered in the air and seemed to us like some emanation from his body.

"What do you want?" he said. "Go away. I do not wish to be watched by you."

Clean clothes, folded and stiff and fresh, grew in stacks around him. They piled up on the ironing board, the floor, the dryer. The radio crackled; he adjusted the antenna.

Catherine pulled me away from the door. "Let's go out," she said.

"I want to stay." I turned to John: "Can we help?"

"No." He turned back to the laundry and his hands became more purposeful, his folding more vigorous and impatient.

But I liked watching John; he was so different from Firdis, who slammed and slung and tossed things: John used such care touching Simone's lingerie, folding the tap pants trimmed with lace, turning bra cups inside each other, his fingers tugging down silky straps. Simone favored silks and crepes—in dusky roses, lilacs, peach. I often thought: Who is this woman, Simone, to wear these fabrics and colors—so chaste, so innocent—next to her body? Who does she think she is? Perhaps John wondered the same thing.

Later, as we were walking down the hall to the kitchen, Catherine suddenly said, "I don't think he likes girls seeing him do the laundry."

I looked at her over my hand. "We watch him cook and clean and do the dishes."

"It's different." She shrugged. "Laundry is beneath him. It's women's work."

On afternoons when she was home, Simone and John huddled together in the kitchen and spoke in low tones, studying menus and seating charts, flower arrangements and butter clovers. The two of them were always scheming some upcoming social triumph.

We pushed open the door—looking for a drink, an approved

snack, some distraction or another—and they both looked up as if intruded upon during some private, occult rite. Foodstuffs were spread on the counter, silver was drying on soft towels, the refrigerator hummed. Simone huffed, straightened her skirt with her long, pale hands and launched an interrogation.

"Have you done your homework, Catherine? Practiced at the barre? Why are your faces dirty? Your hands? You aren't wearing shoes inside the house, are you? Surely I'm seeing things."

We backed away and tiptoed down the hall to Catherine's room, settling for the candy we hoarded in her closet and water straight from the bathroom tap. The latter was ill-advised, but we had both, since arriving in Turkey, developed cast-iron stomachs.

We kept our candy hidden in a shoebox behind Catherine's neatly hung clothes—Peter Pan–collared shirts, pleated tartan skirts, navy blue trousers. Over the summer months a kind of bargain had blossomed silently between John and Catherine. And the candy was part of it; all of it came from him, delivered in secret, payment for some dark thing growing between them.

She told me a little of it that same afternoon. She told me that when he came to her room to deliver laundry, to straighten her bed or dust her dresser, he stayed just a bit longer than the task required. He carried in her white cotton panties, pink leotards and clean tights, collared shirts and school skirts—and all the time, he whispered to her. The whole time, most of it, his hands slid shirts onto hangers, crisp cottons into her dresser. He never stayed more than a few minutes, she said. Perhaps he needed to compose himself for Simone's return, to anticipate the instructions she would insist she'd given him earlier, which would most certainly have come to her under the hair dryer. And yet to Catherine, these moments alone with John had the breadth and substance of hours.

"Your mother is a bitch," he would whisper to her. "A filthy woman, an oppressor, a whore."

Though she was not inclined to disagree, the sound of his accented voice saying these words must have provoked in her some involuntary surge of loyalty, some small instinct to object. I imagine his words accompanied by the sound of fabrics, the shush of cotton, the crinkle of starchy shirts and the vaguely stiff leotards Catherine had by the dozen, which Simone had shipped from Montreal.

John was slight, wiry and strong; he smelled of clean clothes and hair oil and he moved as Simone herself did, glidingly, and was not much for eye contact. If he touched Catherine, which he did not often do, being restrained by some odd chivalry, he left grease marks on the collar of her shirt, across its crisp alabaster front. When he left he would hold out his arms to take the stained garment away and she would slide it off and place it in his hands. She said he always turned his eyes from her body, as if it didn't interest him.

"Your mother," he would murmur, "she is a bad person, she treats people poorly. Inşallah she will go to hell. Do you agree?"

John's English was exceptionally good, though the words came out with odd inflections: ah-gree, he said. Beesh.

"She does not care for you. Orospu. Only for her perfect parties, her china, her position."

Certainly this was true. Simone was peremptory, imperious and snide, always jockeying for position. (What's that thing stuck to the ambassador's backside? went a common joke among my mother's friends. Oh, that? Just Simone Tremblay.) Simone, almost always dressed for some affair: her clothes silky around her frame, her eyes glittering with pleasure—taking in what John had done: the crystal and china, the sprays of orchids and individual ferns set spikily into vases, the polished silver that threw back her reflection, which she bared her teeth into, bending over the table, checking for stray lipstick.

When Catherine was dispatched to the kitchen to assist John in some preparatory task—folding napkins into intricate designs, polishing water glasses or fruit knives—John mouthed things to her behind Simone's straight back, the knobs of her spine visible under a tennis outfit or a thin cotton dress. She heard the words in her head as though he were placing them there, one by one, as carefully as he laid silver on a table. Whore. Slut. Dog. She could read his lips precisely, in the instant when their eyes met, when he compelled her to look at him. She watched him form those words, hearing his voice in her head, and it was as if he were painting Simone in brilliant, poisonous colors, while the woman herself was occupied with some triviality, clicking her pen over the evening's menu, repositioning a blade of greenery.

You could not help but notice the obsession in Ankara with domestic servants. These strangers in our homes—bending, washing, scrubbing, serving—seemed to have a value greater than any amount of actual currency. Among the ladies they were constantly discussed, traded, inherited, loaned, lauded and complained about. And Simone's relationship with John was particularly interesting to the other women in my mother's circle.

Still, the young man they gossiped about, this swarthy, libidinous houseboy, sly-eyed and hostile, was strangely confined by perimeters known only to him. He never touched me, for example, though I certainly wanted him to. I settled for far less, treasuring even the slip of his cool hand against mine in the hallway. Passing me in the corridor leading to Catherine's room, he would turn his body away from mine; he was taut, bladelike, and the suggestion of a mustache above his upper lip reinforced the implication of a sneer. But our hands would incongruously meet, so quickly and deftly it would be hard later to imagine how it had happened, and I would come away with some bit of cellophane or foil curled inside my palm, a thing to be unwrapped later, privately, savored and adorned with meaning—the flavor, the color of the paper, the comic hidden inside like a Chinese fortune.

But John pressed these riches on us with his typical disinterest, with the manner of one paying a debt he is not quite convinced he owes. From time to time he brusquely deposited in Catherine's room paper bags filled with candy or chewing gum, the sickeningly sweet sugared squares called lokum, which we disposed of down the toilet, for fear, of all things, of hurting his feelings.

It's a mystery why he included me. Perhaps he simply saw how easily my silence could be purchased, how eager I was to be included in what went on between them. Generally, if John spoke to me at all, it was by way of instruction or criticism, reminding me to take off my shoes, or wash my hands, not to touch Simone's breakables or his beautifully laid dining table. He was often Simone's intermediary, taking up her causes when she was absent. You would never have said they were united, of course, but I believe John liked the idea of giving us orders, and he sought out opportunities to do so.

In her bedroom, Catherine and I divided up the candy and rationed it out. I tried to pry from her the details of their encounters—when had he come last, what had he said or done? I felt as entitled to his trespasses as I would if they'd been directed at me.

"Do you think I should tell someone?" she asked me that afternoon. "Should I tell my mother?"

The candy was spread between us on the bed, like treasure poured from an undersea chest. The little mound glittered and winked.

I put my hands deep inside the pile: the cool of cellophane and the squish of caramel, hard sour candies colored like jewels and mysterious little bundles we would have to unwrap to identify. To lose all this booty, to give up the thrill of its secret provenance, seemed tragic to me, and stupid.

"Tell Simone?" I said. "No. Why on earth would you?"

Catherine stared at me. I unwrapped a green sour ball and fitted it inside my mouth. "She'd have to fire him," I pointed out. "She'd hate you for it." I sucked vigorously on the candy; artificial lime flavor burst bright stars in my mouth. "But then again," I said slowly, "what if she didn't? What if she didn't do anything?"

Catherine looked around the room. She smoothed the flowered bedspread under her fingers. "It's nothing anyway," she said then. "It isn't anything."

Looking back, perhaps there was a time when Catherine wanted my advice, or even my approval: she was timid by nature, afraid to walk home from the bus stop alone, terrified of the dogs that roamed the streets and the construction workers who muttered at us incomprehensibly when we passed their work site in the mornings, in our tights and school uniforms, carrying our books.

WHEN CATHERINE and I weren't in the alleys, we spent summer afternoons at the pool at the Canadian Residence, lying side by side on the hot tile, our feet splashing gently in the deep end. The sun beat warm strokes along our bodies; surrounding the pool the lawns were emerald green, thick as carpet, bordered with bright flowering hedges. It was lush, almost suffocating, and the trees overhead seemed to close us in, to gather the sky in a perfect sphere above where we lay prone, lethargic and baking. Outside the tall iron gates the city was dirty and hot and bleak, but it seemed to me as distant as Olson Loop. At lunchtime, we pulled apricots from the trees; they came free still warm from the sun, blushing pink, skins soft and furred.

The scritch of a lighter being flicked repeatedly. I had one arm thrown over my face, a sticky apricot stone clenched in the other hand. I widened my fingers and saw my mother—an alien in enormous sunglasses, a wide hat, a skirted bathing suit, on a lounge chair nearby. She was examining the lighter, looking concerned, the unlit cigarette a little white stick resting in the middle of her luridly pink chest. Simone lay beside her under an umbrella, stretching like a cat, scribbling something on a pad of paper.

My mother disliked Simone, though they were friendly socially. Friendly, but by no means friends. There was something between those women, some sporting camaraderie, but it was limned with something distinctly ungenerous. Catherine and I suspected they were united only in the face of what they mutually disapproved of: slouching girls, back-talking girls, loud, silly, inconsiderate, thoughtless girls.

Closing my fingers, I waited for the sunspots to recede and briefly considered the idea of my mother. She swam long, endless-seeming laps, always breaststroke, her chin never dipping below the surface. She wore a bathing cap studded with plastic flowers. Her white legs frog-kicked end to end, her mouth slightly open, sunglasses propped up on her head. Coming out of the water, she toweled herself vigorously all over, even between her legs; she dragged the cap from her head with a big snap. But aside from Simone, she was liked; you couldn't have said she wasn't. I found it surprising, less than pleasing, an ongoing mystery. And those bracelets she'd begun wearing, they drove me crazy. Maybe a dozen thin, scrolled bangles, they clinked and tinkled along her freckled arms. She went around jingling like our cat and seemed to enjoy it, hearing the sounds she made moving, dressing, brushing her hair, shouldering through the world. Catherine had asked for ones like them and Simone had called them common and sniffed—a sound like a kitten sneezing. Catherine could imitate it perfectly.

The two of them were Canadian by birth, Simone and my mother, but my mother was an American now because she'd married one, which was the first thing Simone found objectionable. But my being named Canada—a bizarre patriotic gesture my father had strenuously opposed—this she called "the height of bad taste." Simone never, ever called me by name. Even when I was not around she said: *your friend,* or *that American girl,* or simply *her.* It was a rudeness she wouldn't have tolerated from Catherine but blithely allowed herself. Simone, I believe, put up with our friendship only because it was temporary, because, of course, everything among us was—posts and schools and apartments and houses, certainly friendships. And what Catherine really wanted, I think, was permanence, a house in a place that stood still, and trees and plants that flowered seasonally, predictably, a school she might graduate from, friends who wouldn't ever change or move or leave. She might have become the kind of woman who nurses a vague agoraphobia or one who earns a living from home, putting papers into envelopes. But then perhaps she would have become the prima ballerina Simone was grooming her to be. Even though I know the truth, I still sometimes picture her as a pin on a map, a little figure of a ballerina, like one on a music box she had, spinning gracefully, somewhere in Quebec.

Under the edge of my blue towel—side by side with Catherine's—I kept a little lump, a mound I rested my hand on periodically, palm flat, fingers wide. I edged the towel back and my fingers rustled in the assortment, culling what I wanted from the rest. I slid a fruit pastille—not a black-currant one, those I kept for myself—against the edge of Catherine's hand. She pushed it back gently and I pushed again, insistently.

"Too hot," she hissed. "It's too hot."

"Look what's left."

"You have it."

There was silence, long and scorching; the sun throbbed against my eyelids.

"Really? You don't mind?"

"I wish you would."

I sighed and wriggled on my towel, shifting my shoulders, greedy fingers busy again in the pile. Papers unfolding, quiet as could be—I submerged each crinkle, snap, or tear beneath a cough, a sigh—each sound allowed to dissipate before another was initiated.

The afternoon wore on into early evening, when lights blinked on in the residence and down the hillside and insects began stirring in the trees. My mother and Simone rose from their chairs and began to gather their towels and lotions and hats. A party was being held at the pool that night and the two disappeared into the cabana to shower and paint their faces and change into dresses. Servants began moving up the path with bottles and folding tables and platters of food wrapped in plastic.

Catherine and I watched them, staying right where we were. We knew we would be conscripted into service soon enough—another thing that both our mothers believed in was silent, well-mannered children circulating through parties with trays. Soon the pool lights flickered on and the water brightened to a deep, unnatural shade of blue. We smelled fried pastries and pungent white cheese and heard the clink of liquor bottles and glasses. Music sputtered through speakers hidden in the bushes, and houseboys in dinner jackets began lighting torches around the pool.

My father had returned from a trip that very morning, smelling of the unknown, his shoes uncharacteristically dusty, his eyes tired. He'd changed and gone over to the embassy but I expected him to arrive at any moment. He and my mother had argued about it and she'd won.

Cars began pulling into the driveway and people wandered down the illuminated path to the swimming pool, lifting drinks from trays as they came, chattering and laughing. My mother and Simone emerged from the changing room at last, both in long skirts and silver jewelry, and they glared at us until we retreated from our towels and sat on a low stone wall in the background. We cadged Cokes from the bar and dunked lemon slices down through the ice with paper straws. We braided and unbraided each other's wet, chlorine-scented hair.

Before long, my mother and the other women pressed Mrs. Trotter into reading cards. She was one of my mother's favorite people in Ankara—a *lovely* person, she always said, a *real* person, one of the best. Paige sat curled and barefoot—with her turban, clunky jewelry and knotty, unpainted toes—on a striped chair as they gathered around her. One by one, she built their futures in the shape of a cross, the cards shifted and slid on the plastic chair, seemingly tuned to the women bending over them, the motion of their hips and breasts, their intent, leaning bodies.

Before long my father came, kissed me hello and then settled on a lounge chair and got busy with his pipe. He still looked tired to me and he gave me a smile I'd seen before—it said: I hate this, and you hate this, but we can get through it together. Soon the smell of his tobacco drifted on the night air, lovely, rich and whiskey-dark, purely him. He wore long pants and a dress shirt—the rest of the men were in swimming trunks and the thick, dark-rimmed eyeglasses that were fashionable at the time. Eventually, they all gathered around him for a photograph; Simone was taking it. I heard my father laugh, his voice thick with booze and exhaustion. People congregated by the drinks table; boys in jackets passed trays. I hovered nearby, my back against the low stone wall, watching, smelling the alcohol rising off their glasses. Everything felt a little heady; everyone seemed a little drunk. I shivered; white lights sparkled in the trees, midges and tiny flies swarmed the food. Simone had come for Catherine and now she too was passing drinks, her hair still damp and the back of her shirt stained dark. I'd been overlooked, forgotten.

I watched Catherine skirt the edge of the pool. Lights danced on the water and underneath, the bottom of the pool seemed to undulate in wide, aquamarine ripples. It looked unearthly and beautiful, a place you might elect to drown in.

I was wearing only my American-flag bikini, and goose pimples came up on my arms. Still, I was waiting until someone explicitly instructed me to get dressed. In the dank, chlorinated cool of the dressing room, with its benches and compartments and slatted wooden walls, were my shoes and street clothes. Rolled inside, tight in the middle, was a small stash of John's candy. A breeze moved across the pool, the clustering adults; it blew through the trees and ruffled the flowers. Pink and yellow petals drifted from the trees and made kaleidoscope patterns on the grass. The American Residence was just up the hill from the Canadian one; the gardens met at a discreet fence. I could see their lights, the bunched shadows of their trees.

I tried to catch Catherine's eye. John was standing near her, taking glasses from the tray she held. Simone had lent him to the ambassador's wife for the evening; it wasn't unusual for him to appear in places like this, in homes and at parties where he didn't actually belong. But it always gave me a shiver when he turned up looking both apart and at ease, as though his presence were merely a fateful accident. But there was always about John the implication that he was doing us a great and undeserved favor just by being where he was. As I watched, he spoke into Catherine's ear and she laughed. A hot flush of jealousy skittered along my arms, made my neck itch.

I pushed off the wall I was leaning against and started toward her, meaning to pull her away, to take one of them—which? I have to wonder—from the other. But I never made it. Halfway there, I saw my father lurch up from his chair and stagger toward the men standing for the photograph. Instinctively, the men moved back, shifting clear of him. A glass crashed to the tile; a table went over. Frozen in my place, I watched as his arms windmilled, and then he pitched hard into the pool, his legs scissoring in his long pants, his head striking the concrete edge. There was a sickening noise. He was wearing his dress shoes. A bright red flower grew at the pool's edge. My mother screamed.

PRELUDE TO a marital argument:

My mother and I sat on the edge of a communal well in a small, dirty village on the Antalya coast. Fishing boats and pleasure craft dotted the harbor nearby, none of them the least bit splendid. They bounced on the roughening water, tethers slapping the waves. A storm was gathering, a dark, domed headpiece of clouds in the distance. The tree we were sitting under had jaundiced slowly in the changing light—the yellow of maturing bruises, coming thunder.

My father had been gone well over an hour and my mother was hopping. We had watched streams of people stop at the shabby little mosque nearby to wash their hands at the taps and rub the crumbling mosaic wall with their fingers. But now the square was nearly deserted and fat raindrops had begun to splatter the ground beyond the tree. A goat tied to a rusted bicycle folded its knees solemnly, then lowered its haunches to the ground. My father had disappeared with a man promising to show him some antiquities, undoubtedly looted from a nearby archaeological dig or tomb. I had a Coke my mother bought me from a street vendor, tepid, the bottle filmed with dust, very nearly an artifact in its own right. Bored, I picked at a scab on my knee; I was familiar with this scenario. In the beginning, new to Turkey, we often made weekend trips to tourist attractions and historic sites, and my parents fought habitually about the things he acquired and the manner in which he did it. *These unsavory characters you turn up,* my mother said every time. *You'll have us all killed.*

This morning outside the pillars of Ephesus my father had made contact with a dirty little man who sidled up to us speaking pidgin English: Roman coins, he said. Authentic artifacts. Follow me. My father turned to him with amused eyes and spoke rapidly in Turkish.

Before long the talk quickened and the eyes of the peddler brightened. He knew another man, as it happened. A bargain was struck. It was only a short walk. His wife would make tea. It was the same every time, and my mother and I had watched him go, marching off with the diminutive man, the two of them speaking and laughing and gesturing, until they vanished down the dusty road.

Strange bedfellows, my mother once said to me, in a rare moment of humor. We were sitting on the hill beyond the Virgin Mary's little stone house, gnawing at bread we'd bought earlier that day by the roadside. The waters of the spring below were teeming with pilgrims. Twisted olive trees rustled overhead; the air smelled of oranges and the sea. My mother used a house key to cut a corner of crumbling white cheese; she spoke through a mouthful, her manners momentarily abandoned. *Miniver Cheevy,* she said. Born too late. She trailed off, chewing.

You had to wonder: how did my father find these men, or what was it about him that drew them, these slit-eyed, craven little men, dressed in ragged clothes, with their terrible teeth? They always seemed to recognize each other. Unlike my mother, though, I enjoyed these transactions. I liked the furtive commerce, the way the men glanced over their shoulders and touched my father's sleeve in a pleading way, the way they offered up their bundles of rags and pockets full of coins. And my father's excitement was contagious.

We'd trooped to innumerable dirty houses and apartments, to tumbled burial sites where ragged articles were spread across stone slabs on which chiseled lettering, finger-wide, grown shallow and worn, had faded almost entirely away. Huddled together over ancient epitaphs, my father haggled happily with these men over the price and authenticity of countless dirty, unidentifiable relics. But eventually my mother refused to accompany him.

The rain became serious. The tree was no longer an awning but an honest-to-goodness gutter, sluicing water onto our shoulders and knees.

Raindrops the size of marbles bounced on the dusty ground and the air thickened with the smell of wet stone and dirt. I glanced over at my mother, who sat, her hands folded on her knees and her eyes closed, while water ran in rivulets down her cheeks. The edges of her scarf drooped; her makeup ran. I looked around for a place to get out of the wet, but she said, "Stay put." I closed my eyes against the water; I understood what we were doing. The rain slicked my skin and needled at my sunburned knees; my socks went sloppy and my cheap white tennis shoes soaked through, expanding by at least two sizes. My mother's eyes stay closed, and somehow, between the expression on her face and the streaming water, she managed to look beatific. Which was, of course, the point.

When my father returned, carrying some heavy wrapped thing, he took one look at us and doubled over, hooting with laughter. "You," he said to me. "You, I thought had more sense."

We were back in the car for a while before the rain finally stopped. Mountains rose in the near distance; the sea below was one of those unnatural, natural hues—crystal, cerulean—lapping at an alabaster shore. I was in the backseat, my clothes dried cardboard stiff, reading a lurid version of *Sinbad,* my hand busy between my legs under a blanket, head turned into the fragrant, smoky leather of the seat. The argument was on, held in hushed tones, my mother's voice chilly and hard. My father laughed, which outraged her.

"It isn't safe," my mother said finally. "You disappearing off who knows where, leaving us in the middle of some godforsaken hellhole. One of these days you're going to get your head bashed in."

"Not today," he said, with a smile in his voice. "Sorry to disappoint you."

"Pull over," my mother said after a moment. "Stop the car."

I closed my eyes and stilled my hands on the pages. The car continued to move, snaking along the road; the sunlight was hot on my eyelids, intrusive, insinuating.

"Stop this car this minute." Her voice rose; her teeth were clenched. I heard her fingers scrabbling at the nub of the door lock. But the car gained speed. I smelled sand and salt in my hair, a gritty feeling along my arms and neck, the day's sand and dirt caked into the creases of my skin.

"I'm not kidding," she said.

My father was quiet. I couldn't even hear him breathe—just the hum of the little red car, the noise of air beating against the windows.

Then the car stopped. There was the sensation of it lurching onto the shoulder, the wheels dipping onto the packed earth. The passenger door opened; my mother exited and slammed it behind her. A few hot moments passed.

He said, "I know you're awake."

I sat up and looked around. We were stopped on a cliff, the sea glittering below. In the distance on the other side of the car a hill rose gently, the vegetation sparse among the usual tumble of gray-white stones the size of oranges, and a few whiter ones, more square in shape, that dotted the field. Farther away were the rounded woolly bodies of sheep. I saw the plumed tail of one of the Turkish sheepdogs and the glint of its great spiked collar as it circled its flock in wide arcs.

My mother walked slowly along the roadway. Her scarf lifted in the wind rising from the sea; she swayed along in tight cigarette-style pants. White pants, and I saw the silhouette of her underwear clearly. She was wearing small heels and teetering a little on the uneven surface.

"Look," said my father happily, pointing up the hill outside the passenger window. "Graves. Let's go see."

We got out of the car and started up the hill together. My mother didn't glance back. I was wearing shorts, a sun hat tied below my chin. The grasses were spiky, leaving thin red lashes along my calves. My father moved purposefully but slowly, his eyes on the ground. I'd done this a thousand times with my father: he had infinite patience and we could be there for hours. He bent down and with his handkerchief wiped a slab clean of grit and debris, sheep droppings. The marble was veined and cool to the touch, a surprising contrast in the heat. The lettering was Roman; there were numbers I could almost decipher. My father stood with his hands on his hips and looked down at it. He kicked around gently, found other markers and cleared them off as well. He did this almost reverently, humming a little tune. The bald spot on the top of his head reddened and sweat sprang up on his forehead.

After a while we shared the candy bar he had in his pocket, sitting beside a tomb in the dirt. I made a little wreath of grasses and tiny purple flowers. Anemones, I think; they peppered the field as far as the eye could see. My father licked the chocolate from his fingers, then stood and wandered farther up the hill, and in his absence I experienced a rare moment of spiritual consternation. I had taken the little wreath and placed it on one of the marble slabs. But it occurred to me suddenly that this might be sacrilege—I had sufficient schooling in my mother's faith to grasp this. I removed the wreath from the stone but suddenly was afraid of offending the Roman gods. It went back and forth like this for a while. I put the wreath down; I picked it up.

When my father returned, we walked back down the hill to the car. There's no telling how much time had passed. My mother was sitting in the passenger seat, and when we got in the car she made a small noise in her throat and turned her head away, staring fixedly out the window. I understood she was angry with me as well, that I had committed some betrayal, but certainly not the first one between us.

"And we're off," my father said cheerfully. He started the car and we drove back to the city. Soon the view became monochromatic again, and the pleated hills looked like nothing so much as great swaths of canvas flung out across the land and allowed to gently billow down.

All that had been months earlier, in the summer, when Catherine and I were set free of the chilly schoolroom with its slanted caramel light, the deserted garden, the dirty city and frantic streets, the dense, troubled silences of our city homes. We'd run wild, and not only in the alleys of Ankara. On many weekends we'd also shared the cramped backseat of the Rover, piled high and soft with pillows and blankets, the floor littered with books. We played games—Ghost, I Spy—on endless drives as the road wound along the coast, past jagged peninsulas and villages, past women squatting in fields, past boys driving sheep and cattle, along countless tumbled ruins and fields of scrubby brush.

Sometimes the landscape was ferociously bare, sometimes wild formations of stone and caves jutted startlingly from picturesque meadows. Behind my father we crept together through ancient caves and catacombs, holding ropes strung along damp, streaming walls, crawling in tunnels and passageways, deep into the hearts of rock churches and subterranean cathedrals where our whispers came back strangely shaped, echoing and distorted. In a hotel in Pamukkale, a place too expensive for us to stay in, we swam through ruins they'd flooded to make a swimming pool, chasing each other's kicking legs through cloudy green water, hiding from each other behind submerged stone colonnades. In hot springs nearby, steam rose in columns around our bodies and we scrambled down calcified terraces barefoot, stunned by the whiteness, the amazing, endless, stepping whiteness of the view. We shared small beds in cheap beachside hotels, where sand blew up in mounds against the wooden steps and pilings of the cottages, where snails traveled unmolested along the walls and floors and we played all day in shallow blue water, faces clownish with sun cream.

AFTER THE accident, Bahar's husband came daily to our apartment when he had finished with his patients. My mother, for her own reasons, had not wanted my father treated at the American hospital. Even before the fall, my father had had a reputation for drinking too much, for staggering at parties, for needing to be taken home by the elbows. "Your father is fine," my mother told me the morning after the accident, "but we're telling people he's gone on a trip. So he can recover in peace. It's a little secret." She narrowed her eyes. "You can keep a secret, can't you?"

Bahar's husband, Ali, was big and stocky, a man who loved his beautiful wife, adored his wild boys, dressed immaculately and carried himself with an air of friendly dispassion. He treated my parents' bedroom as if it were a sickroom, tiptoeing in and out, opening the door just wide enough to permit his not-insubstantial body to slide through and then silently closing it. He carried a very expensive-looking satchel; the scratched exterior, its general distress, seemed to enhance its luxury, and I often contrived to touch it when he wasn't looking. Inside the bedroom—even my mother sensed she was unwelcome—I imagine that dressings were changed and medicines dispensed and certain words exchanged. I heard them laughing in there from time to time. Men's laughter—rough and low and secretive.

Later, he and my mother would speak in quiet tones in the hallway, or behind the frosted-glass doors of the living room. He would often poke his head into the kitchen on his way out and say something in Turkish to Firdis, who would giggle insanely and cover her head with her apron. Ali had a strange effect on Firdis: he undid her completely. Firdis was a woman of an indeterminate age and body type, so swathed and swaddled in garments that there was nothing remotely womanly about her shape. Her husband was a kapıcı in

Çankaya and she seemed to have children in litters. When Ali's fleeting, male attentions were turned on her, she reddened and cowered, would knock to the floor some item from the kitchen counter or the mantel, then scramble for it, nearly hysterical, one hand pressed to her mouth.

MY FATHER had been in bed nearly a week, receiving his daily calls from Ali, when my mother and Simone and Catherine and I took a trip together to the baths. In the taxi to the Old City Catherine had the window and I was pressed unhappily between the two women, their thighs tight against mine, the fabric of their respective dresses cool and hot against my bare legs. Simone, so close, with her cakey, creamy smell, wore cotton; my mother had on some slithery synthetic that trapped humidity and made me itch. Every time I slid my hand between our too-close legs to scratch myself, she cut her eyes at me and wriggled a millimeter away. On the far side of the car, Catherine stared out the window. Simone argued furiously with the taxi driver about the route he was taking—in a fumbling patois of Turkish, French and English. Finally, he gave up fighting her and took the road she pointed out, and immediately we were trapped in traffic that seemed unlikely to move again, ever. The noise was earsplitting.

"He should have known there was construction. He should have said so." Simone adjusted her body in the seat, her hips pushed against me; she extracted her arm from her side and reached into her handbag.

"He did, I think," my mother said, but with no discernible note of victory. The cab was steamy with our breath, the mingled chemistry of our bodies, even though the windows were rolled down. The air outside was motionless.

Simone handed a tissue to Catherine and told her to blow her nose. Catherine took the tissue, studied its weave, then bunched it up and held it tightly in her fist.

"This is crazy," said Simone. "It's a hundred and fifty degrees. I'm melting into a puddle." And yet it was like sitting next to a penguin, she was so cool and smart and immaculate.

We were meeting some of the Turkish ladies at the baths; it was their monthly pilgrimage and we'd been invited. The previous night at a function, Simone and my mother had discovered their mutual plans—accidentally, unhappily—and so, for economy's sake, we were sharing a cab.

Simone blew her nose with a kitten-sniff; my mother stared out her window and fingered her bracelets.

"You know, Grace," Simone said suddenly. "Marjorie didn't know anything about Rand's trip. So unexpected. And he must still be recovering from that fall. I asked Marjorie and she was mystified."

Marjorie was the Canadian ambassador's wife. They'd been to a party the night before at the Canadian Residence—all blond wood and oriental furnishings, exotic flower arrangements and food wrapped in seaweed. It made my mother nervous to step foot in there—she felt, I think, a mixture of longing and infidelity. She'd given up her citizenship to marry my father and had never stopped reminding him of it. But she also envied Simone's relationship with Marjorie; I could tell because she called it "sickening" and "shamelessly self-serving."

"Well, why would she?" said my mother. "I can't imagine why she would." She was examining the view outside her window and craned her neck to watch a heated argument taking place nearby over a fender bender.

Simone zipped her patent leather handbag closed. "Oh, Grace," she said with something like a sigh. "Marjorie knows everything. She's completely on the inside. You know it as well as I do."

My mother turned her head and looked across me at Simone. Her face was pink and her nostrils flared slightly.

"Honestly, Simone, I can't imagine what all the interest is. Rand is fine; it was barely a scratch. Besides, men go; they come back. I've never known anyone to notice particularly."

I didn't look at my mother, staring instead at the back of the cabbie's head, where a jagged scar showed beneath the bristly hairs at the nape of his neck.

"Certainly," said Simone, without any certainty at all. "I just don't recall anyone mentioning a trip." She looked at me. "Didn't I ask after him the other day?"

"I forgot," I said. I scratched myself more furiously. My mother lifted her warm polyester hip and edged it away.

On the other side of Simone, Catherine didn't flinch, though Simone was pinching her quite hard, because she had not yet blown her nose. She was studying her shoes, her elbows propped on her knees. What had I told her of all this? For a moment I honestly couldn't remember. I was ashamed of my father's fall at the pool, the same hot shame I would have felt had I myself taken a public spill and scraped my knees. I was embarrassed by his clumsiness, his drunkenness, the bandages and bruises, by his lumbering gait through the apartment on his way to the bathroom. I was not advertising anything about him these days.

How in the world had my mother thought to slip something like this by Simone, with her hound nose for intrigue and deception, her hatred of being excluded? Had she really thought Simone wouldn't follow up? After all, she'd seen the fall with her own eyes, had tended my father while I was closed up in the chlorinated changing room, clutching John's candies in my clammy hands, stuffing them into my mouth like a junkie, the slick of the tile slimy and cold beneath my bare feet. I could hear the adults beyond the thin walls; they were so incompetent, dithering around, half drunk themselves, useless in a crisis.

John had put his sleek head in at one point, while people milled outside; his collar was open, his features obscured by the dim of the changing room. He stared at me for a few long moments. Please, I thought, please. He looked slowly around the room, as though someone else might have been concealed there. When I looked at him, he withdrew his face from the doorway without apology. He had come for Catherine, of course. Not even a calamity, not even my father, his head cracked open, possibly dead, could make him think of me.

When I saw Catherine next—I'd been hustled home by some well-meaning adult, mostly asleep, cried out, exhausted—we both pretended that nothing terrible had happened.

We arrived late at the baths and the women were already in the marble chambers, splayed and naked on low stone slabs; they looked like volunteers for ritual sacrifice. I saw Bahar and Ben Gul and other women I recognized but couldn't name. Everything moved at a crawl and the room was cavernous, the air thick and swampy. Even walking through it felt like an enormous effort, as if we were moving upright against living water. Dark, leathery women edged along the vast perimeter, their limbs stringy, their movements cautious. In shallow marble pools, others hunched in the steam, their slack bellies and arms draped over doughy knees as they worked to locate themselves, all their crevices and hollows, with rough scraps of washcloths. Lining the room were little stone cubicles where you could have a modest amount of privacy, where both hot and cold water spurted forcefully from faucets set deep in the marble walls.

Catherine and I lay cautiously down on the marble slabs. Suddenly, breasts—slick and damp and heavy, entirely unlike the cool, powdered flesh I was familiar with—swung unapologetically against my bare back. A woman began scrubbing me. The sponges felt like steel wool, like the ones Firdis used to scour the kitchen sink. I heard my mother speaking to Bahar in low tones in the pool behind me. I rubbed my own dead skin between my fingers, the grimy, fascinating little balls that came off with the rough sponges.

Bahar was telling my mother about a restaurant she'd recently been to and my mother said she'd like to try it, perhaps when my father returned from his trip.

Bahar laughed. "Very well," she said. "When he returns. But remember please, you already went there with me. Last week, if anyone asks."

Catherine said, "What does she mean by all that?"

I turned my face on the marble and we were eye-to-eye.

"By what?"

We were whispering. Above us, the huge Turkish women talked between the tables in sharp bursts. All the sounds of voices ricocheting around the chamber and hissing steam and running water made it almost impossible to tell who was saying what to whom.

"Your father went away? You never said."

"I thought I did."

"You didn't."

"No?"

"No." Catherine breathed heavily and reached her arms down to brush against the floor. I saw her pale flesh ripple under the force of the scrubbing. "You said he was home in bed indefinitely. You said he was all banged up."

"I don't remember that."

"I do. I remember it specifically."

"Look," I said, and I heard in my voice the heavy, affected exhaustion of a lie. "He went on a trip. I forgot."

"I don't care," she said. "I really don't care. But, still."

She turned her face away and her breathing became even and calm. I thought she'd fallen asleep.

Then she said, "You should say if we aren't going to tell things. You should just say that we're not saying."

My skin tensed over my bones. "You don't tell me every last thing."

"Oh, but I have," she said. "Until now."

I turned my face away on my own bed of marble and closed my eyes. Though I didn't quite believe her, I heard a finality—new, adult, implacable—in her tone. When the women were finished with us and we rose, shaky on our legs, and made for the cubicles to rinse off, we didn't speak. Usually we went together and fought over the cold water, but this time Catherine closed herself into a single stall and left me standing in the steam, my hand outstretched for the door she had just shut behind her.

Simone, wrapped in a towel, sat on the edge of a pool nearby. Her hair, usually so perfect, lacquered and arranged, was pasted stiffly around her pale face. My mother and Bahar were naked, languid and soaking, their big breasts floating on the misty surface like pastries at the bakery.

My mother tilted her head back and looked up at me from that angle, her hair on the marble, her arms outstretched along the edge. Her nipples broke the surface; the water was milky, frothing like foam.

"Lovely, isn't it?" she said, in a drunken tone that seemed to me stagy and put on, overly suggestive.

I went into another stall and closed the door. The pounding water revived me somewhat and I left the suffocating baths and went to the lockers for my clothes. I pulled on my shorts, my dumb shirt, my stupid shoes and went to sit in the lobby. The steaming walls dripped, and everything—my clothes and hair and body—smelled of this water and the dank underground labyrinth of the hamam. Groups of women came out, paid the crone behind the counter and left through the dark tunnel that led to the street. I was parched, my skin flayed and red, my muscles turned to taffy. I drank four tiny glasses of thick, sweet juice that someone would have to pay for and sat there, staring at the slimy floor, waiting for them to emerge.

When they came out—laughing, damp and glowing, scrubbed of

makeup and superfluous skin—it didn't seem they had missed me at all. Outside, in the equally airless afternoon, we wilted into separate taxis and dozed home through the choked streets. What an odd recreation, on such a day. We must have looked as we felt: raw and scoured, tired, for the moment, beyond politeness, beyond questions or recriminations.

AUGUST 1975

4

IN THE LIVING ROOM WHERE BAHAR AND GRACE SIT THE LIGHT IS dimming. Grace's fingers itch for a lamp but the ornate clock on the wall tells her it's too soon. Beside her, Bahar is blond and beautiful—a new shade, the blond, and against her dusky complexion the contrast is stark. Grace sits in silence and inhales the scent that rises from her friend—stale flowers and warm, tanned skin, frequently touched.

In the hallway Firdis is readying for home. Grace hears her taking her things from the closet, moving surreptitiously, like a thief in the house, stealing away.

"Güle güle," Bahar calls. "Çok mersi."

Grace opens her mouth and then shuts it: she is uncomfortable using Bahar's own language in front of her. It makes her feel thick-tongued, strangely vulnerable. She gets to her feet.

"Drink?" she says, instead.

Bahar sighs and checks her wrist, though the time is all around them, ticking, moving too slowly. She half rises and then sits down again.

"Scotch?" she says. "Do you have the good kind?"

"I'm sure we do." Grace crosses to the liquor cabinet, turns the key and finds the bottle. She dislikes scotch but pours them each a glowing glass. She sits back down.

Bahar raises her glass and drinks. She sighs with pleasure; a breath of sweet air escapes her mouth, lingers and then dissipates. "This stuff you Americans have is much better than the shit we find here. And on the black market it is ridiculously expensive. You cannot imagine.

"So," says Bahar, after a pause, "I have a favor to ask of you."

"Shoot."

"Excuse me?"

"Go ahead. Ask." Grace props her legs on the coffee table and shoves an ashtray aside with her foot. "What is it?"

"I was thinking that while Rand is here, while he is recovering, you might help me out someway." Bahar takes a long drink that seems barely to stir the surface of her glass. She sets it down. "Where's the girl?"

"The girl is with her friend, I expect. They run around in the streets like wild Indians. Sometimes I wonder if I should worry."

Bahar nods absently. "That's good," she says. "That's fine." She settles back into the couch and lifts her slender feet next to Grace's.

"Why?"

"No reason. I want to talk to you. You are my good friend. We have had so little time lately. I miss you."

Bahar draws her knees to her chest. She is wearing slim pants and a flowing blouse; the silk gathers around her updrawn knees, floats onto the surface of the sofa. She sighs.

"Here it is, as you say. Ali is here very much now, yes? This is helpful to you, I think. To not have the embarrassment of the American doctors. People asking questions that might be difficult."

Grace senses the stillness of the apartment—Rand is drugged half to death in the other room. A broken rib that punctured a lung, a significant concussion. The American medical facility was closed when he fell; he'd spent the night in the Turkish hospital and then had come home to be cared for by Ali, after some frantic calls to Bahar. It seemed wiser, in those early hours after the accident, to keep his drunken tumble off the radar screens of his superiors. Paige, who had been there that night, had strenuously agreed. It had been her idea to say he'd been called away on business.

"I'm very grateful," she says.

"That's good," says Bahar. "And it's a pleasure to help you. These things are neat in this way, aren't they? I help you, you help me."

"Yes," says Grace. "I was helping before, remember?"

For some little time Grace had been doing favors for Bahar. Her life was distant enough from Bahar's that a real intersection between them was not possible. She was that American woman Bahar played cards with, the one who had asked Ali for a referral to a pediatrician. Just then Bahar was having an affair with her riding teacher, out at the stables in Balgat, a man considerably older than she was, with a rugged and lined face and a wide and smiling mouth. He was charming, with the bandy legs of a lifelong horseman. Grace had met him once at an exhibition at the cavalry grounds where they'd gone as families: Bahar's hooligan boys, Ali, Grace and Rand and Canada. Sitting in crowded bleachers—it was a holiday, some national celebration or commemoration—Bahar rose suddenly from her seat and threaded down through the crush, her bright hair a thing you could follow with your eyes, her big stylish sunglasses propped on her head. She had returned with a man in tow, an upright figure in a uniform, his hair fully white, his posture casual but erect. A man clearly comfortable anywhere, in any situation. Hands were shaken all around.

"Ahmet bey," Bahar had said, by way of introduction.

"Efendi," said Ali and then Rand, each rising slightly from his seat.

The man bowed a little over Grace's hand. Chatting, his eyes strayed to the field, where horses were moving in formation. His gaze was professional, evaluating. Flags snapped in the wind. The day was brilliant, blue and hot. Around them, families opened picnics on their laps, mothers passed food, bright orange soft drinks in bottles.

Bahar's hand rested on the man's forearm; she leaned back against the rail, her summer dress filmy and clinging to her legs. He lit her cigarette, the lighter coming from nowhere, vanishing again into a pocket. A little wreath of smoke circled their heads; Bahar was several inches taller in her heels. The band struck up something stirring.

In the bleachers, Ali turned back to the boys, lifting them by their belts as they scrambled away, up to mischief as always, and bent close to whisper some halfhearted threat or admonishment. Bahar and her friend spoke in Turkish for a few moments. Grace caught only a word here or there; it was still too fast for her.

Turning to her with a quick laugh, the man said, "But we are being rude." He then directed to her some question about the city, and she fumbled for a reply. There was some quality about this man that undid her a little.

Searching for something, she heard herself say, "My daughter, Canada, loves horses. She's always wanted to ride."

"Is it so?" Ahmet said and he swung back to Bahar. "You must bring the girl to the stable with you sometime. Perhaps it is a good distraction for everyone."

Bahar had been looking out over the field; she said without turning, "Yes, I will. What a nice idea."

Grace was suddenly aware of the heat of the day on her shoulders and cheekbones, the warmth of sun through the fabric of her dress, like the sudden flush of a sunburn you hadn't known you had. She'd turned her eyes to the husbands, Ali and Rand, by then engaged in some conversation of their own, Ali pointing to some distant place in the stadium, Rand following his finger. Canada had wandered off somewhere. It astonished her that anyone could miss *this*—this electricity, the shocking radiance of Bahar's smile, the coy tilt of her head. The angle of this man's slim, uniformed body toward hers. To Grace, their studied nonchalance screamed of intimacies.

So, in hidden moments of the day, while ostensibly elsewhere, Bahar was closeted away on the top floor of the Buyuk Ankara hotel, or in Ahmet's trailer at the stables. Often she told Ali she was with Grace—shopping, at the hamam, the zoo—some frivolous but plausible activity. It was Grace's job merely to keep up this pretense at the rare social events where she crossed paths with Ali, to remember that they had been here one day, there the next. And Ali's interest in his wife's whereabouts was negligible, amounting to little more than conversational courtesy: did you have a nice time at this place, or that one? He's a robber, that merchant. I hope you had the dolma, it's very good there. Moving around the apartment in the stultifying daylight hours, without electricity, as Rand recuperated in the bedroom, was maddening, embittering. All day Grace pictured Bahar wrapped in cool linens, running ice cubes along her cheeks and collarbone, her limbs striped with shadow and muscle, while Grace hunted up powdered milk in the kitchen, ferreted out some vital kitchen implement that had grown legs, or wondered vaguely, if at all, where her daughter might be.

But now it seems that Bahar has another favor to ask of Grace and she tucks her shining hair behind her ears. "That is absolutely correct and I do not mean to diminish it. It was very kind, what you did for me. You told Ali we had lunch, is that right? I am very appreciative. Thank you."

Grace looks around the darkening room. Outside the windows she sees lights splashing on; she senses the hum of the city starting up again. The cord of the lamp hangs within reach but she keeps her hands in her lap. On the table in front of her, the amber glass of scotch seems to lose its glimmer, its luster dulls and the light seems to leak away.

"What do you need?" she says. "Tell me and I'll do it."

"Tamam!" says Bahar. "Okay." Her voice is bright with satisfaction but holds not a trace of gratitude—but after all, she is a not a woman accustomed to the word *no*. "Here is what we will do. You will remember what Ali said about the horses, and perhaps also you wish to take Canada off the streets—it is not altogether safe, this running around in Ankara. . . ."

Grace puts her scotch down, pulls her legs onto the sofa and girdles her body with her arms. She presses her cheek against her knee and watches Bahar speak with her hands; she nods in the right places but she has already stopped listening.

SOMETIMES WHEN she is alone in the apartment, as Rand sleeps heavily in the other room, and Canada is off with Catherine, Grace leafs through the photo albums she has meticulously assembled over the years. Always she has the sensation of looking at photographs of strangers. Here she and Rand are leaning against the Rover at a beach in the States; her legs are slim and outstretched, her backside resting on the hood of the car, her hair tied in a scarf with the wind a nearly visible thing—the fabric fans out from her face like a cowl. She is smiling. Another picture has Canada standing between her legs, Grace's hands putting weight on her shoulders, both their faces flushed and freckled. It must be Rand behind the camera.

She remembers that trip well. Some months before orders had come, while they were living on Olson Loop, they took a weekend drive to Rehoboth Beach. The car wheezed over a great, cabled bridge, along endlessly flat roads until the sea came into view, announcing itself subtly, with just a change of light. Finally, the green gave way, revealing a pure glint in the distance. It was as though the world had leveled off, been smoothed by a spatula. There was something lively playing on the radio.

Rand was in a good mood, banging his hands on the steering wheel, tamping a cigarette, his profile clean and slender: he smelled pleasingly of drugstore aftershave. In the backseat, Canada slept, fists balled, lengthening legs pulled to her chin. The Rover, red on the outside, caramel leather on the inside, was finned in the rear and the front, a cheerful little car they had shipped from Germany. Rand loved that car like some people love small dogs. He talked baby talk to the dashboard, and somehow coaxed from it an unnatural longevity.

The place, when they arrived, was clearly army-issue: a long line of barracks, the quarters only nominally converted from their original purpose—a tiny kitchenette had been added, a room lined with bunk beds, a master bedroom the size of a closet. The beach was over a rise of dune and the water concealed a fierce, churning undertow. There was no television, no phone and a rusted showerhead around the back where Grace made Canada strip after the beach: she pushed her under the hard, stinging spray while Canada cowered, covering herself, hands everywhere, trying to fend off the water.

The days became a long, pleasant blur, punctuated by small events: Canada sat on a wasp one afternoon while looking through the grass for four-leaf clovers and they waited the requisite period of time to determine whether she was allergic. Grace was caught in the undertow one morning and went ass over teacup into the surf, her thin white legs sticking up as though she were doing a handstand, for laughs. Rand had thought it hilarious, though Grace had been thoroughly shaken and become cautious of the water.

At the waterline ghostly sand crabs scuttled at high speeds, surprised by the ebbing waves, and Canada chased them, first their little white bodies and then the trail of bubbles they left behind: her hands scrabbled through the wet sand after them with occasional success.

There was a small store on the property, a short walk across the sandy compound, where a meager assortment of groceries could be found and a disproportionately large selection of beer; they carried cigarettes and squishy packages of bread, playing cards, bottles of suntan lotion. In the evenings Grace made meals of peanut butter sandwiches, hot dogs and potato chips. Rand drank steadily at the kitchen table, his hands shuffling cards, dealing out hands of blackjack for himself and Canada. A bare bulb over the table spotlighted ancient stains and spidery fissures in the Formica.

Rand also did card tricks for Canada at the scarred table, her freckled legs pulled up on the chair, her forehead furrowed. He fanned out cards: passing his hands over them, shuffling them deftly, cutting the stack clean as a knife and then miraculously discovering hers in the deck. He also had a sleight in which a saltcellar disappeared right through the table, a napkin swirling over it in graceful folds. At the end, his hand came down with a crash, flattening the empty napkin onto the table, making the furniture, and the audience, jump. Where had it gone? He would never say. Grace, watching that trick more than a decade before, had been delighted. Canada adored it too.

At night they slept under army blankets—stiff and green, smelling of mildew, the sheets coarse as sandpaper. If Grace rolled toward Rand he rolled away, either feigning sleep or lost in a drunken fugue. If his hand touched her hip it was accidental, or in the brush of a dream. Grace fell asleep to his sounds, his snoring, interrupted and confused, his wide nostrils and bare broad chest, stippled with hair. During those long nights she found him inexplicably repulsive and desirable, both.

Edie and Greg had come along on that trip to the beach, though to look at the photograph album you would not know it. During the day Edie and Grace set up camp near the dunes, by the tall, waving beach grasses. They carried down a small cooler filled with Thermoses and sandwiches, then spread their blankets and paraphernalia around them in ever widening circles, taking over the nearly empty stretch of beach, inch by inch. They made jokes about soldierly conduct, about encroaching on neighboring territories, though there were no neighbors to speak of, no enemy camps to overtake. Far down the beach were the shimmering mirages of other little lands like their own, other bases and provinces, with figures that acted out their own miniature plays and maneuvers—running, splashing, roughhousing, all in slow motion.

Edie and Grace had no umbrella and they lay mostly with their shirts across their faces, using their hands to anchor them against the wind. Still, the sand blew and infiltrated and formed a thin film on their bodies, a second, gritty skin that resisted water or scrubbing. The feeling accompanied them throughout the trip and even later; after they'd returned home and taken many hot baths, both women thought they still felt it on their bodies and imagined that it lingered even in the weave and nap of clothing that had stayed behind, folded away in drawers on Olson Loop.

Rand and Greg walked endlessly, restlessly, up and down the beach, fading in and out of sight, behind dunes and curves of coast, strangely unfamiliar in their civilian clothes, their casual short-sleeved shirts and rolled-up trousers, their bare feet. They returned from time to time with pockets full of beach treasure—green glass, bits of driftwood and shells, battered starfish and urchins. They emptied their pockets for Canada's scrutiny and then left again, as though on the trail of something more significant.

Edie and Grace spoke casually, loopingly, of inconsequential things—dinners and lunches and possible shopping trips they might take to nearby tourist towns. Saltwater taffy and shellfish, the famous migrating ponies. They drank from the shared red plastic cap of the Thermos, powdered lemonade with slivers of ice cubes swimming in it. The taste was stale and metallic, and as the day passed it grew watery and gritty with sand.

Grace rose to her elbows from time to time and shaded her eyes to watch Canada playing at the shore. When Edie fell asleep, Grace would get up and begin some project with Canada, a sand castle or a catalog of her beach treasures. But before long Grace would grow bored and wander away, scuffing her feet in the surf, wading ankle-deep but not an inch more. The undertow had given her a good fright. She stared out at the flat gray-green water and waited for Edie to wake from her catnap. Edie grew darker by the day. The sand on her skin shimmered like a golden dust; on Grace's arms it was nowhere near as sultry, it gathered aggressively, dirtily, in the creases of her elbows and at the hollow of her throat.

"What do they talk about, I wonder," Edie said one afternoon, propped up on her arms, watching Canada gather and mound sand in some mysterious design.

The men were visible, but barely, in the distance. Rand's sun hat moved down the beach jauntily; he bent to pick something up and resumed walking.

"I can't imagine," Grace said. They seemed to have nothing in common, these men, yet they had spent the days together quite easily. Grace knew that Rand thought Greg weak and ineffectual, and if his career was stalled, Rand clearly felt it was entirely through some fault of his own. Though, of course, being Rand, he wouldn't discuss it with her in any detail. It was Greg who had championed this trip, had needled and coaxed Edie until at last she'd packed a small bag and stood reluctantly in the sunlight beside the car, looking as if she might at any moment make a dash for the shadows, for the comforting gloom of her own house.

"She's very self-sufficient," Edie said then, presumably referring to Canada. Grace felt a quick, skittering shiver of remorse.

"She's had to be, I guess." Though really, Grace did not have to guess at this. It troubled her: Canada's odd independence, her satisfaction with her own manufactured amusements.

"You should have one," Grace said then, thinking to change the subject.

Edie was quiet. A seagull landed nearby and hopped gracelessly around their encampment. Grace sat up on the bright beach towel and drew her sandy knees up to her chin. "Sorry," she said after a moment. "That was thoughtless."

Edie shook her head back and forth. "No," she said. "It's fine."

They sat there in the sand and pretended to watch Canada mucking near the waterline.

"Well, why not?" said Grace, finally. "You want to, right?" She spoke slowly, feeling the distinct sensation of crossing a boundary.

Edie laughed and it sounded quick and harsh, a little like the gulls crying overhead.

"Two people have to be interested," she said after a while. "At least that's what I continue to tell Greg. Unless I've missed something important. Have I?"

Edie stood abruptly and began to shake out her towel: sand flew wildly, a tiny storm of it blew in their faces, stung their eyes, stuck in their sunblock.

"God," said Edie, brushing her hands at her face, "I'm such a clod. Sorry."

She turned her face away and her hair fell across it: she stayed that way, her features, her expression, hidden.

Grace rose and began to pick up their things. She replaced the cap on the Thermos, refolded a half-eaten sandwich in wax paper, shrugged her shirt on. She glanced down the beach, but the men were nowhere in sight. She called to Canada, who looked up at her strangely, her eyes taking in the packed bundles and rolled towels, their fully dressed bodies. It was hours before the time they usually went in.

They walked back slowly. Canada trailed them, whining. The noise of her spade dragging in the sand seemed designed to make Grace angry, to register her unhappiness at the turn the day was taking. Grace thought about Greg, his unfailing pleasantness, his rather antiquated chivalry with both her and Edie. He was a man who rose from his seat when a woman entered a room and stood until she had situated herself. He had a habit of laughing with his mouth closed, as though he was ashamed of his teeth—for no reason Grace could discern. He treated Edie as though she were exceptionally brittle, not designed to withstand any but the gentlest handling. Beside him Rand seemed coarse and overlarge, too loud, a bit rough-edged.

On their last night at the beach Edie had dropped a glass, it was plastic and merely bounced across the floor but Edie had burst alarmingly into tears and stood sobbing in the middle of the kitchen. After a moment she said, "You don't know what I'm up against."

"No?" Grace said. "What?" She had not moved from the sink; her hands were deep in soapy water.

The wind moved outside, banging the flimsy screen door. The men were still on the beach; they'd taken Canada to watch the sunset.

"Tell me," she said, but she kept her back to Edie and her eyes on the dishes.

After a long moment, Edie said, "I mean do you really think we've been here cooling our heels for two years because they've for-gotten about us? Hardly. They're trying to think of somewhere to stash us, someplace remote and horrible. They just haven't come up with anything suitably dreadful yet."

Grace finished wiping a plate and inserted it into the dish rack. She turned around. "I'm not sure what you're saying."

"Of course I want children, Grace. It's killing me not to have a baby. Maybe I could live with it if I had one. Maybe this would be bearable."

"Then why not? Is there a problem?"

Edie looked up at her, her face wet and angry. "He's not inter-ested in me," she said. "That's it. Not even slightly interested."

"Oh well," Grace said. "I can't say Rand is all that enthralled with me either."

Edie picked up the glass from the floor and set it carefully down on the counter. "And that's not all," she said. "He'll never be pro-moted. He'll never advance. His career is shot."

"Edie," Grace said, "I am utterly lost."

They stood there in the kitchen and looked at each other. Grace heard the cheap clock keeping track on the wall behind her. A child, someone else's, she hoped, screamed outside.

"It's all my fault," Edie said. "I'm not the right kind of wife. They all think I'm completely unsuitable."

"That isn't true," Grace said. "I know it's not."

Regardless of what Edie had meant, what Grace felt just then was almost maternal—maybe the closest thing to it she'd known. She felt the need to console or make right. The feeling would haunt her: so unexpected and foreign, so obviously misplaced. She held Edie's small brown shoulders as she knelt weeping on the linoleum, stroking her hair and speaking nonsense, until Greg's face appeared at the doorway—he saw them there and turned away without a sound, his expression suddenly weary but utterly without surprise.

5

CATHERINE AND I WERE DOWN THE HILL, PERCHED ON HER kitchen counter, daring each other to eat butter straight from the refrigerator. In the background, John hovered, muttering to himself, polishing an ornate silver tea service. The smell of chemicals was acrid and strong. Sunlight came through the kitchen in a wide aisle, like light through a church.

We'd been shaving our arms with Simone's razor—an act we would come to regret—and we both rubbed unconsciously at them, feeling the fresh smoothness of the skin. Our fingers kept returning there, the way a tongue will to an abscess or a cavity.

I was flipping the pages of a book I'd nicked from my mother's shelves called *The Officer's Wife,* some thirty years old. Catherine and I had been having a lot of superior fun with it: the book advised young military brides on the nuances of proper conduct, on military etiquette and how to have parties:

You are your husband's ambassador, it said. *Never underestimate your responsibility for his advancement! Your home, how you conduct yourself, the gracious way you entertain, the admirable deportment of your children—all these things are critical to his career. Let us not forget the example of one busy young wife who forgot to write a proper thank-you note to the wife of a superior officer—this gaffe would stymie her poor husband, and hinder his advancement, for years to come.*

"Listen," I said. " 'Take a large polished pumpkin and fill it with blue morning glories. At the last moment, sprinkle the flowers with ice that has been crushed to a sparkling powder—the effect is one of glistening dew.'"

Catherine was tentatively licking butter from a knife; she made a noise.

"Or," I said, "'Crystal cocktail glasses filled with crushed ice, holding a small fruit cup, can be made very attractive by tinting the ice with a few drops of crème de menthe.' Let's do that."

We were bored. The heat was still fierce during the day but no one was offering to take us to the pool. At night, now, tired of tossing and turning, I often crept into my parents' bedroom and watched my father sleep. I'd become obsessed with the idea of his death, and couldn't seem to count on his ability to keep breathing. These thoughts gnawed at me, making sleep impossible. They drove me from bed, propelled me down the hallway—raised on tiptoes when I passed the den where my mother had taken to sleeping—and compelled me to stand beside the bed. I'm just checking, I told myself every night. Just checking.

Lying huge under the white sheets, my father dwarfed the bed, his belly rising and falling with his inhalations. They seemed steady enough while I stood there, one hand on the pineapple shape of the bedstead finial, toes curling against the prayer rug under my feet. The bandages on his head were getting smaller: at first he'd looked mummified, his entire head enveloped in muslin. Now there was just a small white patch on the side of his head, above his right ear, though a terrible yellow bruise remained along his cheek, and I knew his ribs were taped beneath the bedclothes. He lay with his mouth open and his breath was strong and stale. On the bedside table were a glass of water, a small brigade of pill bottles, extra bandages. Every afternoon Ali came by to change them, to prod around with his delicate fingers and announce progress. Ali was a kind, cheerful man, ever an optimist, an accomplished smoother-over of uncomfortable situations. He patted my head reassuringly; he slipped forbidden pieces of gum into my pockets.

During these examinations my mother sat in the living room, wan, quiet and angry. I sensed this—it did not take a genius—and gave her a wide berth. She smoked relentlessly, sitting in a brocade chair with her arms stiff and her legs crossed. Sometimes Bahar was there as well, doubling the smoke and thickening the general air of tension. The two sat mostly in silence, though from time to time there was a harsh laugh or a flurry of whispering.

Lately even Firdis had been working with exaggerated caution, taking baby steps down the hallway, moving in such a falsely solicitous way that it made me want to scream. She'd developed a habit of standing too close, cornering me, her broad dark face at a level with my own as she shook her head back and forth, making tsking noises. "Poor Baba," she would say, with a very grave expression. "Poor, poor Baba."

I extricated myself ungraciously, my stomach turning over, face afire. I couldn't stand Firdis; her dank smell, her oily hands. She liked to grab my cheeks and tug at them, saying, "Çok güzel, çok güzel." I was not çok güzel—very beautiful—anyone could see that. I stayed shut inside my room, rereading books, memorizing epic poems.

At night, standing in the dark, I watched my father for what seemed like hours. The room was full of his breathing and his intermittent snores. The furniture seemed close and vaguely alive. The shapes grew as familiar in the dark as they were in daylight, a low silhouette of jutting corners and angles, of bedposts and window edges, the glowing trinkets on my mother's vanity, a white smile of doily edging the bedside lamp.

But during the daylight hours Catherine and I had taken to harassing John, to being underfoot in the kitchen and following him around making nuisances of ourselves. Since my father's accident, something imperceptible had shifted in our triad. Now John brushed against Catherine more than ever, his hand touched her waist and when she stepped away from him her face was flushed pink and her eyes avoided mine.

"'Suggested Luncheon Menus,'" I read. "Fruit cup. Broiled chicken. Tomato-avocado salad. Jellied consommé. Spinach ring."

Catherine brushed wisps of hair from her face, which she had pulled back in a tight ponytail, the way Simone liked it. Catherine's face was elfish and pale, but still beautiful. I should have been used to it but it was a continuing, unhappy surprise. When we stood side by side in the mirror, I concentrated on Catherine's features instead of my own, her broad forehead and delicate nose, her wide mouth and perfect teeth. What would it be like in there—moored inside Catherine's flawless self?

The phone rang and John answered it in the kitchen. He spoke in Turkish into the receiver, and Catherine and I went through the refrigerator, looking for ingredients we could transform into something else.

John had begun letting us do foolish things, probably dangerous things, in his kitchen. He let us use Simone's food coloring to tint ice and butter and mayonnaise. He let us make hollandaise sauce and selections from *The Officer's Wife*'s list of "Twenty-five Suggested Appetizers." Seeded green grapes, split and filled with Gruyère cheese. Seasoned cream cheese wrapped in dried beef funnels. Celery stuffed with Roquefort. He let us arrange the table in the way the book advised: we manufactured Easter luncheons and festive Mexican-themed teas and we speared all sorts of things with Simone's fancy ruffled toothpicks. We devoted an entire afternoon to the "Dresden Bouquet" salad, reputedly a luncheon favorite at the Argyle. We followed the directions to the letter:

The cauliflower is first boiled; then the flowerets are separated and each tinted with food coloring in delicate shades of blue, pink, orchid, green and yellow. The bouquet is placed in a basket of lettuce or rose leaves and French dressing is poured over all.

Had she known about any of this, Simone would have had a litter, so all the evidence had to be completely eradicated from the kitchen before she returned home. Into a bag it went, unceremoniously: the colored vegetables, the sparkling greenish ice, the tiny, perfect stacks of cheeses and olives. John helped us do it, fussily and with little humor, never making a noise about the waste. We carried the garbage out to the broiling alley behind the apartment building, skirting the little Turkish girls jumping rope and the kapıcı, introspective as ever, busy with his ear.

Catherine hummed while we cleaned, a piece of disco music that was forever coming out of John's radio. Often, in the kitchen on those long afternoons, they seemed like a very young married couple, slightly built and similarly boyish, moving around each other with ease, handing things to each other, exchanging smiles when they bumped.

School would be starting soon and though we wouldn't have admitted it, we were looking forward to it. We missed the regimentation of days, the structure of lessons, the odd comfort of queuing for everything. We were tired of being left to our own devices; perhaps we were even amazed by what we'd gotten up to.

John ended his conversation and put the phone down. He took the things Catherine was holding and began to stack them and return them to the refrigerator. I was watching his hands touch Catherine's as he did it—the dusk against the white, the almost indiscernible caress of his fingers on hers.

"Your cat is finished," he said.

A moment passed before I realized he was talking to me. It happened so rarely. "I beg your pardon?" I said. "I'm sorry, what?"

"The cat is gone. Firdis let him go."

"Let him go? What do you mean let him go? Go where?"

John shrugged. He clearly had no interest in the cat or what had happened to it.

"He doesn't go out," I said. "Never."

John ignored me. He put the food away; he returned to the silverware. The matter was closed as far he was concerned and my panic made no impression on him.

It took Catherine to extract the details from him. That morning, while my father lay in bed recuperating, Firdis had let Pasha escape. Apparently, he'd slipped out while she was taking bread from the kapıcı and arguing with him about the state of the fruit he'd brought.

Pasha, the cat we'd rescued from the street, now liked to sit on the edge of the balcony and look down disdainfully on the place he had come from. He'd grown up to be massive and imperious: a Persian cat of some kind, with snow-white fur and mismatched eyes and a terrible disposition. I was perpetually covered with claw marks, the result of trying to love him and make him love me back. Pasha had strange habits. He would snooze twenty-three hours a day on the sofa in the living room, in a patch of sun, until something stirred him and he would spring up and fly hysterically around the room, skidding on the hardwood floors, ricocheting off furniture in a blur of white angora. When he sat on the balcony, flicking his tail gently, quiet and contemptuous, his chest would puff out like the feathery breast of a great white bird.

I made Catherine come with me to look for Pasha. He couldn't have gone far, I thought, surely he would be somewhere on our street, a place I knew like the back of my own hand. It was her idea to bring John.

"He can ask people," she said. "He can help."

John said, "I do not care about this stupid cat."

Nonetheless, he came. He walked behind us, with his hands in his pockets, and made not even the slightest pretense of looking for any cat.

Once in a while that summer we tagged along with John on errands he was dispatched to do for Simone. We were never expressly invited, but he made no move to stop us. Striding ahead of us through the streets, we had the impression that he wanted not to be seen in our company. We always had to hustle to keep up, to maintain sight of his slim, straight back, the triangular wings of his arms jammed casually into his pockets. His cool never left him, never burned off in the heat of the day, it could not be shaken by irate crowds or crabby shopkeepers. He brushed away the goods held out to him, lifted his chin sharply and kept moving, sliding through the solid mass of bodies like a wraith.

On this day, as we walked through Gasi Osman Paşa calling out for the cat, John hung back and studied the trees and the sidewalks. He whistled from time to time, but only to himself. He checked his wristwatch occasionally. The neighborhood sprawled across several hills and there were a thousand places to look. Catherine and I crawled under cars and opened trash cans; we looked in the glittering coal heap and walked the empty field where children sledded in the winter—we'd done it once or twice ourselves, until some Turkish boys had taken our sled from us and flung it into the street. We yelled ourselves hoarse, and by the end our feet hurt and my eyes stung with tears I could not allow myself to shed in front of John. We walked all the way to the Russians, where we stood and stared at their gates, at the stiff-legged men with guns who strode back and forth behind them.

My mother had driven me by this compound once or twice but I had never seen it so closely. I had always imagined the Kremlin looking like this, huge and fortified and angry at the world. The whole thing was several city blocks, invisible from the street, sealed off by a huge surrounding wall. The Russians lived and worked inside; my father said they weren't allowed out. I had a vague idea that what all of us were doing in Turkey, and what our fathers did all day, had something to do with the people who lived behind those walls.

Catherine and I had always been fascinated by the Russian compound, by the very idea of it. Standing there in the broad daylight,
glimpsing the facade through the heavy gates, gave me a shivery
kind of pleasure. In light of what we'd been told—about the confinement of its inhabitants, the secrecy of their lives—we felt freer,
more independent and less shut-in ourselves. In Catherine's room,
we'd even manufactured a lovely Russian girl named Vassilissa, who
peered out from the window of her prison and dreamed of walking
around in the streets as we did: eating apple tarts from the bakery,
buying ice cream cones from the street vendors. She always went
about in a fur coat, saying, da, da, da, which was the only Russian
word we knew, aside from *koshka,* for cat, and we didn't allow Vassilissa to have one of those. We didn't think Russians kept cats.

John slipped away, into a store, and Catherine and I stood near
the gates, trying to get our bearings. The air smelled of ripe fruit
from a vendor across the street, where flies swarmed on mounds of
dark plums and apricots. Catherine leaned against a thin tree and
took a stone out of her shoe. When John came back, he was eating a
plum, catching the bright juice in his hand. He steadied Catherine's
elbow as she shook out her other shoe, then he held the bitten plum
up to her mouth. Purple juice dripped lazily onto the sidewalk and I
looked away.

The buildings there were a little larger and set farther apart. My
mother had a Turkish acquaintance who lived nearby, an unmarried
woman who slept at night in an enormous hammock under a blanket
of rescued cats, surrounded by flowering tropical plants. Perhaps
Pasha might find his way there, to Ben Gul; her name meant a thousand roses. My mother had taken me to her one afternoon to have
my ears pierced, and the woman came at me in the kitchen with a
darning needle and ice cubes. The procedure did not go smoothly—
I was fidgeting, Ben Gul said—and my mother fainted inconve-
niently in the middle, going limp against the counter that held the

coffeepot and then sliding down it luxuriously, her eyes blinking like a butterfly's wings. While Ben Gul attended to her, the darning needle remained halfway through my ear, quivering in the cartilage. I looked around the kitchen (I could see the tip of the needle out of the corner of my eye): an orange cat was sitting on top of the refrigerator; a collage of cherry pits adhered to the counter; on the floor underneath the stool they put me on was a cat turd, dried and nearly fluffy with age, which moved with the motion of the air in the room, rolling gently back and forth. Ben Gul fanned at my mother's face with a fluted coffee filter. In the end, I had holes that didn't match, and wearing earrings made me look asymmetrical and strange.

We didn't find Pasha until we'd walked almost all the way home. By then John was in front of us, annoyed at the turn the day had taken and no doubt thinking of Simone and what she'd have in store for him when he returned. I was planning to sit outside our building, on the front steps, holding a can of cat food as long as necessary. All night if I had to. It was John who spotted Pasha at the deep end of an alley several blocks from the apartment. Some Turkish boys had found him first. It was stunning what they'd done to him. He was pinned against the fence in the corner of the alley; his lovely fur had been ripped out in hunks, and a match had been taken to his tail; they had probably killed him with stones at the end, for the ground around him was littered with rocks. He was such a dignified creature, Pasha, so pompous and regal. The twisted creature we saw—claws extended, mouth frozen in a silent yowl—might have been unidentifiable were it not for the little belled collar on his neck.

"Was this your cat?" John said, and he put out his arm to hold Catherine back. He didn't have to—neither of us was going to go any closer.

"Don't look," he said to her and then spun her around so that she faced the street. Standing there, my own legs did something strange—they both turned to rubber and wanted to run; my whole body quivered with those competing instincts—the need for speed and movement and the desire to fall screaming to the ground. I wanted to break and throw and destroy things: kill people, tear down buildings, desecrate mosques.

We left his body there. Neither of us was brave enough to pick him up, and John would not even consider it. Then we walked home in silence, shaking, too horrified for words.

It speaks to the state of things in our house that when I told my mother, she shook her head as if confused and went first to look for him in the living room, then under my bed and finally, out on the balcony. Then she came back and said, "Now tell me this again."

6

GRACE SETS HER ELBOWS ON HER DRESSING TABLE. IT IS SEVEN o'clock but the day seems to be ceding nothing to evening, not in terms of temperature. Her evening gloves—clean, pearl buttoned— are folded on the edge of the table. Her mother's silver dresser set sits at a neat slant in the center of the vanity—a white-bristled brush, a rattling mirror—each with similarly patterned reliefs: voluptuous Victorian women and cherubic babies, frolicking in tarnished sterling.

The dressing mirror hangs on hinges between two carved wooden posts. It reflects in the background the double bed she used to share with Rand, a four-poster with pineapple carvings, a peaked headboard. A nubby chenille bedspread, two flat pillows, her bedside lamp, now casting pools of light on the tatted doily. Rand is bulkily asleep, the air stale with his breathing: the whole room needs a good airing out.

Grace is forty years old today. Right now, this very minute. Forty.

She hears stuttering flamenco notes from the other side of the wall, from the den, where she has been sleeping, where Canada sits now with her classical guitar teacher. Another elusive Turkish name. Grace shakes her head a little, attempts a laugh. She tries it for the mirror. Wrinkles. No. Parentheses. They stack up on either side of her mouth when she smiles. She runs a hand down the left side of her nose, her fingernail in the slice that runs from the edge of her nostril to her chin. Funny. She hadn't thought she'd laughed all that much.

Dear Edie, she writes in her head, *I'm ancient, how about you?*

Grace forces herself back to the mirror. She leans forward and examines her face. The changes are both imperceptible and obvious; she contemplates the incongruity of that, holding a powder puff in one hand.

Among other things, Grace cannot bring herself to mention this newest disgrace of Rand's to Edie: the details seem shameful, and it's as if they reflect even more poorly on her than on her husband. Reputations here are built on such shifting sands; the potential for disgrace seems to lurk around every corner. Now the women's eyes seem to study her, evaluate her and find her wanting. Still, it's been surprisingly easy to sell the story of his trip to the embassy people; they are all so immersed in their own secrecies that it doesn't faze them when one of their number disappears without explanation. Grace mattes her face with powder, buffs it from the tiny lines, where it gathers, cakes. She's never felt quite as pale as she does in this country. She brushes out her hair in hard, strong strokes, then twists it behind her head in a knot. She is wearing her slip and underwear, the thin silky straps slip from her shoulders, the sheath of it hugs her belly, the wide lace hem is tight against her thighs.

She hears the door of the den open; the lesson has ended. Now she'll listen to Canada's fingers picking little riffs, practicing, for the next week. Strings buzzing, the notes jarring and discordant, but once in a while she'll hear a pretty little thing, a little Latin waterfall of strings. She gets up to write a check, shrugs her robe on. She hears Canada's footsteps padding down the hall, the front door opening and closing. Heading for Catherine's down the street, no doubt, which is where Grace is going too in a few hours, for a party Simone is giving. Grace sighs at the thought of it and opens the door to face the guitar teacher, a man whose fingers seem too wide and thick to produce the agile sounds she hears from his instrument: "Malaguena" and "Adagio," other swift, familiar pieces. With Grace he is obsequious; in the den with Canada, the door closed, his voice rises, admonishing, threatening. Grace knows he takes her fingers and stretches them across the frets—*so,* she hears him say, and *so.* Canada's fingers, when she catches a glimpse of them, are raw and calloused and each pad carries a short, deep stripe left by the cat gut.

She cannot turn up the checkbook and Firdis has gone for the day, on the bus home to Çankaya, where her husband is a kapıcı in a better apartment building than this one. Why, oh why, can't this woman leave things where they belong?

In apologetic gestures, she communicates all this to the guitar teacher, who bows his concession but is clearly displeased. He sucks his belly in and lifts his guitar through the door. She hears him humph on the landing, and curse in English as the case bangs against the rail.

Grace pads down the narrow corridor, past the closets (neither bedroom has its own; they line the hallway, little boxes, hardly deep enough for the shoulders of Rand's suits and uniforms), past the postage-stamp-size kitchen, where three grown people cannot stand comfortably. The curtains on the balcony door hang in the still air; Firdis has left the door cracked, despite what Grace tells her, and now the kitchen smells of the city. There is a phrase the Americans like to throw around, about apartment hunting: Mutfak utfak, ama farketmez. The kitchen is too small, but it doesn't matter. In the beginning, they like the way it sounds—almost naughty, a silly little phrase, nearly rhyming. But now it does matter. You can't turn around without touching something—the tiny round table, the avocado-green refrigerator. It makes Grace itch to stand in there, where the smell of Firdis and her cooking gathers and coils, invisible and inescapable.

Grace dreads tonight's party. She steps down the hall to the closet at the far end and studies its contents. Dressing for Simone—perfect, meticulous, climbing Simone—is always perilous. She'll have Catherine in a princess dress, passing canapés and clearing glasses—Catherine, with her squared shoulders and lowered head, her remote eyes, her polite, murmuring answers. What do they have in common, those two girls? Catherine's behavior is always impeccable but she often seems to Grace more like a mannequin than a child—almost too beautiful, too perfect and robotic to love. Simone is grooming Catherine for a career in ballet, carting her to lessons, choreographing recitals, terrorizing the teacher. Everyone has heard about Simone's own career in dance, but the general suspicion is that the stories are highly exaggerated. Also, she has installed a barre in the hallway, Grace heard recently.

Simone's parties are all the same: dully elegant, engineered by that houseboy she holds in such suspiciously high regard. John is not his name, of course, but it's what Simone chooses to call him. So classically, so perfectly Simone.

Grace selects a dress—pale, simple, unremarkable—and returns to her room. She would very much like to know where the checkbook has got off to; there is something about Firdis's reordering of her household that strikes her lately as proprietary, presumptuous. She imagines Canada will be down the hill tonight as well—that she will run into her own daughter at a party. She anticipates being amazed by her good manners, her helpfulness—the Simone effect—enviable, but not, as far as she can see, replicable.

Before she leaves she wakes Rand and doses him with pills. He is very nearly better now, though Grace can hardly bear to look at him. When she does, she cannot help but think of Bahar and

Ahmet, and all the imagined details of their trysts. In recent weeks, Bahar has become breezy and distant, and since her appearance at card games can no longer be counted on, Grace's attendance has slipped as well.

AT THE party later, Grace's eyes find Catherine standing by the balcony doors, a macramé plant holder dangling behind her, cradling a potted ivy. Catherine's head is raised to John's and he leans near her, whispering, a tray upheld on one palm, the other hand shielding his mouth. The black shoulder of his jacket presses the ruffled cap of Catherine's sleeve, flattening it, and the girl's expression is wholly unreadable. Her own daughter is nowhere in sight.

Grace studies them for a moment and then turns away, with the feeling that her attention—and that alone—is interrupting something private. They seem engrossed and strangely complicit, the two of them—an island, the party lapping at them gently but without consequence.

Grace catches Simone's eye then; she is standing by the doorway in a cluster of men in dress uniform. In her expression and the angle of her body, her bright smile and fluttering hands, is a kind of antic, half-hysterical vivacity. Something passes between the two women then and Simone turns her head away. Then she touches the shoulder of a man in a tuxedo and glides toward Grace, her dress the color of champagne, rustling softly around her ankles.

"Having a nice time?" she says. "Single girl out on the town."

Grace smiles tightly. "Lovely. I'm forgetting what it's like to be married."

"No such luck though, right?" says Simone. Her eyes are heavily lined, her lips sugary pink. "Unless you've killed him and not told us how you've gotten away with it. Which would be dreadfully mean of you." She wags a finger. "Unforgivably so."

"Don't worry," says Grace, "you'll be the first to know."

"Will I?" she says, ever so lightly. Her head swivels, surveying the room. "Sometimes I think I don't know a blessed thing. I feel totally out in the cold half the time."

Grace sets her glass down on the piano. Simone deftly slides a napkin beneath it and then, rubbing her fingers together, brings some small pearls of moisture from the glass to her lips. "I mean, you and Bahar are so chummy these days, and Rand has been off on one of his superimportant missions. It seems like years since we've seen him."

"Yes," says Grace, "I know what you mean."

"Maybe we should play bridge? Just us English-speaking girls? I can't stand all the language nonsense, personally. I always feel as if they're making jokes at my expense."

"Really?" says Grace. "I think they've been quite gracious."

Simone smiles. "Well, they like you, don't they? You fit in so well, you're so awfully good that way. It's a talent of yours I envy. Always flattering them and currying favor. Complimenting their awful decorating, that terrible hair, their spoiled children. You're the real diplomat, Grace. We could all take lessons."

Grace touches her hand to her warm face and laughs. But it comes a beat too late and Simone pinches her upper arm, as if to suggest she was just being mischievous. As if either of them thought her capable of it.

"And now," she says brightly, "I must go whip the help into shape. That fellow visiting from Riyadh is stag too, so I've put you next to him. Do try to behave yourself, though—we wouldn't want any nasty rumors started." She laughs. "I mean we're totally full up in that department already, don't you think?"

Later that night, Grace opens the door to the bedroom where Rand is sleeping—she's a little tipsy, the evening has been filled with questions that were a little too piercing, a little too hard to deflect—and finds Canada standing half asleep, rocking a little on her feet, at the foot of the bed. The air in the room is sticky with alcoholic breathing. (Rand is sneaking booze again; she's begun to find smeary glasses behind the curtains and underneath the bed.) She takes Canada back to bed, pulls the covers around her shoulders and sits there for a moment in her dress and tight shoes, looking around her daughter's unfamiliar room.

After a while she gets up and walks into the den. She unfolds the blanket from the back of the rough tweed couch and props a pillow against its hard wooden arms. The space is cramped; her knees knock against the coffee table if she shifts position in any dramatic way. Still, she sleeps soundly enough. The things she would like to say to Rand she keeps to herself. The fear she saw in his eyes those first few days is gone. Now he is defensive and falsely jolly. How does he remember that night anyway? She hasn't asked and doesn't intend to. He's gracefully held up the story: water-slick tile, the confusion of lights and darkness, a freak accident, one that might have happened to anyone. A bump on the head, and then the call in the night, the secret business he'd suddenly been called away on. In fact, she'd overheard him on the phone with some superior in the States a few days earlier, telling this very same story. Their pretenses have coincided again, conveniently, and to his benefit.

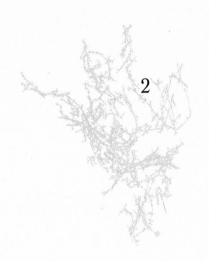

2

SEPTEMBER 1975

7

IN SEPTEMBER SCHOOL BEGAN. CATHERINE AND I MET IN FRONT of my apartment and walked together to the bus stop at the end of the street. The building next to ours was still under construction; the workmen stood around drinking coffee, eating simits over a fire in a rusted barrel. The flames licked up into the morning air and the men shouted at us, as they always did, when we crossed the street to walk on the rough wall that bordered the vineyard. I replied with an expression John used routinely with beggar children, and offered the corresponding hand gesture. Their laughter carried across the street, followed us all the way down to the corner, where we waited under spreading trees. Turkish schoolchildren in their uniforms drifted by in twos and threes, the boys in short pants, the girls in dark skirts and white blouses, chattering. Standing there, kicking at the ground, I held all of them responsible for Pasha's death. My mother had offered to get another kitten, but her callousness about it infuriated me. I was not speaking to Firdis, either. I often dreamed about Pasha and the way we had found him—tortured, mutilated, discarded.

Both Catherine and I attended a private school at the British Embassy, though I had lobbied hard for the American school on the base. My mother wouldn't hear of it: she had strong, ingrained ideas about the inferiority of American education. Our school was housed on the British Embassy grounds in a low-slung, modernish building with glass windows tinted the color of Coca-Cola in bottles. A cricket pitch was being laid behind the school and above that sat the embassy and the Anglican Church, which we'd attended with some regularity when we first arrived in Ankara. The embassy also had a swimming pool in which we were obligated to take morning lessons—regardless of the weather. It was nothing like the Canadian pool and we dreaded it. The water was glacial, the changing rooms moldy and cramped. We crowded in on chilly mornings before classes, when both air and water were far too cold, and swam straight through the first frost. We stood shivering at the edge in bathing caps and regulation navy one-pieces, toes curling, goose pimples peppering our skin, while the swimming mistress, a thick, squeaky woman with no common sense, wetly shrilled a whistle. She called to us in nasal English syllables to: "Crack it, girls. It's worse standing here than it is in the water."

But it wasn't. The water was bone chilling, breath stealing. We swam, still shivering, always shivering, up and down the roped-off lanes, until our turns mercifully ended and we scurried into the changing rooms to paste our clothes back on, wring out frigid suits and pull off leaky bathing caps. We passed the boys walking in a line back down the hill, all of them skinny and sharp featured, whispering to one another, reaching out with bony hands to grab someone's hair, a sleeve, the hem of a skirt. Hands were slapped, there were urgent, thrilled whispers of, "Stop it. Cut it out. Don't." Our two lines were parallel for only a few moments, but in those instants a range of sophisticated interactions occurred: sweets changed hands, plans were formed, threats were made and met.

The school was a gathering of embassy children from all over the world. We followed the English curriculum, studying Latin and algebra and literature and French. We segregated ourselves, the boys and the girls, steering well clear of one another except when we were forced to mingle—for dancing lessons or field days or the production of plays. *Toad of Toad Hall* was planned for the winter pageant and I was to play Rat, a role of which I was terrifically proud but which I pretended, with elaborate weariness, to feel was a great, unwelcome chore.

At lunch Catherine and I sat on the hill above the cricket pitch and spoke idly of the boys. They did not, for the most part, interest us. They ran wildly around on the pitch below, fighting with one another and kicking soccer balls around, running up the hill occasionally to torment us with profanities and innuendo.

Every day Catherine wore a long grosgrain ribbon in her hair, very old-fashioned, and a blouse with a Peter Pan collar. Her legs were smooth and pale, like the marble limbs of statues I had seen with my father. I knew that Simone picked out her clothes for her and laid them out on the bed every evening. I was left to myself in this regard and as a result I generally looked very silly, or messy, or dirty. In the mornings my mother brushed my hair, which was long and dark and horribly tangled. The ritual often ended in tears, and in the second week of school it concluded with the back of my mother's silver hairbrush smashing into my mouth. I went to school humiliated and frightened, and had hidden my bloody mouth—I was certain teeth were loose—from everyone, including Catherine. I kept my mouth closed and went to the bathroom three times to cry.

After school, I walked up the hill slowly and was surprised when I reached the top to find my mother waiting there. She and Bahar were spending the afternoons together, visiting the orphanage or driving to the outlying villages to help teach English to the local schoolchildren.

But there she was on that afternoon, sitting in the red Rover, wearing sunglasses and a headscarf, her face puffy. She was smoking a cigarette out the window, and when I climbed into the car she grabbed me fiercely. Her chin dug into my shoulder; she knocked the breath clean out of me.

"I'm sorry," she said wildly. "I'm so sorry. I'm just having a terrible time right now." She pulled her scarf away from her face. "I must be a terrible, rotten, miserable mother."

It was not my mother's custom to apologize to children. But I heard her usual, overdramatic manner, her desire to be placated and comforted. Most of all, she was fishing to be told that she was not as bad as that, not as bad as she said.

And it was soon after that that I was allowed to begin horseback riding lessons.

GETTING TO the American base, Balgat, required a long drive down unpaved roads, past Atatürk's tomb—a huge memorial and mausoleum that could be seen from virtually everywhere in the city. While Catherine went to ballet after school, my mother began driving me there and I learned to ride on a vaulting saddle and eventually on an actual saddle on an actual horse. I had campaigned for years to ride. I'd been told it was too expensive, or inconvenient or impractical.

"It's simply convenient now," she'd said when I asked. "Bahar's friend has offered to teach you. It's very kind of him. Say thank you."

On a horse Ahmet looked like a statue you might find crowning a monument; striding around the ring, he slapped his tall boots with a whip and called out to me that he could see Atatürk's tomb between my backside and the saddle, which was his way of scolding me. "Sit it down," he said, "or I will glue it to the saddle. I have done it before."

While he taught me in the big dusty ring, my mother sometimes watched from a white bench nearby. But on many days she never even left the car. Bahar was usually there as well, cantering her big chestnut horse over red and white barrels in the jumping ring. Beyond the ring were long stretches of open land, scrubby green fields that rose up to the horizon.

The stables soon occupied almost all my free time. I loved being there—the big heads of the horses hanging over their stalls looking for sugar and peppermints, the smell of hay and oats and the extraordinary, matchless feeling of being aloft, of flying around the ring. I learned to tack and groom, to fall and remount, to clean saddles and bridles, to muck out stalls. Often we did not get home until well after dark. It must have been exceptionally boring for my mother, who eventually, as the weather turned, began spending the whole time in the car, reading travel brochures and writing letters. In the late afternoons Bahar and Ahmet bey often sat together in the little trailer near the entrance that served as his office. It had a couch and a lamp, a big desk on which he did paperwork and a hot plate. They consumed huge quantities of tea in there, and you could often hear their laughter through the flimsy walls.

Sometimes in the afternoons, while she waited, my mother would obsessively plan trips to points of artistic or cultural or archaeological interest. Perhaps this distracted her. When I opened the car door and slid inside, she would go on and on about her plans, pushing pictures under my nose and telling me to look at this or that, to think of the history, the significance, to appreciate the opportunity we had to see these places. I could not have been less interested.

The car was filled up with her—the cigarettes and Arpège, the smell of laundered clothes and the noise of those bracelets moving on her wrists—and it overwhelmed and infuriated me. I rode home with my nose pressed against the cold glass, counting telephone poles or yellow automobiles, whatever I had arbitrarily chosen, ignoring her.

Meanwhile, my father recovered. His driver brought to the apartment large stacks of paperwork and other documents and he began moving around, slowly at first, but with increasing strength and humor. I had never seen so much of him.

It was growing colder, the leaves had turned and the air was perfumed with woodsmoke from the fires that burned on the streets, and with the hot smell of street food—roasting lamb and sesame and bread. Swimming at school stopped—even the hearty British drew the line somewhere—and Catherine and I sat above the cricket pitch with our skirts pulled over our knees and our hands under our sweaters for warmth. We wore our heavier tights and watched the boys' exertions below us, their white breath mingling in the air, their shoes making a faint noise on the frost. Inside, the school smelled of coats and scarves and gloves—of damp wool and sweet sweat, of chalk and the pages of books, the breezy perfume our Latin teacher wore.

We said to each other: Hic, haec, hoc. Huius, huius, huius. Agricola, agricolarum. Amo, amas, amat. We were both struggling with Latin pluperfect, but Catherine's French was exquisite, compliments of Simone's insistence on speaking French at the dinner table.

When our afternoons were free, which was rarely, we went to Catherine's apartment. We had plowed through the entire text of *The Officer's Wife,* had followed many of its recipes and drilled each other on matters of protocol. Though we did it laughingly, disdainfully, I think we both harbored the vague notion that these skills might one day be valuable. We thought we might end up like our mothers—leading the same glamorous, vagabond lives, traveling in diplomatic circles.

Catherine's father, like mine, was not around much. He was an attaché, with sloping shoulders and nicotine-stained fingers. When he was home he was quiet and unobtrusive and Simone bossed him around mercilessly; he had the air of a man who'd been long neutered. It was clear that Simone did not need a husband, except in the most desultory of ways, and she moved through the world with an off-putting competence, battering down walls with the force of her personality. What Simone did all day, and what my mother occupied herself with, was somewhat obscure. They overlapped in social circles and sometimes played cards together. But Simone was tight with the Canadian ambassador's wife and had wrangled a little position as her social secretary: she spent a few afternoons a week penning invitations and thank-you notes, which on the surface seemed beneath her but was actually a social leg up, a way of knowing nearly everything.

"All serving of food is from the left, and dishes are removed from the right. It's not rocket science, and since the ambassador will be here you will please take pains to do it correctly."

We overheard Simone as we slid into the apartment, already taking off our shoes. She called us in: she was in the dining room with John, who stood with his hands folded at his back and his feet apart like a soldier at attention.

"Girls," she said. "I'm glad you're here."

Catherine and I glanced at each other in the hallway; being summoned by Simone was ever a thing to dread.

She wore a red and white striped day dress and low-heeled shoes; she looked like an awning or a deck chair, and her creamy skin carried two spots of bright blush on the cheekbones. They were a little riveting, those two apple-colored circles.

"You're gaping," she said to me, very snappily. "Don't gape. How's your father?"

The whole time she was fussing around the table, moving a salad fork a centimeter to the right, examining a water goblet for streaks.

"Fine," I said.

"Has he come back?"

I considered this for a moment.

"No," I said finally, uncertainly. I wasn't sure if I was allowed to say that at that very moment, he probably was in our apartment; I had seen him just hours earlier, going through papers in his dressing gown.

Simone narrowed her eyes. "Really?" she said. "It's very mysterious. No one's seen hide nor hair of him since he took that nasty fall." She paused. "Your father is one of those people who really shouldn't drink."

It did not trouble Simone at all to say things like this—she was extraordinarily tactless, though I believe she thought herself forthright.

She stared at me for a moment. I heard John shift position, ever so slightly. I glanced over; he might have been made of wood. Then she brushed her hands together brusquely and said to Catherine, "I need you dressed this evening. I've hung it up on the closet door. Put it on and brush your hair. Better yet, have John do your hair. You'll make a botch of it. You'll pass canapés during cocktails and then have dinner in the kitchen."

We all stood there for a beat until she clapped her hands and said, "Well? That's all. Don't stand around like automatons, go do something productive."

"Jesus," said Catherine under her breath, as we escaped down the hallway. "What a cunt."

"A what?" I said.

"It's a very bad word," she said. "Maybe the worst. John told it to me. He says it all the time."

"What is it in Turkish?"

"Amcyk."

"Huh," I said. I rolled it around in my head, committing it to memory.

"What else did he tell you?"

That afternoon I learned all the foul language John had taught Catherine, all the native profanities, the colorful insults and curses he used to describe Simone. Cross-legged on Catherine's twin beds, with her neat dresser holding her matching comb and hairbrush and mirror, the ruffled lamp on her bedside table, her pictures in little silver frames, we quizzed each other on the terrible words John whispered to her, all the vulgar things we had known to be true about Simone, but had only, until then, had one inadequate set of words for. The whole time we talked, she fingered a string of rough blue beads like the ones my mother had at home. I had never seen them before.

John had given Catherine a few pieces of jewelry—a bracelet with an evil eye bead, a Maşallah pendant like the one my mother wore around her neck. Catherine had given some of these to me to hold and I kept them taped inside the lid of an orange plastic record player. I looked at them often in secret, touching the graceful strokes of the Arabic symbol, or putting the beads to my tongue, feeling the strange protrusion of the blue eye, the cool, lacy metal of the silver. Neither of us wanted to be seen with these items but I hoarded them like a dragon's treasure, as if they were gifts from my own boyfriend.

Later, while Catherine bathed, I helped Simone set the dinner table: you would have thought that the precise positioning of salad forks was a matter of life and death. When I returned to Catherine's room, John was standing behind her at the dressing table, brushing her hair—gently lifting the dark weight of it and hefting it in his hand. He pulled the brush through it in long, slow, sleepy strokes. I thought of my mother yanking through mine that morning and how that had ended and I saw the tenderness in his touch and then, suddenly, the way he pulled her head back hard and bent his face over hers. He was about to say something; his lips parted. He saw me in the mirror then and his hands moved away. He stepped back, laid the brush down on the table and left the room. Unhurried, unfazed.

Boyfriend. I used that word, ribbing Catherine.

"Is that what you think?" she said, rising from the vanity and bending into the closet. That hair swung around and whisked across her face. Her dress was hanging on the door—a childish confection, cherry-colored, with ribbons and smocking.

I shrugged my shoulders. "No," I said. "Maybe." I folded a candy wrapper into a tiny square, then folded it again.

"You like him," I said. I was fishing, of course. "I can tell."

"Then you're stupid," she said quickly. "I hate him. I can't stand the sight of him. He makes my skin crawl." She'd been holding a pair of ballet shoes in her hand and she threw them, hard, against the dresser, knocking the music box to the floor and setting off that tinkling little *Nutcracker* tune.

"Damn it," she said. "God, god, god damn it." She crawled over on her knees and snapped the lid closed with such force that the ballerina was nearly decapitated. Honestly, I had not thought her capable of such passion.

"Maybe you should tell your mother," I said to her. "Maybe you should."

She wasn't looking at me, but down at the pink tea roses that scrolled her bedspread; she traced a vine with her finger. "I did."

"You did? When? What happened?" Why hadn't she told me this? It irritated me.

"Nothing happened is what happened."

"What did you tell her?"

"I told her he touched me. She said I was silly, of course he touched me. She said I had an overactive imagination. She said you give me too many dirty books."

I was offended but still, somehow, not entirely displeased. "I told you she wouldn't care," I said.

THE WORKINGS of Catherine's home remained mysterious, an enigma I could never quite unwrap, not entirely. Once after school we came quietly past the living room and saw a terrible and strange thing. Though it was broad daylight, the blinds were drawn and the room was dim. Simone was on the couch, her shoes were off and her feet lay in John's slender hands. Her shoes were askew under the glass coffee table. There was something soft and French playing on the stereo. John was crouched in front of her, rubbing her bare feet, while Simone breathed softly, like a sleeping animal, her eyes closed. We stood at the edge of the door, frozen. Then I felt Catherine's hand on my shoulder, pulling me away.

John didn't look up when he heard us, nothing in his posture suggested he knew we were there—but he did. We slipped silently away, down the hall to Catherine's room. She shut the bedroom door behind us and stood breathing heavily, her straight back flush against the frame.

"What?" I said.

She shrugged.

We didn't say it aloud but it could not have been worse had we found her naked, with her breasts bared and her legs splayed, bone-bright against the black leather.

A while later we heard Simone humming in the hallway, the rustle as she gathered her bag and fussed in the foyer. The scent of her—musky and floral—drifted under the door.

Simone, as you would expect, was militant about privacy, about the sanctity of her room. Had we ever been caught in there, the punishment would have been dreadful. But John had license and slid inside often, carrying laundry or sheets or dusting cloths, shutting the door softly behind him. He must have made her bed and cleaned the fragrant bathroom—the bath rail trailing a jungle of silk stockings and hand-washables, the vanity lined with expensive lipsticks and cut-glass bottles, the whole place saturated with the luxurious, concentrated scent of Simone and her myriad toiletries.

Sometimes we saw him coming out of the bedroom, with empty hands and a glowering face. If we met in the hallway, near one of Simone's ugly, incomprehensible paintings, he might glare at us, say something under his breath. His expression didn't soften as it landed on Catherine but seemed instead to resolve.

And soon, not long after we saw them together in the living room, Catherine and John began stealing things from Simone's bedroom, from her drawers and bathroom—perfumes and lipsticks, silver spoons and tiny glass figurines. They didn't stash these in Catherine's room, but instead gave them to me to keep. I do not remember our discussing this, or that I asked any questions; I'm sure I didn't, as I wanted only to be included. I took these trinkets home as I had taken the jewelry, hidden under my clothes or in my coat, and kept them under my bed, inside board games or in the back of my closet in the hallway.

My father returned to the embassy and a small scar on his forehead was all that remained of those weeks and the lies we had told to protect him, to protect us. It all seemed tied to the changing season—the new coolness, strange smells on the air, the scent of horses and schoolbooks and powdered milk. Gusts of wind traveled the alleys behind the apartment building, gathering up dirt and swirling it down the length of the alley in tiny funnels of grime and debris, sending cats scattering. Leaves dropped from the plane trees along the far end of the street and we jumped into them, crunching them to bits under the soles of our shoes and tossing them wildly at each other, fat fistfuls of crackling brown confetti.

My mother was overly bright and cheerful for a stretch of time, driving me to the stables and venturing past the parking lot, wrapped tight in scarves and woolens, watching me circle the ring. Ali came to the apartment less frequently now, only for social visits with my father. They'd become friends during his convalescence. In the afternoons they drank scotch together in the living room, smoking their pipes and speaking, I imagined, of politics and rising anti-American sentiment.

OCTOBER 1975

8

ON A BRISK AFTERNOON GRACE SITS IN THE PARKING LOT ABOVE the stables at Balgat, running the heat on high and smelling the stale, recycled air pumping from the vents. She smokes through a crack in the window and stares out at the banked dirt in front of the fender. With one hand she fingers a rip in the leather seat; it started small, but she has been worrying it to ruin. It's been over a month now that she has been coming here in the afternoons, providing flimsy cover for Bahar and Ahmet, waiting out their private moments.

When a knock comes at the passenger window, she jumps. She sees Ahmet's face leaning down to the glass, his cloud of prematurely white hair, his knuckles resting in a fist on the window. She leans across the seat and cranks the glass down.

"Hello," he says. "Merhaba."

"Merhaba." She drops the cigarette out the window and looks up at him, aware of his scent of horse and something else, less definable, like the smell of sun and wind.

"Come down," he says. "She is cleaning stalls, it will be a bit. I'll make tea."

He is holding a saddle, the pommel of it resting on his knee. He hefts it up and adjusts it against his body.

"It's all right," she says. "I'll wait."

She lifts the book that is sitting spine-up on the dash and gestures with it, to indicate that she's occupied. His face disappears from the window and she thinks for a moment that she's insulted him, that he's gone off in a huff. But he has merely stepped to the other side of the car, and now he opens the door, extending his free hand to help her out.

"Please," he says. "Sit with me."

In his trailer, where she has been before only for moments at a time, there is the gathered scent of horse and leather and sugary tea. On a plastic tray by the hot plate are a bowl of lump sugar and mugs, three limp carrots, a snaffle bit. The trailer is overly warm; there is the buzzing, electric sound of a space heater, Turkish voices coming from a radio on his desk. She sits cautiously on a stained floral couch; a thin spotted kitten sleeps at one end, its paws twitching in dreams.

"Thank you," she says. She accepts the tea and holds it between her hands; steam rises.

"She is doing well here," he says to her. "Canada."

Grace nods: she too has been surprised by Canada's aptitude for this, her uncharacteristic display of discipline. "It's good for her, I think."

She is startled to find that she means it. She had hated this mightily, being manipulated by Bahar, more or less forced to bring Canada here, part of Bahar's romantic subterfuge. Bahar had said to her, "I can only take so many riding lessons a week. There is a limit, and Ali may become suspicious. But if you are there, and the girl, then my time is more easily explained. I am helping you, translating and so forth." Of course Ahmet's English is quite perfect; no translation is required.

He watches her now, one hip resting on the corner of his desk, the saddle balanced on his knee. Grace has noticed in Canada all the markings of a schoolgirl crush on this man—her high color and tittering laughter, her willingness to attempt all manner of dangerous, absurd, unnatural-seeming things. As Grace drives her home her daughter is warm-faced and pensive, smelling all over of animals, her eyes distant, her posture hunched and inimical.

"Bahar is a beautiful woman," Ahmet says then, thoughtfully.

He rubs his hands along the smooth, worn seat of the saddle. The tea shimmies in the mug Grace holds.

"She is also a very selfish woman. But I think you know this."

Grace looks up at him, surprised. "I'm afraid I don't know what you mean."

"I think you might," he says. He rises from the desk and places the saddle over the arm of the couch. He sits down beside her, dislodging the kitten, which mews and repositions itself. "She has said to me what this is about. I am aware of the circumstances."

"What circumstances are those?"

Ahmet hesitates for a moment. He rests his hand lightly on her knee. "That your husband drinks too much and injured himself. That there is the matter of keeping this unfortunate event quiet, that Bahar's husband is caring for him. I hope he is doing well."

He rattles these off, his fingers drumming a little beat on her knee. She stares at his hands. They are finely shaped, roughened by work and weather.

She says, "Canada has wanted riding lessons for some time. I've been meaning to do it."

His eyes are the color of cognac, and, actually, the eyes of a dog she remembers from childhood, a freckled spaniel called Brigadier.

"Well," he says. "Then it has worked out for everyone. You will continue with the lessons then, in spite of Bahar?"

"In spite of Bahar what?" she asks.

"Have you not seen her lately?" He takes his hand from her leg and begins rubbing his palms on his knees—he is wearing slim-fitting britches and tall boots, his feet look surprisingly small and delicate.

Grace has not, actually. She telephoned several times but couldn't raise her. She assumed they had merely been missing each other at the stable.

"Bahar is a woman who changes her mind very frequently. I have not seen her recently. Maybe a week, maybe more."

Grace considers this. She recalls the sketchy answers the housekeeper has given on the telephone, the way her English suddenly deteriorated.

"What does that mean?"

"It means she is tiring of this place, or not. It means she will come back or she won't. It means someone has to exercise that horse of hers. I do not know, precisely, what it means. Only Bahar does." He laughs, a low sound but not a harsh one, and then rises and shakes a cigarette from a pack on the desk. He holds it out to her and she takes it, pulling off her glove to fit it into her mouth, reaching forward for the light he offers.

Sitting stiffly on the couch, inhaling the harsh Turkish tobacco, Grace realizes she is furious. She is angry with nearly everyone—with Rand, for being such a jackass, with Bahar for using her so badly and with herself for allowing it, for going along the way she does, the way she always has. Sometimes, lately, she even feels as though she might be the woman her daughter imagines she is—irritable, middle-aged, beneath interest. Now she sees in Canada that look with which children will inevitably come to regard parents, as though she suddenly recognizes in her mother every despicable, hidden thing. Grace is disgusted with herself, with all of them, and she stands abruptly, putting the mug down hard on the table, watching the tea slosh over the sides and pool on the surface. Ahmet leans forward on the couch, palms pressed together in front of his face.

"I understand," he says quietly.

"I doubt it," she says, turning to leave.

"You are welcome anytime," he says to her, as she opens the door and the brisk air rushes in. "Come back anytime."

She stands outside the trailer catching her breath. The sky is clear, the air scented autumn gold and red; fallen leaves, still soft, dying only at their very edges, litter the uneven concrete. Around the corner, the stables are quiet except for the sound of the horses' mingled breath, their huffing, indecipherable conversations.

Grace thinks of that terrible party she'd been to at Simone's and of the sound the hairbrush made slamming into Canada's teeth the following morning. She'd had a rare hangover; there had been too many questions the evening before and too much innuendo. Paige Trotter had come up on her at the party, just after Simone had glided away. Grace was relieved to see her.

"This is dreadful," Grace told her, her eyes on Simone's back. "I'm a terrible fraud." She was aware of John and Catherine, whom she had just seen disappear into the kitchen together, and of Canada—who was hiding behind the grand piano with what looked like a brandy snifter.

Paige laughed. "Well, it does take some practice."

Paige observed the room appraisingly and popped a canapé into her wide, bright mouth. She smiled as John passed—there he was again, out of thin air—and lifted a fluted glass from his tray. Then she touched her hand to his sleeve to halt him and spoke to him in Turkish. He nodded, replied softly, the whole cant and affect of his body surprisingly deferential. As he moved away, threading effortlessly through the mass of bodies, Paige turned to Grace and looked at her through decorative, jewel-rimmed spectacles.

"Buck up," she said. "You presume people are more interested in you than they are. It's a common mistake. Look at this lot. Do you really think they give a damn where your husband is? Do you think they care if you tell them the truth? That's a bit of an arrogance, if you don't mind my saying."

They were standing then beside the perfectly arranged dinner table. At each setting was a cut-glass bowl of glittering ice, tinted Aegean blue; fat pink shrimp nestled close around the rim.

"Look," said Paige. "John has discovered food coloring."

"Even he knows I'm lying," said Grace. "The damn houseboy."

"Oh well," Paige said. "If anyone does, it's him. But he's got his own secrets, that one. He couldn't be less interested in yours."

"What is it about him that makes me so uncomfortable?" Grace asked. "And that girl. I get a shiver every time I see them together. Doesn't Simone notice?"

Paige shrugged. "Don't let your imagination run away with you."

Grace surveyed the table. The flowers and the shimmering silver, the glowing tapers, the snowy linen. "My, but Firdis is a clod," she said. "This is so beautiful."

"Isn't it exquisite?" Paige said. "Don't you want to just smash it to bits?"

And then the next morning, while brushing Canada's hair out, Grace had noticed a tiny bluish bruise in the place Simone's fingers had been. The woman had actually pinched her. Grace's head throbbed; her eyelids felt fat as slugs. She had not liked Simone's insinuating tone; the whole situation had her jumpy as a cat.

Grace was thinking about this, all of it, while she was tugging the brush through Canada's horrendous rat's nest, wondering, Did she sleep in chewing gum? And just then Canada had snapped her head around, whining that Grace was yanking her bald, and in that instant, which seemed in retrospect frozen and wide, full of opportunities for withdrawals and retractions, Grace had not stilled the brush—not slowed it at all.

9

SIMONE WAS WILD. SHE BANGED THROUGH THE APARTMENT, slamming doors and tearing through the contents of drawers. We heard silverware clanging, cabinet doors opening and closing with force. We heard her swear—unusual, for Simone hated vulgarity. No, that's not entirely true: she hated it in others.

Sitting on the twin beds in Catherine's room, we were folding her leotards into little pink squares. We had accumulated several cubes on the bedspread. Catherine looked up and our eyes met.

"What is she looking for?" I whispered. Though the door was closed we took no chances—we suspected Simone of having supernatural hearing, as well as eyes in the back of her head.

"I don't know."

In my mind I inventoried the things of Simone's that were hidden in my room—stray bits of cutlery and camisoles, a crystal saltcellar, pieces of costume jewelry. Why did they do it? They each had their own reasons, I suppose, but part of it must have been to drive her a little mad, to shake her composure.

Simone opened the door to the room and stood there in the doorway. Her hair was mussed and her expression stormy—she looked like a woman who had been on a killing spree, or was contemplating one.

"I'm missing my diamond earrings," she said. "The good ones your father gave me for our anniversary. Have you taken them?"

"No," Catherine said with total self-possession. Simone no longer had the power to rattle her. She had taken something of John's too, I saw then, some of his coolness, his disdain.

"Well, if they don't turn up by this evening there's going to be serious trouble." What could Simone have meant by that? She certainly couldn't have been offering amnesty.

Catherine shrugged. She patted the stack of leotards and smiled. "You must have misplaced them."

"When have you known me to misplace something?"

There was a moment of impasse; they observed each other.

I said, "Did you look in your jewelry box?"

Simone's eyes slid to me and narrowed. "Yes," she said. "Of course I have. Were you two playing dress-up?"

"We don't play dress-up," Catherine said calmly. "We haven't in ages."

"That's true," I said. "We're too old for that."

But we had done, and not so long ago. Harem girls and bedouin brides, favored daughters of the caliph—whirling in filmy bits and pieces taken from Simone's bedroom, scarves tucked into our waists and necklaces strung round our foreheads, fat stolen jewels of topaz and amethyst and aquamarine, like great glittering tears, dangling in our eyes.

Simone closed the door with a bang; the noise took a moment to die away. I looked at Catherine.

"Diamond earrings?" I said. "You took her earrings?"

"She left them by the sink in the kitchen. Stupid cow." Catherine began plaiting a bit of her hair. Her expression was serene.

"Where are they?"

"John sold them, down on Tunali. She pays him next to nothing; his family is so poor you can't imagine."

"Are you kidding me? Are you crazy?" They'd obviously lost their minds.

"Relax," she said. "They're gone anyway."

"She's going to kill you. I can't imagine what she'll do to him."

"Calm down," she said. "She'll never know."

"Have you met your mother?"

"I don't care," said Catherine, in that new, preternaturally calm voice. "I don't care at all."

But I was terrified: I pictured Simone storming up the hill to our apartment and rummaging around in my room. I thought about whether or not my mother would let her. I couldn't decide.

"I'm getting rid of it all," I said. "Today."

"Do what you want."

I stood up. "Jesus," I said. "Good God."

Catherine smiled. She said, "Avallah."

Really, what could Catherine have known of John's family? We lived like kings in Turkey. I did not need my mother to point this out to me, though she liked to. Once, my father had taken his driver Kadir home and I had been along in the car. The poverty, the difference in our situations, shocked me—their tin-roofed house was little more than a run-in shed, open to the street; there were hordes of dirty, barefoot children, a fire burning in a rusted barrel. It struck me that Kadir was ashamed for us to see where he lived—even me, a mere child, no one of the least importance.

But my father climbed from the car as though it were the easiest thing in the world, as if anyone could do it, and let the children swarm him. They rummaged through his pockets—which contained, it turned out, all manner of small, delightful, mysterious American things, made of sugar and plastic—and then he sat down on a box in the courtyard, mindless of his suit, his coat, his shoes, and they crawled into his lap and he made them giggle and blush, the girls and boys alike. Somehow nearly an hour passed in this way—all of us sitting on upturned boxes in the packed-dirt yard, shadows flickering on the corrugated tin roof, my father and Kadir speaking in Turkish and English—until the light was entirely gone and then my father sighed and climbed to his feet and shook Kadir's hand. We got back into the car and drove home through the dark streets. We climbed back through the hills of Ankara into the bright sections, the warm hotels and restaurants and shops, and my father pulled me near him on the seat and when I turned my face into his collar he smelled of smoke and all those children's bodies and himself, all of it together.

Yet, I had never thought of John outside of Simone's apartment, beyond her clutches. Certainly he left at night and returned early in the morning, but in my memories he was always there, ever busy. I had never considered where he lived or that he might have a family waiting for him—brothers, sisters, aunts, a mother. It was beyond my imagination.

Then, sometime in October, he took Catherine home to his family: they rode in a dolmuş—a kind of shared taxi—through the city and into a section of it she could not satisfactorily describe. I was shocked to learn that Catherine and John had left the apartment together. I pictured the two of them side by side in broad daylight, how he would have shepherded her through the traffic and the surging crowds. She was always nervous in crowds, and disliked the noise and the closeness, the shoving and coarse talk of the merchants and shoppers. When I imagined them together, out in the world, I was half mad with jealousy. I saw his hand comforting her elbow, his mouth close at her ear.

The winding streets always confused Catherine, though the city was laid out like a map in my mind—the hills of Gasi Osman Paşa, the twisting ascent to Çankaya above the botanical gardens and the British Embassy, the descent into the business district or the longer drive through the gates of the Old City, where we sometimes went to the baths.

I questioned her mercilessly about that trip:

How had they gotten out?

Quite easily, she said. Through the front door.

Where had Simone been?

At the dressmaker.

When was this trip?

I don't quite remember; not so very long ago.

But I wanted to know every detail: the condition of the seats in the dolmuş, the markings of the animals they would have seen, every smell and shadow and hue of the day. But she was different by then and it was no longer only Simone who could not reach her. This was a new Catherine: taciturn, superior, dismissive.

It was fine, she said. Nothing too interesting. She had lately begun observing herself in the mirror and I remember her braiding her hair, looking at me in the glass.

I pressed her to tell me about his family, his home, his manner around them. "Why in the world do you want to know?" she asked. I thought, not for the first time, that he was wasting himself on her.

"We had tea with his mother and about a hundred other smelly old women," she told me finally, her fingers still busy in her hair. "All of them look just like your mother's maid."

Something dark and thick rose in my throat. "What did you talk about? How did he act? Where did Simone think you were?"

But by then she had pulled the curtains around the two of them, and I was outside, searching for even a chink of light, the briefest admittance to their private world.

"I thought you hated him," I said.

She put the brush down then and turned around. It was as if she hadn't heard me. "Those women crawl all over him," she said, and a thrilled amazement crept into her voice. "Patting him and patting him, kissing his cheeks."

But quickly her voice grew adult again. "But really, it was terrible," she said. "The place smelled to high heaven."

How like Simone Catherine was at times. How had I not seen it before?

We grew sick of each other, and the subject, and we wandered out into the kitchen and watched John prepare borek for the evening. I sat on the counter; she helped him. I despised seeing them together, working side by side, Catherine rolling the little cigars filled with spinach and cheese, John frying them in spitting grease, then draining them on paper towels laid on the counter. They whistled the same stupid little tune.

"He simply worships me," she would say from time to time. And her nose would wrinkle with the thought of it. Her face would flush pink and she would make her hands busy. My whole body would go squirmy with hatred.

On the afternoon I'm thinking of, Catherine was wearing a crepey cotton shirt with a crocheted inset at the neck—we both had them, they were sold downtown and my mother had given in and bought them for us. Mine was red checked, Catherine's blue. They had wide bat sleeves that ended in a point, edged with crochet work. Catherine's sleeve was dragging in the bowl that held the filling, then dripping shreds of cheese and spinach across the counter and onto the polished floor. I thought for a moment to tell her but instead closed my mouth. I was sitting on the counter, banging my heels against the wood. John stepped away from the heat of the stove, lifted Catherine's arm by the elbow and held it up to show her the mess she'd made. To accommodate this she had to drop her shoulder and let her arm be twisted up unnaturally, but she didn't protest or pull away. Instead, her mouth formed a little o of surprise and then they laughed together, bodies bent toward each other. Then, while I watched, he bent his silky head and put the end of her sleeve in his mouth, pulling it through his teeth. He drew the wet point from his lips and let it fall against her skin. For a moment I almost felt it: the dampness of the crochet against my inner elbow, the idea of his mouth brushing my skin.

I pushed off the counter and slammed out through the swinging kitchen door. I nearly collided with Simone, who was standing there, quiet as a statue. My breath was coming in ragged little gasps.

"What is it?" she said. Why did concern or interest from Simone always sound the same—so treacly, so poisonous? She moved her thin eyebrows, one at a time; they twitched like pale, prehistoric millipedes.

"It's too hot in there."

She watched me carefully; we were standing close to each other. I saw the freckling on her neck, the way the skin there was getting papery. She put her hand out and touched the place where my heart was pounding. I don't believe she'd ever laid a hand on me before.

MECCA LIES south of Ankara. In the afternoons, John knelt on a small prayer rug in the laundry room, facing the alley. He bent with his hands outstretched on the faded rug, his forehead to the ground. I often came across him in this position, the sun pulsing through the small window onto his prostrate form. Passing the open door, I barely even glanced at him. His voice was low and muttering, and the words ran together. 'Allah' was the only one I could isolate.

Then one afternoon, there was Catherine, bent similarly, with a dresser scarf over her head, alone in the aisle between the twin beds in her room, muttering something at first I couldn't make out. No, then I recognized it: she was reciting the Lord's Prayer, but in a singsong voice, jamming all the words together.

I stood and watched her for a moment. Her blinds were closed; the light came in striped and angled. She was wearing a leotard and tights; the soles of her feet were gray.

"What's this?"

"Ikindi Namazý," she said. Her head was touching the floor as John's did; it looked exceptionally uncomfortable.

"Which is?" My voice must have held an edge of discomfort, of nervous superiority, the unease that comes of finding a familiar person engaged in an utterly foreign activity.

"Afternoon prayer." She sat up on her heels and pulled the scarf from her head. "Not to be confused with sabah, öğle, akşam, or yatsı."

"I don't think they say the Our Father. I'm pretty sure it appears nowhere in the Koran."

"Technically no," she said. "But my Arabic's a little iffy."

I sank down on her bed. Catherine had rosary beads, for heaven's sake. She could rattle off Hail Marys like nobody's business. I stared at her, her slim shape, the not-quite-flatness of her chest beneath the bubblegum-colored leotard, her legs sheathed in those pig-pink tights.

She showed me a book he'd given her with a tattered blue cover. She had been keeping it under her pillow.

"What?" I said. "You're converting? Give me a break."

"Maybe," she said. "Who knows."

"Uh-huh," I said.

I opened the book randomly. I read this: " 'As a young child, the angel Jibreel visited Muhammad, ripped his chest open, removed his heart, extracted a blood clot, and returned him to normalcy.' Wow. Great stuff."

"Oh, shut up," she said.

Neither of us said anything for a long time. I couldn't remember the last time John had given us candy, or we had done something secretive together, just the two of us.

"Hey," I said. "Want to go up to the garden? Throw rocks at the construction site?"

"Not so much," she said. "I think I want to read."

She took the book back from me and flipped through the pages. I picked up the copy of *The Officer's Wife;* it was sitting on her bedside table, sandwiched among a collection of boarding-school books.

I read out loud: " 'Detailed Weekly Schedule for Household with One Maid. Monday—general cleaning of the house. Collect laundry, dry cleaning and leather to be polished. Inspection. Tuesday—laundry. Iron silk underwear. Wednesday—defrost Frigidaire.' "

Catherine said, "Do you mind?"

" 'Thursday—clean stove, breadbox, cake box. Friday—clean silver. Polish flatware one week and hollow ware the next.' What's hollow ware?"

"Fine," she said. She riffled pages. " 'The five pillars of Islam. Belief in the oneness of God and the finality of the prophethood of Muhammad. Establishment of the daily prayers. Almsgiving to the needy. Self-purification through fasting. The pilgrimage to Mecca.' "

" 'An inspection of the house once a week is essential, no matter what a jewel your maid may be. All the more reason if she is lax or inexperienced. A close inspection tones up the morale of a household, lets a servant know you have your finger on the pulse of the household, that you know what the score is.' " I stopped. "Like Simone, I guess."

"She doesn't know the score," said Catherine. She paused and read on for a moment. Then she looked up.

"For instance, she's been giving alms to the needy, and she certainly doesn't know that. Listen: 'there is none worthy of worship except God and Muhammad is the messenger of God. That's Shahada.' "

"Simone is giving alms to the needy how exactly?"

"Her earrings, for one. A few other things."

I snapped the book shut. "You're going to get in serious trouble here. I hate to be the one to break it to you."

"We're saving money to go somewhere."

"Whose money? We who?"

Catherine lifted her hands. The book was open on her lap; she was sitting Indian-style. "There's somewhere we want to go," she said. "John and I. Mecca, maybe. Istanbul. Somewhere."

"Mecca?" I said. "You and the houseboy are going to Mecca? That's rich."

Catherine shot me a look. She closed the book with a bang. She said, "We're done here, right?"

Of course I was struck stupid by the romance of it—the hazy idea of the two of them running off through the city, traveling through the countryside, along the seashore, through poppy fields and olive groves and miles of ocher-colored nothingness. I was dazzled by the lyricism of trains, by the mechanics of shared meals and too little money and highly improper sleeping arrangements.

The next day, I threw myself into riding, into life among horses, into the dusty otherworld of Balgat. I polished saddles and bridles and crusty bits. My fingers were striped with cuts from baling wire; I stank of manure and the wet, brown, sticky sweet of oats. I mucked out stalls and threw hay bales from the loft onto the concrete strip below; my back ached, I grew stronger. There were older girls at Balgat then, slinky, lanky teenage girls who went to the American school on the base and rode their expensive horses with finesse. They allowed me to pal around with them in a distant way; they admitted me to the fringes of their hysteria, their debauched laughter. Everything about them, everything they did, reeked of sex and mystery. Up in the hayloft they furthered international relations with the grooms via cross-cultural sex games in which more was insinuated than accomplished. Some afternoons I was allowed to sit with them and listen, though what went on was largely incomprehensible to me. We perched on hay bales, some stacked as high as the ceiling: the boards gaped beneath our feet and below we heard the movement of the animals, glimpsed a sleek curve of wither or ducking neck. Looking down was dizzying, a distinct sensation of danger. The loft was dark; the air danced with insects and was warm with the powerfully green aroma of hay. Blades of it pricked ankles and arms and the light from the one small window made everything glow golden, glancing off polished black boots and hard hats, the corn-silk hair of the girls, the bare, honeyed flesh of their breasts in dipping sweaters. The grooms slouched and leered, huddled together, occasionally stretching their long, dark arms and legs in a pretense of ease, exchanging studied, offhand remarks that no one understood.

At school Catherine wrinkled her nose when I sat down beside her. The look on her face made me think of her mother.

When a horse went wild one day and tore loose through the barn, slipped in a river of muck and tea-colored urine and ripped his knee wide and bloody, I stayed long past dark, after my mother had gone, holding the stripped, flayed skin together while Ahmet repaired it carefully with a long and vicious-looking needle. We knelt together in the warm straw, only a lantern illuminating the wound and the deep corners of the stall. The wind whipped around the buildings outside, leaves blew in against our faces, and Uğurlu—it meant Lucky—stamped and shivered, his skin fluttering like black silk across the great scaffold of his bones. Ahmet murmured quietly, clucking with his tongue, putting his big hands on the horse's leg to still him.

He looked up at me once and said, "He wasn't today, was he? Uğurlu?"

Ahmet finished, smearing ointment on Uğurlu's sewn-up foreleg, patting his soft, blowing nose, and then he took up the lantern and went for something else. I stood freezing in the dark, clinging to Uğurlu's huge, warm neck. It seemed like a long time there: my arms around the steaming heat of his body, my voice reaching for his fur-lined ear. The scent of what Ahmet had concocted reached me long before he returned: molasses and bran and steam, apples and something else, something heady and milky and powerful.

He winked at me; the heavy, sloshing bucket was no struggle for him. He put the lantern and the bucket down in the straw. "Sahlep for horses," he said. "For comfort."

He saw my face in the flickering light. "Poppies?" he said. "You've heard of poppies? Opium? No? Taste."

I put my finger in the dark bucket and tasted oats, sickly sweet with molasses and hot milk, and something else that tasted strangely of sleep. I pulled my finger from my mouth to say this but Uğurlu's head was there at my shoulder, impatient and nuzzling. He pushed me aside and buried his great, white-splashed nose in the bucket.

We closed up the stall against the wind and Ahmet drove me home. My hands were stained with Betadine and blood, his ancient car chugged reluctantly into Gasi Osman Paşa; we rode mostly in silence. In the flickering night light of the city, half dozing, I watched his hands on the wheel, his stern, hawkish profile facing forward.

Riding is like driving a car, he always said, never look down. Look to where you're going, not where you are. I fell asleep on the seat beside him and he half carried me upstairs: his coat smelled of rubbing alcohol and that sweet, sleepy mash and I was happy in his arms; I pretended to be far more drowsy and helpless than I was.

NOVEMBER 1975

10

SHIVERING, GRACE SIPS SAHLEP FROM A MUG BY THE SIDE OF THE riding ring. It's November now and the wind is bitter, whining around the corners of the buildings: the sky seems like an enormous pewter serving tray, etched with tarnish. Ahmet has brewed the drink for her in his trailer—powdered orchid root mixed with hot milk and cinnamon. It tastes warm, exotic, and the ingredients look a bit like an illegal substance; the orchid root is ground to a fine powder, like pale, sugary sand. It is a common remedy for sore throats and coughs but today Grace feels quite well. She wears boots and a long sheepskin coat, a style borrowed from Bahar. *Kismet* is a word you hear often in Turkey.

This is what Ahmet calls it, their meeting as they have, here at this dilapidated stable with the two dusty rings, the swaybacked fences, the peeling row of bleachers between two scrawny trees. The stables are shaped in a long **L**; the rows of stalls meet in a neat right angle.

This year she is ahead of schedule: she has mailed her Christmas cards and begun to hang the ones she has received around the fireplace, a custom that bewilders Firdis. Sitting bundled by the ring, her legs drawn up and tucked inside her coat, Grace watches Ahmet canter easily around on Bahar's horse, in a fisherman's sweater and tan britches, his hands in leather gloves, his legs tight against the saddle. To the left, in the distance, is Atatürk's tomb, a stark, somber memorial with columns and long stretches of flat marble: there's the impression, the dark, glassine look, of water.

And where is Bahar? It's been weeks since Grace has heard from her and each day that passes without word brings a kind of relief. Now, during the days, while Canada is in school, Grace is at the stables, huddled in the trailer with Ahmet. She cannot help but feel a kind of comparison, a need to measure up against Bahar's exotic beauty and fashion, her polished demeanor, her chilly wit.

Not that Ahmet has touched her. But there is a growing sense of comfort and well-being, an ease she hasn't felt in years. It is like suddenly breathing without a catch in one's chest, after having become entirely used to one. She thinks: I've never really been at rest with anyone. And she believes that here, in this shabby little trailer with a near stranger—who remains, no matter how many hours they talk, seductively unfamiliar—she is being fully and entirely herself.

They speak of all sorts of things, of his wife, who is ill, of Rand, who has gone back to the embassy and fallen into his usual routine. They talk of Canada, of Grace's inability to reach her in any significant way.

Sometimes Grace thinks to call out to her, when she hears her key in the lock, if she is sitting in the living room, reading, leafing through a magazine, or thinking through a menu. But on the rare occasions she's given in to this urge, the outcome has been less than encouraging. Canada stands in front of her, hands locked behind her back, expression not exactly friendly. Innocent questions are met with monosyllables and her feet are in constant motion, shuffling on the parquet—itching, it seems, to be gone. Grace gives up. If this is growing up, then so be it. If this is what teenagers are like, shades of what's ahead of her, fine.

Ahmet laughs at this, but remotely, as he has no children of his own. He talks of serving in the cavalry, and of horses, always of horses. This is a lovely thing about him, his way with animals, his gentle authority. Perhaps Bahar felt like this as well, that she would like nothing more than to be a creature in his competent care, subject to the warmth of his practiced hands. Everything else is so tangled, so knotty and intricate; there is beauty in the simplicity of animals, and in Ahmet's manner around them—his hand running down a foreleg, feeling for heat, the gentle clucking noise he makes in his throat, the way the horses duck supple heads into his sure hands. Their needs seem so elemental.

"Tell me about your husband, this marriage you have," Ahmet asks. Grace sees in his quiet, knowing manner, his drowsy-eyed glance, his quick flash of teeth, that many women have found him irresistible. He does not hide that and it does not detract from his charm. On the contrary.

"My maid is pregnant," she says instead. "It's quite a conundrum. I can't imagine doing without her. Isn't that awful? She seems to want me to help somehow." Grace laughs; it is a nervous, vulnerable sound.

Ahmet looks at her over his tea. He is assembling a bridle in his lap; he seems not to need to look to do it. The leather pieces, jumbled, darkly slick with oil, come together like a puzzle ring in the market.

"Your husband," he says gently. "What is he like?"

Really, what is there to say? Grace travels the facts in her mind: the details of her life, each isolated in a particular city, an apartment, each connected and influenced by trivial facts—a south-facing window, an unpredictable elevator, a fruit stand on the corner. She sees her life in these small aspects, thinks of her shoes traveling uneven sidewalks, the noise of new languages in her ears like an assault, the fright of assimilating, and of adapting, always adapting. New people, new obligations, new social structures to decipher and navigate— places where the smallest misstep holds the potential for irreversible disaster.

They'd met on a blind date and she'd pursued him; it's not a fact she can overlook. She had wanted to shake off her childhood, the tight, icy little Canadian town and her father's magnificent, untempered disapproval. But Rand had had a different sort of life—the youngest in a houseful of sisters, and the women, smothering, pink and lacy, forever smelling of biscuits, had kept him like a pet. He'd not much wanted marriage, or children; he had not wanted a household's worth of furniture and bric-a-brac.

Still, there had been moments, drives through the Alps and wine and cassoulet, dancing and easy laughter. Christmases and holidays had been captured in photographs; there were gingerbread villages and pillow talk, cathedrals and ruins. Once, they had punted down a sun-speckled river, under a dreamy canopy of greenery. Always, of course, there was talk of his career, of who needed to be buttered or snubbed, feted or one-upped, letters she'd helped write requesting better posts or positions, people she hated whom she had cozied up to nonetheless, time spent studying protocols and hierarchies. It seemed like years of striking flimsy bargains, of walking on tiptoe and selling out, a little flesh at a time; hardly noticeable, barely missed.

But all she can think to say to Ahmet is, "It's terribly complicated."

"Ah," he says, putting aside the bridle, flashing that smile of his. "Perhaps less so than you think."

While they visit, Canada is absorbed in the daily activities of the stable: she's become a companion to the Turkish grooms—rough trade, these young men, with their bad teeth and uneasy grins, drooping trousers, cheap shoes. At Ahmet's instruction they teach Canada to care for the animals, but their manner with her is not exactly willing or generous. Grace sees them exchanging looks over Canada's bent head, as she leans to clean a hoof or bandage a leg, looks that might be construed as lewd or unfriendly, signaling that she is an intruder, unwelcome, and forced on them. But Grace doesn't bring this to Ahmet's attention. She doesn't want to make something of nothing, or in any way threaten the time they spend together. Nor does it escape her that Canada doesn't like her new friendship with Ahmet. She's not altogether displeased by the look on Canada's face when she finds them together, which she reads as bitter surprise.

Sometimes lately, provoked by an astonishing new boldness, she stands behind him and rubs at the knots in his shoulders, feeling the wool of his sweater beneath her fingers, and under it, the contour of bone and muscle. Though he is older, Ahmet's body seems younger than Rand's. Ahmet is slender framed, almost lupine, and she imagines that his back is covered with soft hair, but the idea does not repulse her, not at all. He moves his shoulders under her touch, not making sounds of enjoyment—which would seem a weakness on his part, a thing she would not like—but turning his neck from side to side like an animal, putting against her fingers the places he wants attended. She closes her eyes and feels his skin under her hands, the knobs of his spine: she inhales the lovely mixed-up scent of him. She thinks of the previous week, when Paige Trotter had found the shape of a bird in her coffee grounds. Look, she'd said, a wish your heart desires.

And one autumn day Ahmet catches her hand with his own, bringing it down across his shoulder to his face. He breathes against her palm, warm air brushes her skin; he puts each of her fingers to his lips.

"Grace," he says, "I think you are making your life more complicated."

It isn't clear what he means. She stands motionless behind him, her hand frozen in his, her knees locked.

"I mean," he says, and his grip loosens, letting her hand fall awkwardly away, "that for a woman who desires simplicity, you have a way of tangling things."

Grace pulls her hand back; she rubs her palms against her hips. She hears herself breathing and strives to quiet it.

"Don't misunderstand," he says.

"Have you heard from Bahar?" Grace feels suddenly breathless; the air has turned to glass.

"She was here," he says after a moment's pause.

"When?"

"Recently."

Grace steps away from him; her hand still holds the warmth of his. Her face is hot, her skin itches. She drags a hand down the side of her face and then begins to tidy the papers on his desk, to shuffle them together: invoices and bills in illegible scripts, Turkish handwriting— with its cedillas and breves, ogoneks and carons—scrawled across slips of colored paper.

"Please don't do that," he says. "Please sit down."

She perches on the arm of the sofa; it creaks under her weight.

"I should go," she says, but makes no move to.

"It's not as you think," he says, after a moment. "Bahar is not a woman who knows what she wants. She is always changing her thoughts. She does not expect that those of others might change as well."

"What do you mean?"

He sighs. Grace studies his face for clues as to what he is thinking. He seems tired. She wonders if she has misjudged again, if this man she has decided to fall in love with is a cad, if she has made, or is on the road to making, a monumental fool of herself.

She thinks of an argument she had with Rand just this morning; how willing she's been in recent weeks to provoke him, to instigate trouble. She's been reckless and impulsive—calling things the way she sees them, for once. She'd looked at him standing in the doorway of the apartment, his eyes puffy, the map of broken capillaries around his nose more prominent than usual. His shirt was pressed and he smelled of that familiar amalgam of his—liquor and aftershave, too much alcohol altogether.

"Straighten up," she said. "Pull yourself together. I'm sick to death of it."

He looked confused—when did she ever speak to him like that? He kept his hand on the doorknob, staring at her.

"What's wrong with you?"

"Me?" she said. "Nothing I can think of. Except being married to you, in this hellhole, with little to no modern conveniences, the stink of this city, the gamesmanship, the craziness—I'm fed up."

He shifted on the step in his polished shoes and rubbed his red face with one big hand. His eyes were watery and he fell back to brace himself against the wall. Hung over, as usual, and badly. "You couldn't possibly understand the pressure I'm under," he said. "You have absolutely no idea." He assumed a familiar posture: a man supremely misunderstood, colossally unappreciated.

It infuriated her. "Of course I don't. How could I? It's all so bloody important. So classified. So triple top secret. I'd tell you but I'd have to kill you. Honestly, Rand, what a bore you are. All of you. Can't you see it?"

What had seemed glamorous about it all those years ago—promises of intrigue and romance, exotic locales, matters of national security—now seemed like an almanac's advertisement for some quackery, a charlatan outfit promising eternal youth in a bottle.

Of course, she'd been thinking of Ahmet, saying all that to him. Thinking of the drive to Balgat in the morning air, escaping the gunmetal pall of the city, the long uphill drive through the rocky landscape, the parking lot with the stable nestled below, where the days held a new kind of possibility, the bright electricity of hope.

Standing in the trailer, Grace feels a sudden surge of regret and anxiety, an edgy, discomfiting energy. She feels a nerve twitch at the corner of her mouth and claps her hand to it.

"Ah well," Ahmet says, and gets to his feet. "It doesn't matter."

"Do you love her?" Grace is surprised at herself; though the words are out, she had not really expected to hear them.

"Bahar?" he says, and this strikes her as deliberate obtuseness, stalling.

He walks to his desk and begins to rearrange the very papers he has asked her not to touch. "That is complicated," he says, after a minor eternity.

"Oh," she breathes. "I see."

It's then that he kisses her. He steps across the room and pulls her close to his chest—that familiar, fraying, horsey sweater—and bites at her lips and neck. His breath smells of tobacco and crushed orchids; his body against hers is lithe and solid, shockingly present.

As he pushes her down on the couch, the kitten—bigger now, proprietary—cries out and leaps to the ground. The telephone rings, quivering against the papers it rests on; Ahmet reaches up and pulls the curtains closed across the window. They rattle together along the rod, a cheap floral pattern in waxy fabric, the ring of the metal hooks; the dimming room.

11

THE BUS RATTLED, THAT FIRST COLD SATURDAY, INTO THE OLDER part of the city, left the main thoroughfare and entered a poor, run-down neighborhood. Bouncing along on the torn green seats, we peered out the thick windows. There was no laughter, no chatter, we were locked in our private miseries, mute and helpless.

My mother had signed me up for charity visits to the Turkish orphanage. The idea had struck her when she and Bahar visited there, and nothing I did or said could dissuade her. Some girls my age from the American base were along and a few other unfortunates, some of whom I knew from school. All the mothers had cooked this up together; clearly it had been coming for some time. But not Catherine, of course, for Simone, with her fear of germs and the unwashed foreign masses, would never, ever have enlisted her in this.

Kate, who was the headmaster's daughter from my school, was the only person who spoke on the drive. She sat slumped in the rear of the bus, her oily hair hanging around her face, her big, chapped hands dangling between her knees.

"Bloody buggering orphans," she said and then fell silent.

The orphanage was on the corner of two streets, a spreading brick monstrosity held fast behind barbed-wire fencing. Around it, the streets were quiet and depressed. Uncollected garbage gathered in heaps in the gutters and stringy cats stood atop them like royalty, kneading refuse, arching their backs. Not a living human soul was evident. The buckling roofs of the houses seemed verging on collapse and the streets we traveled were barely paved. The bus sank into a pothole, lurched and stuttered, then gained momentum and sped too fast into the drive. We stood up, involuntarily, clutching the backs of the seats and stared unbelievingly through the windshield.

The gates were huge, rusted and Gothic, overgrown with bushes and greenery, and they swung open slowly, creakily, just wide enough to admit the big yellow bus. The road curved through a small passage, branches snatched at the roof and windows and then there was a sudden noise like gunfire—we'd blown a tire.

The bus rolled to a pitchy stop. For long moments no one moved. The driver stood and gestured us off; he was already rolling a cigarette and violently cursing the roads, the tire, us, our mothers and their mothers. We hesitated, looking around for things we hadn't brought, adjusting our socks and sweaters. We came down the steps at last, rubbing at ourselves and stretching—delay tactics—and clustered together in a sympathetic knot. Suddenly, standing in front of the grim, peeling doors of the orphanage, we were all friends.

Then they were flung open—not a speck of light escaped, blackness gaped in the background—and several bright, fluttery church ladies came tripping down the stone steps to greet us, flapping their arms: they would split us up, one announced, take us to the playground, the nursery. *How lovely it was that we had come. How kind. What nice children we were.*

We went off casting desperate looks at one another, checking our watches and glancing back at the bus as if it might disappear and leave us there . . . stranded, forever. Already, the driver had the tire off and was studying it, perplexedly, as if considering whether all of them, all four, were really absolutely essential. Perhaps everyone was wondering, as I was, if this was part of some more diabolical plan our mothers had concocted to get rid of us.

Inside, the hallways were narrow and dark, plaster peeled from the walls and we scurried to keep up with the women striding ahead of us. The only sound was that of our shoes echoing on the tiled floors. For safety's sake we kept our hands at our sides or stuffed deep in our pockets; the whole building and all the air trapped inside it seemed contagious. The matron led us immediately to the nursery—large and dim, it was lit only with naked bulbs, filled with the cloying smell of souring formula, of unwashed diapers and unhappiness.

Metal cribs stretched along the walls, quiet women standing among them here or there, heads bent, hands reaching. Inside the cribs, the babies lay like forgotten dolls, lost on beaches of cheap plastic—dark shocks of hair, diapers held shut with masking tape, rosebud lips coated with pasty white film. The babies either howled despairingly or lay utterly still. It was as though human touch were foreign to them, completely without meaning. We moved around the room in silence, looking into the barred cribs, unable, unwilling to utter the cooing noises that seemed expected of us.

We escaped outside finally—sneaking off one by one, with assorted excuses—to a small, dilapidated playground at one side of the building. The swing set had one working swing, its rubber seat nearly frayed through on one end. The slide listed so dramatically you had to climb it sideways.

At the orphanage Kate and I stayed together—on that first morning and subsequent ones—though we were not really friends. I was wary of her; she was the kind of girl who liked to hide other people's clothes in the changing room after swimming. More than once she had taken knickers from the younger girls and hidden them inside her own things. Then later, on the playground, she would display them to the boys, while their mortified owner shrieked and cried and chased after her with flailing arms. She could be as cruel, and as inventive, as any boy.

Kate wanted nothing to do with the orphans. She had no compunction about this—it did not embarrass her at all to seem uncharitable.

She could have joined the others, who after the second Saturday began avoiding the matrons—it turned out that the other girls were all earning a badge for Girl Guides—but for some reason she seemed to prefer my company. The others played marbles under the shade of a tree near the entrance and watched the driver roll and smoke cigarettes until it was time to leave. He could get through about fifteen before he would let anyone back on the bus.

So Kate and I sat together, taking turns on the lone swing, and waited out the mornings. A small girl began hanging around us, an orphan named Aynur, maybe six or seven years old. She smelled of old milk and clothes that had not been washed; she wore plastic sandals with torn bindings and mismatched socks.

"Go away," Kate would say to her, kicking her feet in Aynur's direction. "Scram."

Aynur ignored her. She sat at our feet in the dirt and moved rocks from one place to another. This seemed to absorb her completely. It is fair to say that the orphans wanted no more to do with us than we did with them. Most of the children Aynur's age vanished when we arrived, leaving the playground deserted.

"Why doesn't she go with her friends?" Kate would say. "What does she want with us?"

Nothing much, it seemed. She played silently at our feet, following at a safe distance if we moved from one piece of broken equipment to another.

"Hey," Kate said once. "What are you doing here anyway? Where are your parents?"

Aynur barely looked up. She was sucking loudly on her sleeve, playing with her rocks and clumps of dirt.

"Don't," I said, for no real reason.

"Don't what? I bet she doesn't speak a single bloody word of English. Hey, ugly little girl, tell us something. Is your mother a dirty

Turkish whore? And is your father, by any chance, a donkey-fucking pig?"

Aynur smiled up at her, pleased with the sudden attention and Kate's new conversational tone. Encouraged, Kate continued. She had an extraordinarily foul vocabulary.

Aynur was an unsatisfactory victim, oblivious to abuse, and eventually Kate pushed off the swing and grabbed for her hand. "Show us around," she said, gesturing indiscriminately, "Show us something. We want to bakmak. Look. Bakmak istiyoruz."

Aynur scrambled to her feet, thrilled.

The playground was at the back of the building, pressed up against the fence that bordered the deserted residential street. The orphanage itself was brick faced, tall and wide: beyond it, the rest of the city, its crammed buildings and crazed bustle and occasional beauty, might not have existed at all. But the few trees were golden, the sky was smoke and a brisk wind stirred the dirt around our feet. Led by Aynur, we wandered around the side of the building where thick bushes and trees obscured the windows. Quickly we came face-to-face with the undergrowth. Above, the stone building rose several severe stories.

Aynur pointed, showing us a trampled little path through the bushes. The trail was clearly well used—bottle tops and candy wrappers on the ground, a doll's plastic head crushed flat, the marks of a toy car etching its soft pink scalp—but the path was made for children her size, not ours.

"Capital," said Kate. "A secret passage." She bent her gangly body and ducked down through the undergrowth. "Come on," she said to me, peering over her shoulder. "Crack it."

We nearly walked smack into the building, it came up so quickly. The cool, greening stone was suddenly right in front of us. It was claustrophobic in there and more than a little spooky—the dank stone in our faces and the dense tangle of bushes behind.

I half turned away. "This is stupid," I said. "I'm going back."

Kate's fingers snatched at my jacket. "She's showing us something," she said. "Don't be such an invertebrate."

On Aynur's heels, we shoved through the thick vegetation alongside the building until we came to a tiny window set nearly into the ground. Thick iron bars, reddened with rust, crossed it in narrow **X**s.

"Look," Kate said with pleasure. "A dungeon."

She leaned down beside Aynur and gripped the bars with her hands. She motioned me to do the same; next to her, Aynur was nodding her head, her features working busily.

"Bozuk," said Aynur, pointing.

Bozuk. I couldn't think what it meant. I crouched down beside Kate. The window was filthy with grime, but a smeary patch had been cleared in the middle, as if made by someone's sleeve, rubbed in circles. It took a moment for my eyes to adjust.

It was a basement of some kind, a large room without a stick of furniture; a single bulb swung from the ceiling, the light it threw dusty and yellow. For a few moments I saw nothing—then a flash of white near the far corner. I squinted and the room came clear. I heard Kate's intake of breath, the low whistle as she let it out.

"Now, that's something," she said.

There were maybe a dozen children, all of different ages, some wearing diapers, the rest in little more than rags. Children nearly our own age were naked but for diapers; a girl with huge breasts rocked herself, backed flat and terrified against the wall, her face twisting in monstrous expressions. And there were children Aynur's size as well; one was hitting his head repeatedly against the wall, as if he had been doing it for years.

Infants like the ones we'd seen in the nursery lay marooned in the middle of the room, on the concrete floor, their faces slack. There were no mattresses, no cribs. Everywhere we saw contorted limbs and faces, the walls were smeared with dark streaks and once our eyes adjusted it all became unmistakable: puddles on the floor, garbage in the webbed corners. In the middle of an opposite wall was a heavy door with a window set up high and bars like the ones we leaned on.

Bozuk. Broken.

"Bozuk," said Kate. "No fucking joke."

She patted Aynur on the head and then, slowly at first, she began to kick the bars on the window. The sound rang out and she kicked faster and faster, wildly. Aynur shrieked with joy; the rusted metal quivered and sang. The children in the room looked up, and a few rose and staggered to the window. They reeled there below us, pointing, gabbling noiselessly. I felt as if I'd swallowed a stone. Suddenly, I was in a film my mother would never have allowed me to watch.

Aynur glanced at Kate for approval and then grabbed the bars and began to shake them. I snatched quickly, clumsily, at her hands, trying to pull them away, but they were claws, her grip deathly, and her face moved in parody of the expressions that gazed up at us. The room below erupted. Some of the children opened their mouths in noiseless howls. One grabbed his head and shook it violently. The girl with long, horrible breasts held them up in her hands; her lips babbled and drooled and she grinned up, showing toothless gums. I heard Kate whistle again. I could imagine, I could very nearly taste, the smell in there.

I dragged Aynur away. Her laughter was like bells pealing. Clear of the undergrowth, standing up straight again, I took her and shook her hard by the shoulders; she was frail under my hands but suddenly grotesque. Shabby, ugly, demonic. How had I ever felt sorry for her? Kate came rustling out a few moments later, her face flushed, hair tangled with leaves. She uncurled her body and put her hands on her hips.

"Good show," she said. "I bet they do that all the time, the little monsters."

I glanced down at Aynur; she'd sidled over to Kate and taken her hand.

"Sik sik?" I said. "Siz?" I pointed back through the undergrowth, toward the window. "Oraya?" Often. You. There.

"Evet." She nodded furiously. "Bize. Hep." Us. All the time.

"Bloody hell," Kate said, clearly pleased. And on the bus that day, through the teeming Ankara streets, she whistled all the way home.

That night I dreamed of secret children, hidden away in the crevices of our tiny apartment; they peered out from the depths of my closet: stolen, disfigured and forgotten. Children for whom no one would ever go looking.

I did not go to the orphanage again. My mother seemed to lose interest in the whole business and several Saturdays came and went before she noticed I was still at home and underfoot.

"DID YOU know that Ahmet has offered to teach me to ride as well?" my mother said one evening as we drove home from the stables. "Wouldn't that be fun?"

No. It would not.

The electricity was back full-time and it had become darker in the afternoons. By the time we left Balgat the city was illuminated, and it seemed we were driving from pitch blackness behind us—it gathered coldly at the skirts of our taillights—straight into a low, distant skyline, into a galaxy of multicolored constellations.

It was then, in that fuzzy time period, while everything was in its seasonal flux—we were unearthing winter tights and testing coats for fit and suitability, finding mismatched mittens and thinking prematurely of Christmas—that she began her full-fledged pursuit of Ahmet.

I already hated my mother's intrusion into my world at Balgat; her gawky movements around the animals, her silly laugh and fresh way with Ahmet, her proprietary gestures and glances.

The day of her third lesson I caught her slipping out of his trailer as I came around the corner, her face flustered and triumphant. That very afternoon he had put her up on Uğurlu—beautiful Uğurlu, with the perfectly sewn scar on his knee, the one Ahmet and I had made together. I saw his hand adjusting her leg as he did mine, his palm at the small of her back. She was wearing blue jeans and tennis shoes and giggled as she sat up there, hunched over and terrified.

"That was fun," she said to me.

"It didn't look fun," I said. "You looked petrified."

"Ahmet said I did very well."

I snorted, turned away and stared fixedly out the window, jabbing the glass with my index finger as we drove. I heard her sigh beside me and then she turned up the radio and began to hum along. She sounded so pleased with herself that I wanted to strangle her.

It was only November but there was a sprinkling of Christmas cards taped around our fireplace, occasionally fluttering in some unseen movement of air across the room. At school, in the basement of the Anglican church, we were practicing for our pageant. Catherine was excused from the production because it interfered with her ballet: I almost never saw her anymore. During recess she sat above the cricket pitch wrapped in her blue woolen coat, staring off into space. I was spending time with Kate—she was Toad, the star of our play—and we developed an alliance based on that, that and a mutual, newfound desire to be cruel to Catherine.

Kate invited me home for lunch. Hers was a real house with a walled garden in a neighborhood some distance from ours. Directly across the street was a public school behind a chain-link fence. The schoolyard was dirt and there was no play equipment, not a bit more comforting than the orphanage. While we walked from the bus, she yelled obscenities at the boys who ran to the fence and clung there, their fingers and toes jammed between the diamond-shaped links. Girls jumped rope frenetically behind them, singing out rhymes.

Like the orphans, and the children on the sledding hill, the boys who had killed Pasha, they seemed to us like children of a different species.

Kate's mother, the headmistress of our school, made us egg and chips, the oilcloth on the table stained with vinegar droppings and dehydrated egg yolk. At an upright piano in the other room her younger brother banged out the first bars of "Eleanor Rigby," over and over again.

Kate, as ever, was fierce and fearless. She proudly showed me her bra—undoubtedly a hand-me-down, grimy pink with a thousand escaping nubs of elastic. When she pulled up her shirt in the back to show me, I saw her underwear coming out of her trousers: it too was dingy and less than new-looking. Inside, the house was dirty and wild. Her mother—so sedate in the classroom, moving around at the pace of a luxury liner—banged pans and swore, slung dishes on the table and cuffed her children with great, swatting paws. Everyone ignored her.

After lunch Kate took me into the garden behind the house and we climbed into the low tree that grew against the wall.

Kate leaned back against the trunk, her legs straddling the crotch of the tree, fingers plucking at her eyelashes. Freckles splotched her face and arms. "So tell me about that odd girl you're friends with," she said. "The Canadian? Catherine, her majesty."

I shrugged. The bark rubbed at my back, my feet were slipping from the tree limb I had been given to sit on, a flimsy one; Kate took the sturdiest.

"Miss Priss," said Kate, and made a sour face. She lifted her feet an inch or so and pointed her toes; she fluttered her hands around her face. "Pas de who cares," she said. "She makes me sick."

In the garden that bordered Kate's house a dirty sheep was running around willy-nilly, butting at the stone wall, bleating. "Shut up," she yelled, and snapped a branch from the tree we were sitting in and hurled it, hard, over the wall. It bounced off the sheep's back and skittered across the dirt.

"Are you still friends? I thought you two were like this." Kate twisted two of her long fingers together, like a vine against a tree. "Bobbseys."

"Not really," I said. "Our mothers are friends."

"That's good," said Kate. She mimed smoking a cigarette, holding a twig to her mouth, drawing it away, breathing out like a stage actress. "I hate her."

The noise of the school across the street was buffered by the house between us. The wind scuffed leaves across the garden floor. A door on Kate's house banged loudly. Through a cracked window I heard her sister, Josephine, screaming obscenities at her brother.

"Do you know why that sheep is yellow?" she said matter-of-factly. "It's piss. It sleeps in its piss. Shit too. If you want to come back at Kurban Bayramı they're going to kill it. Everyone says they run around like this afterward." Her index finger made lazy circles in the air. "I can't wait."

I took a breath. "I could tell you some stuff about Catherine."

I FOUND my mother sitting at her vanity table holding a scrap of lilac lace in her hands, turning it over and holding it up as though thinking about its fit, considering measurements. My mother and Simone were about the same size but Simone was taller and my mother wore more demure and matronly underthings—full slips and satiny nightgowns that buttoned at the neck.

Firdis had uncovered some small items of Simone's and they'd begun turning up around the house—on the china cabinet, on my dresser, in a kitchen drawer—wherever she thought they best belonged. I had not thrown these things away as I'd threatened Catherine I would.

"Does this look at all familiar to you?" my mother said. The room was quite dim, with only the bedside lamp illuminating the dark mahogany and the polished floor. The white bedspread gave off a pinkish glow. "I found it in my drawer."

I shrugged, shook my head. I was standing in the doorway, my feet angled for escape.

"Really?" she said. "It's not at all mine."

I made a noise of disavowal, gathered myself for motion. She was still carefully studying the lace-trimmed camisole.

"Wait," she said. She dropped it ostentatiously on the dresser top and turned. "How are you?" she said.

"Okay," I said. "Fine, thanks."

There was a pause; she was waiting for me to elaborate, but even her interest made me uneasy.

She sighed heavily. "Fine," she said. "Be uncommunicative. It isn't like I'm not used to it." She put her hand to her head. "Do you like my hair like this? What do you think?"

I looked and noticed that she'd had it cut: it was quite short, probably stylish.

"It's okay."

For a moment it seemed she was thinking. Then she threw her infamous silver hairbrush hard across the room. It skittered on the floorboards and disappeared under the bed.

"It's funny," she said, after the noise subsided. Her voice was flat, as though nothing out of the ordinary had happened. "I used to think it was your father's job that made him this way. But maybe he was like this all along. Maybe it's genetic."

Any mention of my father piqued my interest; I stood shifting in the doorway.

"The apple doesn't fall far from the tree," she said thoughtfully. "I guess you come by it honestly."

"Come by what?"

She began arranging her hair, backcombing it, moving one short piece from side to side, examining the effect. She waved a hand. "You're very like him, you know."

"Like him how?"

"Oh," she said, "lots of ways. Sneaky, secretive. Always up to something furtive. I live here too, you know. I'm not blind."

She lifted the camisole with her smallest finger and dangled it. It settled against the air, faintly shimmering. "How do you think this got into my drawer?" she asked.

"Firdis?" I said. It must have been, anyway. How it got into the apartment was another question.

"The two of you," she said. "You and your father. You're always against me. I don't think you've ever once been on my side. I'm your mother, for heaven's sake." She looked past me with distant eyes, as though cataloging these betrayals.

When I was smaller I would sometimes—rarely—come upon my parents standing together in an embrace, my mother's head tilted back, smiling up at him. I would hurl myself frantically between them, wrestling into the middle of the hug, grasping my father's legs with my arms, using my body to lever them apart.

"How you presume," my mother said, studying herself in the mirror. "You always have. That I'll always be here for you. That nothing will ever change. But people's feelings change all the time. For no good reason. Mine change for you too."

She began to cry softly then, bare shoulders shuddering. The strap of her slip fell from one shoulder. How I despised her when she did this; I pivoted and left the room. Her voice followed me down the hall.

"You think it's easy for me? This is not fair to me, any of it. And I'm so tired. I'm just so goddamn tired."

THREE DAYS later, when my mother was out on an errand—to the Old City, she'd said, for some sahlep to send to Edie—Firdis was rearranging her drawers. (I had already removed Simone's trinkets from the apartment—the ones I could remember and locate. I'd given them to Kate, who secreted them somewhere in her untidy room. I had the impression that virtually anything could be concealed in that household—people, animals, medium-size explosions.) Firdis had the drawers turned upside down on the floor and was squatting there, her broad hands refolding nightgowns and underthings. She'd made several piles on the bed and I saw that a thin sheaf of papers sat between two stacks of silky polyester.

It was his handwriting I recognized first; I'd seen it so often. And the paper, torn from a pad, with the heading ANKARA HUNT AND SADDLE CLUB. These pads were everywhere in Ahmet's office, and one always poked from his breast pocket: he took notes on them and made lists of things that needed ordering or replacing. The papers were bound together with a bit of silk ribbon. I picked them up and skimmed them. Some were completely benign; you would wonder why she'd kept them. Tuesday? said one, and nothing more. But others were more incriminating.

Firdis, looking up at my expression from her place on the floor, said, "Okay? Tamam? Hasta mısın?" Yes, I was sick. I had never felt quite so sick.

I left carrying those letters. For days I moved them regularly, from inside my pillowcase to under my mattress, from the pages of a book to the interior of my right winter boot. For a while I could not think of a place in the apartment where Firdis did not go, or a thing she did not interfere with. I hated her for it, for her relentless exposure of our secrets.

But in the end, the place I settled on for the letters seemed safe as houses.

I HADN'T stopped seeing Catherine entirely. Some afternoons I would still wander down the hill and climb the stairs to her apartment, but the distance between us was widening. When I was around her I felt oddly detached, as if perhaps she were something I'd been sent to study and I would later report back to my superiors what I'd learned—albeit embellished and darkened.

One afternoon Kate and I put into motion a plan we'd hatched sitting in the tree in her backyard. We invited Catherine to play with us at Kate's house after school. I'd approached her at lunch above the cricket pitch several days before, my heart speeding, my stomach churning. I felt a quick surge of pleasure when she agreed: she seemed so hesitant, so grateful. She'd shaken her hair, nodded her head—and she looked, at that moment, more like the girl I used to know. So, on the designated afternoon, we sat on the bus together, the three of us, talking intermittently. Kate was full of plans, the games we were going to play, the things she would show Catherine. She was so false and friendly; I admired how guileless she seemed.

"We'll have sweets," Kate said. "I have tons. I'll show you how to play something on the piano. Maybe you can stay for supper."

Catherine nodded slightly; her hair swung. "I'd have to check," she said.

"Grand," Kate said. "It'll be grand."

The streets slid by. Behind us, boys hissed and fought in furious whispers. Kate grabbed my hand beneath the seat and squeezed it hard. I saw Catherine's face in profile, she sat on the edge of her seat, turned slightly backward toward us; her mouth looked carved and what I read there, in the brief moment I studied her, was a cautious hope.

When the bus arrived at Kate's stop, we hung back as Catherine climbed down. We stalled, pretending to struggle with our coats and books. From the window, I saw Catherine on the sidewalk, adjusting her book bag, leaning down to straighten her tights around her ankles. She looked up for us, her eyes scanning the windows.

"I'm not getting off here today," Kate called to the driver. "Keep going."

Kate and I sank back into our seats, squeezing each other tight, collapsing, gasping, with laughter. The doors wheezed closed and we left Catherine standing on that strange Ankara street corner, a long, terrifying distance from home.

Of course, I'd told Kate about Catherine's terror of the city, of the confusing streets and too-similar buildings and neighborhoods; her fear of the crowds and the dogs, the flea-bitten animals and plaintive beggars, the guttural language she seemed unable to master. I had made fun of all this, sitting in the tree in Kate's backyard. I'd exaggerated it for her benefit. But I hadn't exaggerated by much.

We spent the rest of the afternoon in alternating states of horror and joy; Kate and I would look at each other, put our hands to our mouths, and simply fall apart laughing.

"Maybe she'll be eaten by dogs," said Kate, "or kidnapped by white slavers."

We were standing on the balcony of my apartment, where we had ended up, looking down over the alleys Catherine and I used to frequent. Kate was peeling an orange and a film of rind and pith grew under her already dirty fingernails. She dropped pieces onto the ground below the balcony and leaned dangerously far out over the railing, spitting seeds in the general direction of a tattered stray cat.

In truth I had not thought much beyond the moment when the bus pulled away and Catherine's figure had receded, then disappeared. How would she get home? She had never been to Kate's house. In my mind I drew a little map: right down this street and left at the hill, past the corner grocery that carried Tipitip gum and then up to the far side of our hill, where she would have to walk along the opposite side of the buildings Kate and I were facing and then climb the long, wide steps to get to my street. Would she know this? Would she figure it out?

All evening I was jumpy and irritable. Once Kate had gone home—strolling easily down the street in her too-short trousers, her stringy hair flattened against her back, swinging her mannish hands—the thrill of the episode dissipated entirely. Through dinner and home-work and bedtime I waited for the phone to ring, for Simone to call, telling my mother what we'd done. She would ring looking for Catherine, wondering if she had come home with me from school, or worse, declaring her missing, lost or savaged. I thought of Pasha in the alley, what had happened to him. Catherine was no savvier, no more suited for those streets than he was: she could easily have been eaten by dogs or kidnapped by white slavers.

But that isn't what happened.

12

GRACE IS IN THE CLOSET, PUSHING AMONG THE HANGERS FOR AN evening dress. She's studying things she knows all too well, wondering if one or another might take on miraculously different properties this particular evening. Disheartened by the row of stale dresses and seeking distraction, she kneels for a moment and snaps open the latches of Rand's suitcase. It's an old habit, looking inside this suitcase, as if she might learn something about her husband that she doesn't already know. The locks are finely filmed with dust and it surprises her: to realize he hasn't traveled despite the story she's told. In fact, her husband has been altogether too present of late. It was an enormous relief to have him finally return to the embassy, to go off in the mornings as men should, leaving the house a breathable, habitable place again.

The heavy lid of the case flies upward and Grace peers into it a little absently, her mind on the upcoming party—Ahmet will be there—with no particular expectations. Inside is the usual masculine assortment of toiletries and pressed shirts and laundered underwear, which always return, she knows from experience, in exactly the same order and condition in which they left. What this signifies, she's not quite sure. But what she finds now—lying alongside the carefully folded shorts and undershirts, his stack of handkerchiefs, a tin of shoe polish—is a complete surprise. She lifts the notes from

Ahmet and holds them lightly; she leans back on her heels and thinks.

But she is not as horrified as she might be. She doesn't really believe Rand has looked in there lately. The question is, who is responsible? There are only two possibilities: her daughter, or her maid, both of them given to the same kind of prying and ransacking. They are both competent poachers and trespassers. Those items she believes are Simone's, for example, that have recently turned up around the apartment. Some of them she easily recognizes: that camisole was most certainly Simone's. She knew that well before she questioned Canada about it. And it doesn't really bother her that Simone is missing her things. In a way, she thinks, it rather serves her right. Is she becoming a little more permissive of late? Grace senses in herself a new willingness to cut everyone some slack. She assumes Canada's light-fingeredness has something to do with her new friendship with the headmaster's daughter; perhaps a kind of passing adolescent rebellion. It's also possible, she supposes, flipping through the incriminating little sheaf of papers, that Canada intended her father to find these letters, but Grace finds this neither alarms nor shocks her, not really.

She gets to her feet, taking the letters and leaving the suitcase open. She wanders down the hall to the bedroom and pulls open the top drawer of her vanity. She drops the letters inside—exactly where they'd been—and pushes the heavy wooden piece back into place: it slides in reluctantly, with a muffled little shriek. She doesn't bother to seek out a more secure hiding spot. There had been a time in their marriage when she might have wanted Rand to find her out, but she is no longer such an ingenue. Some years earlier, in another foreign country, she'd swallowed a fistful of pills—enough to make her dopey, but certainly not enough to do harm—and staged herself on a chaise under a sunny window. She had spilled a few tablets onto the coffee table and taken care that Canada was elsewhere. Rand had come in three sheets to the wind that evening, evaluated the room for a moment and then sternly instructed her not to be so dramatic. He'd called her, if she remembers correctly, childish and inconsiderate.

She leaves the letters in the bedroom and returns to the closet to examine the dresses—the view, the selection, is exactly the same as when she left it. Disappointing.

STANDING IN Paige's kitchen, swiping ineffectually at a sticky countertop, Grace listens for Ahmet's arrival. Simone's houseboy slinks about, opening the refrigerator and closing it again, fetching things from cabinets, acting perfectly at home. He detaches one of Paige's cats from a curtain and tosses it none too gently out of the room. Paige herself is engaged in making drinks—using a blender and salt and a counter's worth of exotic ingredients. She is consulting a book propped against the toaster.

"How," says Grace, once John has left the room, "did you pry him away from Simone? And for God's sake, why?"

The blender slaughters ice cubes; a chartreuse froth bubbles up in the pitcher. Paige tastes the mixture with her finger and grimaces. "He's useful," she says. "And Simone loves to have him where she isn't going to be, in case you haven't noticed. He's like a familiar, sent by some horrible witch who's otherwise occupied—baking children and so on."

"He gives me the shivers."

"Taste this? I think it's absolutely poisonous." She hands Grace a glass. "Of course he gives you the shivers, he entirely intends to."

"Why would he?" Grace pours the drink into the sink. "Battery acid. Please throw it away."

"I think someone will drink it," she says, "don't you? Hand me down those big glasses? Those. Oh, Grace, you must find him a little sexy. That's all part of his appeal."

"Not as far as I'm concerned. He's oily."

"Really? Well, I daresay Simone would not agree. Speaking of your type, has he arrived?"

"Is Bahar coming?" Grace turns on the taps at the sink and runs cool water on her wrists.

"Please," says Paige. "I might invite your lover and your husband to the same party but never your lover, your husband and your lover's former lover. Though I did hear from her. Just back from some cosmopolitan jaunt. Have you seen her?"

Grace has, actually, just the week before. Still, she thinks she will keep the details to herself. She looks at Paige with affection. Her hostess is flushed, valiant, drinking the blender concoction, washing it down with swigs of scotch from the bottle.

"Briefly," she says, and stretches past her for the scotch; she screws the cap back onto the bottle.

She hears Ahmet's voice at the door just then: his big laugh, the noise of greetings and the bustle of coats and scarves coming off, being swept away by obedient children stationed for that purpose. She senses Paige's eyes, kind and shrewd.

"I'm fine," she says to her. "Just fine."

But that is not entirely true.

Two days before, Bahar had stood arch and knowing in her doorway, filling it up with silver-tipped fur, clearly amused.

"So what have we been up to?" she said, and then, before Grace could think of a sidestep or a retort, she went on. "Forget it anyway. I am very busy at the moment and this is not a matter on which a friendship should be broken. Look, I've brought baklava. Shall I come in?"

She held up a box tied with red string. When Grace stepped back, she breezed in as if no time had passed at all and threw herself down on the couch in the living room, pulling off her trendy shoes and sighing as she dropped them one at a time.

"Much better," she said. "Now, I wish to discuss another thing which has come up. We will not talk about this silly business with the horse man; it is a subject I am quite weary of. I am very happy for you, et cetera, et cetera."

Grace had taken a seat, warily, and she studied Bahar. She couldn't imagine where Bahar had come across this information, though it did not much surprise her that she had. Bahar took a cigarette from the silver case on the table and began tapping it briskly against her watch. "Ali tells me you have come to him with the matter of your pregnant maid and this procedure you have in mind. Perhaps he has told you it is a bit late for that remedy?"

Grace nodded. She had been fretting about it nonstop, and Firdis, though not appreciably changed in bulk, was given to bursting into wet, snotty tears at the slightest provocation. Firdis had presented the problem to Grace as if it was hers to solve, and she was eventually made to understand that it was, if she wished to keep her household running smoothly. And Grace could not, she was ashamed to admit, imagine getting by without Firdis. She was maid, cook, babysitter, negotiator and intermediary. Grace had made some gentle inquiries at the American hospital but they had rebuffed her smartly. Even Ali had been less than encouraging; he had, in fact, been brusque. Grace considered Bahar in her living room and inventoried her feelings on the matter.

"I believe his words were: that ship has sailed," Grace said. "She should have come to me much earlier. Or I should have noticed something."

Bahar smiled and leaned forward; she wagged her unlit cigarette in Grace's direction. "That is true, except I was thinking the other day and there is this interesting something that occurs to me."

"Which is?"

"Some while ago, I remember you are telling me about this friend of yours from America—a friend who is also in the military. When you told me about this friend you mentioned this friend has a lack of a baby problem, which is a difficulty for her. Remember this? Yes, well, I remembered it as well. And so I think, Do we have a solution to the problems of not one person but two, perhaps even more?" Bahar leaned back, beaming: she opened her hands at Grace. "Voilà."

Grace had stared at her. "Voilà, what?"

The music filters in from Paige's living room. Voices—men's and women's, a shout of laughter, glasses clinking. Grace imagines Ahmet moving through the party—ever easy, ever relaxed. He will kiss the offered cheeks—skin creamed with rouge, matte with powder—shake men's hands. He will surely encounter Rand there and they will step to the bar together, touch glasses and toss back a drink. Ahmet will be wholly untroubled; it does not concern him at all to be in this position. He had affected the very same nonchalance running into Ali at the cavalry grounds. Once, in her own home, she watched as Ahmet held a match to her husband's pipe and Rand bent forward to meet his cupped hands, their bodies and faces drawn quite close and momentarily illuminated. It was merely a gesture, of course, a nicety between gentlemen—you would see such a thing every day between strangers on a train. But it had made her neck prickle.

Still, Grace stays where she is, leaning against the counter, even after Paige has left the kitchen carrying her sloshing glasses. She lingers in the kitchen for some time, listening to the party, considering Bahar's proposal and what she, Grace, has said or done to lead them all here.

It was certainly true that she'd described Edie to Bahar, she'd mentioned the time on Olson Loop, the interminable days and the incessant wild noise of the children. It had been months earlier, when the two of them had walked the Ankara streets together, had lunched in small cafés and spoken of their lives, in the way that one will bring a new friend up to date. Bahar had said once, while folding a grape leaf neatly between her fingers, "This sounds like a strange woman. This staying in the house all day, in the dark, polishing silver and saying rosaries and whatnot. It seems very, very dull."

Grace had tried to explain. The heat and the circling street, the smell of burning grass and hamburgers, the stoop-women, the men returning in the evenings smelling of beer and cramped offices, picking at their dinners—stuffed peppers and meat loaves, rice pilafs and mixed vegetables—then throwing their feet, in damp black dress socks, onto the inherited coffee tables and falling asleep in front of the news. But Bahar was unimpressed. It seemed to offend her, their shared impotence, all those helpless, commiserating hours. And so perhaps Grace had revealed such a thing, in the hopes of distracting her new friend, of excusing their behavior. My friend was sad, she might have said, she would so like to have a child.

"Don't you wish to help your good friend?" Bahar said. She leaned forward, conspiratorially, "This could be arranged. I have seen such things happen. It is not novel. Ali himself has facilitated such matters. It is a supply-and-demand type of business, like any other."

"Business?" said Grace.

"Arrangement."

"You've done this before," Grace said, and it dawned on her suddenly. "The trips. The orphanage."

Bahar did not move a perfect muscle for a long moment. Then she sighed. "Are you so naïve?" she said. "I had thought you had seen what I had to show you. I thought you were not just another selfish American." And then Bahar lit the cigarette with a twisted mouth, as if she'd been driven to it, and regarded the room with a disgusted expression.

"You've shown me things?"

"That people suffer and children have no homes. I took you to these places."

Grace exhaled. "So?"

"So indeed. I am fixing this in a small way. I am helping people, saving the children."

Grace remembered standing on Tunali with Bahar on that sweltering afternoon. A street vendor had held up a glittering bracelet. The sun struck it hard, sending prisms into her eyes. "You said: I went to get rid of a baby."

"Did I?" Bahar's hands moved; scarves of smoke drifted languorously away. She stubbed the cigarette out in a crystal ashtray and shoved it away with the heel of her hand. It thudded heavily across the table. "I am so glad I am quitting these things. They are that bird on your neck, that albatross." She leaned back and then forward again, just as quickly. "I am merely presenting an opportunity to do something good. To do a charity."

Grace lit another cigarette and smoked in silence for a moment. "So this is all the traveling?"

Bahar shrugged her shoulders. She was wearing a soft sweater nearly the color of her summer skin.

"Listen," she said. "You were at the orphanage, you sent your girl there. Where do you think those children come from? They come from families like those of Firdis. Families who can't afford to feed their children, not on what you foreigners pay them."

"So," said Grace, "money is involved?"

Bahar made a huffing noise. "Consideration," she said. "Consideration for your maid, who is very poor, as we know. Of course, a small amount of consideration for Ali, who will go out of his way to make this possible."

"My maid wants to sell her baby and you're going to arrange it?" said Grace.

"That surprises me," said Bahar. "Perhaps I made a mistake in you. In sending Ali here to care for this troublesome husband of yours. In being so quiet about all this scandal"—she waved a hand in the air—"you and the horse teacher, everything."

"I thought we were friends," Grace said, and to her own ears the words sounded pathetic.

Bahar smiled, and her voice turned a little emphatic: "We are friends. Yes, we are. This is exactly what I'm saying. Will you listen?"

"All right," said Grace—suppressing a desire to get up, to leave the room, the city, the country. "Go on."

But then Bahar rose abruptly from the sofa in a cloud of perfume. She crossed the room and kissed Grace on both cheeks, bending to reach her. "You think about it," she said. "Ali has already discussed it with Firdis and she is very much in agreement. She likes the idea very much. She is çok grateful."

"Really? What about her husband?" said Grace. She turned around in her chair as if expecting to find Firdis standing there, nodding furiously. "It can't exactly be ethical."

Bahar looked down at her; her hair moved softly around her face. "The husband will not know," she said. "That is not necessary. There are always mishaps with babies and births. It is a dangerous business when one is poor. And I think," she went on, "that I will not broach the topic of morality at the moment. I will not use a word such as *hypocrisy,* because that would not be in the spirit of our friendship." She glanced at her watch. "Bok," she said. "Shit. I must dash. We will speak again soon. You see what your friend thinks at least. What can be the harm in that?"

And so Grace had made a few furtive phone calls from Bahar's apartment, while Bahar sat nearby like a voluptuary or a sultana, with her cat-ate-the-cream expression, her knees tucked beneath her. And Edie had been nothing but overjoyed; she had not hesitated for a moment. Grace thought of the woman she knew—though barely, really, when she thought about it—sitting with her chilly bowls of tapioca and her sun-starved house, her milquetoast husband and downy thighs, and of the words that came through the line across the cities and deserts between them, into Bahar's opulent living room: How much? No, never mind how much. How long?

And hearing Edie's gratitude, brushing away her thanks, Grace had felt (she couldn't say she hadn't) the magnanimous sensation of having given a showy and extravagant gift.

This, of all things, she's kept from Paige—though she has confided far more, on infinitely more personal subjects. But she wonders, standing in that woman's grease-filmed kitchen, pouring careless fingers of scotch into a smeared glass, listening to the party rise in volume, what Paige and Bahar might have to say to each other about her. After all, they have known each other for some time. It was Paige, in fact, who'd introduced them, who had taken Grace into the group of Turkish and embassy ladies and advertised the benefits of afternoon card games and pleasant, uncomplicated female society.

DECEMBER 1975

13

WHEN CATHERINE TURNED UP AT SCHOOL AFTER OUR PRANK, I couldn't bear her not looking at me, the tilt of her head when she joined the queue in the courtyard, the way she held her books protectively to her chest. Kate stood behind me in line, jabbing me in the ribs and snorting with laughter. I angled my body away from her. Quit, I said. She kept on; her breath was warm on my neck and her long, witchy fingers dug into my side.

At lunch, Catherine turned her body away as I approached and kept her eyes fastened on her apple, rubbing at it with her sleeve. I ate with Kate and the younger children, sitting on the edge of the sandpit, all of us kicking at a line of ants. Kate built obstacles for the ants to navigate, bits of sticks and stones, a plastic shovel, a young Swedish girl's hair clip, the last of which she took roughly, provoking indignant tears that drew no adult attention. Eventually the smaller children gathered around her to watch, even the little Swedish girl with the flyaway curls, her tears drying in rivulets on her fat cheeks. She snuck her hand inside Kate's and Kate shook it away. She was too busy for comforting and she disdained tears; they moved her not at all.

I watched Catherine, seated above the pitch where we used to huddle, picking at her food. Leaves scudded across the dirt, rustling. I heard the boys' shouts. They were out of sight, down the steep hill

in the pitch. I pressed my knees together and warmed my hands between my thighs; my tights were faded and scratchy, covered in pills
and the beginnings of ladders.

"Look," Kate said. She pointed at the ground. She was trying to
break the line, the strict linear formation the ants seemed bent on
maintaining. It was shaping up into a little battle. She put the hair
clip down and the ants swarmed over and then around it, falling
back immediately into their configuration. It didn't matter what she
did, even when she stomped on a cluster of them, the rest scrambled
over the corpses of their comrades and rejoined the line. "Plucky
buggers," she said. "Un-bloody-deterrable."

We moved the little hurdles so the ants had to turn right and left
quickly to scale each peak. We made a little mountain range of sum-
mits, forcing the ants to backtrack and zigzag, which they did with
no sign of frustration. We eventually gave up and crushed them under our shoes. Catherine never looked over, even when Kate worked
the younger children into a frenzy, encouraging them to scream,
"Die, commie ants. Die!" This, eventually, did bring the glowering
attention of a teacher and we were all marched back inside, in a line
much more ragged and reluctant than that of our victims. I looked
over at Kate, saw her face glowing pink with cruelty and happiness.

"Well, they were red ants."

Later, when I walked home from the bus alone—Simone had
picked Catherine up and whisked her off—I kicked along the crumbling sidewalk and constructed an apology. I had plenty of experience apologizing, but only at my mother's command, under threat of
violence, being frog-marched out to a relative or a guest with her
hand under my elbow. Walking down to Catherine's apartment, I
felt unusually grown-up: perhaps I even imagined a mending of our
friendship that afternoon, that we might sit around in the kitchen,
hoisted up onto the counter, watching John cut fruit or brew tea. He

might show us a new way to fold napkins or to ribbon a lemon the way he did, in one beautiful, curling strip.

I climbed the steps to the second floor of her building, holding the grubby orange rail tight in my hand, dragging myself along it until I reached the landing. I stood outside the front door and inhaled. I set my back straight and raised my fist to knock. My palms were wet and my thighs itched furiously beneath my tights. I took a moment to compose myself, scratching between my legs with a fingernail and thinking of what I would say.

The door swung inward suddenly and John stood there in profile, holding a bag of garbage in one hand. He was not looking at me but had his face turned inside while he worked his sock-feet into his shoes, which were lined up with the other family members' on a small rush mat just inside the door. I cleared my throat.

His head turned and we looked at each other, both of us quite surprised. He straightened his back and stared at me, the bag of garbage dangled from his hand.

"Sen!" he said. Then he laughed. It was not a pleasant noise, though it held traces of genuine amusement.

"Is Catherine home?"

He didn't say anything for a long moment. Then he stepped out into the hall, forcing me to move back, and shut the door softly behind him. He was standing very close. I smelled clove cigarettes on his breath and lemon on his hands. He kept a lemon half beside the sink and brushed his fingers against it to freshen them—another little compulsion of his.

Perhaps it seems strange that just then, in that instant of overcloseness and intimacy, when I saw lucidly every perfection and imperfection of his face, in that deserted, echoing stairwell, I thought for a moment that he might finally kiss me.

He put his hand up and touched his crow-black hair, patting it gently. His eyes slid around the landing and he looked down the stairs: empty. The entire building was quiet as a tomb. Even the kapıcı's wife and her bucket were nowhere in sight.

Looking at him, I found that I could barely, barely breathe.

He spoke very clearly, softly, in perfect English. He said, "You people care for nothing. You are like animals. And you. You are an ugly stupid girl. I have always said this."

Then he slapped me. Hard.

He said, "Now go away and don't come back."

My legs went weak. I put a hand to my scalded cheek.

He looked at me for a moment. "Stupid girl. Go cry somewhere else. Go to your mother maybe, who will not care either."

And then he turned and opened the door, leaving the garbage on the mat, and went back inside. The door clicked firmly behind him.

Walking home, I kicked around at the obsidian fragments in the hollow midway up the hill. The Turkish children were always using these as missiles, hurling them at one another, and early last spring, when there had been a sudden snowstorm and we'd gone sledding, Catherine and I had both come home with our faces and clothes streaked with inky-black marks, our mittens irredeemable. My mother had thrown me in the bath and scrubbed violently at my head, her short, square nails raking my scalp.

It was growing dark. I picked up a piece of coal and crumbled it in my glove; it fell apart in shiny, iridescent bits. These trailed me uphill, like bread after the woodcutter's children. In apartment buildings across the street, lights flickered on, illuminating kitchens and the shapes of women inside them. They seemed to move slowly, almost as if choreographed, bending and reaching, gesturing, lowering their heads. One side of my face felt as if it were glowing; my knees shook.

At the top of the hill I stood across the street from my apartment building. I rested my back against the vineyard wall and looked up at our windows. The living room curtains were open and through the sheers I could see brighter patches that indicated lamplight. I imagined the circumference of the room as I knew it: the couch backed against the window, the two bergère chairs alongside an occasional table, the fireplace, the desk in the corner, the other small grouping of table and chairs. The room was lit, but inside, nothing moved or shifted or seemed remotely lifelike. I wondered if my mother was in there; I pictured her little halo of smoke, her dark cap of hair, her absent eyes.

Ugly, he'd said. I had known it of course; I'd often seen his eyes pass over me without any recognition at all. Once, walking with my mother on Tunali, we passed him near the carpet merchants. He was standing, passing the time with a young man his own age, both of them smoking. He carried a string bag heavy with fruit, a loaf of bread protruding between the handles. My mother was several paces ahead, studying the cases in a jeweler's window. Drawing beside them, I had lingered for a moment, pretending to fumble in my pocket, to make some legitimate business of loitering there on the street. But the moment wore on without his turning, though his companion's eyes passed over me briefly before resting on the traffic beyond—cars crawling by, horns screaming, boisterous Turks conducting their daily traffic squabbles. I heard John speaking rapidly in Turkish and that familiar, derisive laugh of his. People shoved past me, annoyed; I saw my mother turn to scan the crowd. I put my hand up finally, to touch his sleeve, planning in my head some expression of surprise, some adult exclamation of greeting. But when I touched him he turned his head only briefly in my direction, his eyes fastened on that sleeve. Then he shook my hand away severely, the gesture automatic, utterly dismissive. He made a quick hissing noise, as he did in the alley behind Catherine's apartment when cats had gotten into the garbage. "Hayır," he said coldly, as he would to a beggar, and then he moved away from the shop door with his purchases, falling into pace with the crowd.

It was now fully, completely dark. Dogs barked in the near distance. These packs took over the streets at night: shadowy mongrels, all ribs and yellow eyes, raggedly joined and scavenging the city, low, desperate noises in their throats. As if reciting from some script they'd been given, our parents had terrified us with stories of excruciating shots in the stomach, dozens of them, with needles big as loaves of bread. If the shots came too late, they'd warned, we'd die of thirst as we struggled against our own disintegrating brains, petrified of water. It sounded like some gruesome tale from Greek mythology. Still, I stood there, imagining that the barking grew closer. The throbbing in my cheek subsided and was replaced with the heat of humiliation, which I felt all over. I touched my hands to the cold stone wall behind me, feeling its valleys and bumps, the unique roughness of its surface. Above, in my living room, someone drew the curtains and the window went dim. A few minutes passed and then headlights appeared in the distance, their beams rising as they climbed the hill at the far end of the street. I sank into the shadows and froze.

The car stopped opposite where I stood, beside the low iron railing of our building; it was the long blue station wagon that carried my father around the city. The driver's door opened and the interior of the car was suddenly illuminated; I saw his bulky figure in the backseat, his head bent into his hands. Kadir stood beside the open door and stared into the distance beyond the car. My father stayed hunched inside. For a long moment nothing happened. Then my father got out and grasped Kadir's hand. I heard them exchange words; there was low, comradely laughter. Kadir climbed back into the car and drove away, the lights bounced back down the hill.

My father steadied a hand against the gate and stood looking up at the same windows I was observing. He seemed to gather himself to go inside. I heard him huff out air, bring it back in. Then he fumbled in his pockets and began to fiddle with something. I heard his lighter flick, the plastic noise of the tobacco pouch opening. He swore in a language I didn't recognize.

I tried to make myself smaller, remembering the giveaway rustle my winter coat made when I moved. I held perfectly still. I wanted to watch him for hours.

He managed to get the pipe lit and then turned on his heel, swaying a little. The dogs set up again and he lifted his head for a moment and listened.

He said, "I know you're there."

I stayed where I was, silent, still. There was a long pause. Then he laughed.

"Canada," he said. "Come out. I know it's you."

I ran across the street and threw myself against his warm, liquory body. He held me tight; I lifted my head for air, trying to breathe without complaining. The bowl of the hot pipe brushed my ear but I didn't even squeak.

"Where have you been?" he said. "Who hurt you?"

I shook my head into his chest and he said wonderingly, "Where do you go? What do you do?"

Rhetorical questions, clearly. He lifted me off my feet and hugged me close. I put my shoes on top of his and he danced me a few steps, the smell of Captain Black drawing a warm circle around us. He staggered and I stepped down from his shoes and took his elbow.

"How did you know it was me?" I led him up the walkway, pushing open the door to the yellow light of the lobby, looking up at the long flight of steps ahead of us.

He tapped his temple with one finger. "Intuition," he said. And then, after a boozy pause: "I know my girl. I'd know you anywhere."

I walked with him up the steps and he said, "So, what's your old mother up to? No good as usual?"

"I'll never tell."

He thought we looked out for each other, my mother and I. I

didn't bother to tell him otherwise. I didn't really hold him account-able for things he didn't do, or even the ones he did. The morning my mother had hit me with the hairbrush he'd been home, still recovering from his fall, moving somewhere about in the apartment. After the brush landed there had been a long moment of shock, and my mother and I were motionless, frozen and staring at each other. I swung back to the mirror: my lip was split. Blood flooded my mouth; in the mir-ror I saw myself open it to scream. My mother quickly touched her hands to her mouth, to her ears, and left the room. Then I heard his footsteps, moving somewhere—coming, going. I flew down the hall-way, down the narrow space between the closets, around the corner past the black rotary telephone, in pursuit of his rounded, hurrying back. But he didn't stop, and it was only when I reached him in the doorway of the bathroom, when he was obviously involved in some decision—interfere or not—that he finally looked at me.

"God," he said, but not really to me. He was speaking to the air, the closets, the kitchen. And then he turned, limped into the bath-room and closed the door behind him. "No," I wailed at the door. "No. No. No."

His voice came from behind it, thin and helpless. It said, "I'm sorry," and "I can't." He turned on the water, drowning me out.

Now I had him at hand and I gripped his elbow. His shoes kicked and scuffed at the risers of the stairs. "Listen, have I told you about Suppiluliumas? Probably the greatest of the Hittite kings? No, I didn't think so. He ruled four decades and refortified the citadel at Boğazköy. It's spectacular. Would you like to see it?"

"Yes," I said. "Sure."

He patted my hand. "I'm fine," he said. He extricated his elbow and braced himself on the railing. "I'm going to show you amazing things. Stick with me, kid."

I watched him fumble in his pocket for the key. "Okay," he said, when he'd found it. "Onward. Morituri te salutant."

He looked down at me and grinned; it seemed we stood for a moment before we tackled the last, steep staircase. The stinging in my cheek was a dull, steady throb and I was terrified of the vast, blind love I felt for him.

The next morning, before daylight, he left the house without saying goodbye. Later that day it began to snow.

14

FAST ASLEEP, GRACE HEARS THE PHONE RING FROM THE hallway—its panicked midnight sound of emergency and distress. But for Grace, indoctrinated as she is, that noise always means the same thing and it is no longer so alarming. Soon Rand is moving around, and she rises from the couch and finds her slippers and meets him in the hallway. She senses rather than hears Canada in her bedroom, awakened by the noise, always sensitive to her father's movements.

In the hall, Rand is nearly dressed, in a suit designed for warmer weather, and he's struggling with his tie.

"Let me," Grace says. She's still half asleep but her fingers know the job and do it automatically.

She stands with him in the drafty hallway near the mirror and the coatrack and the telephone and finds she wants to say something to him, something he will remember.

But he beats her to it. He says, "Will you finish this thing? This business with the riding teacher? Everything else?"

She doesn't argue or deny it or fumble for explanations. She just says, "It isn't what you think anyway."

She shrugs inside her dressing gown. The space between them seems enormous—but it's merely the breadth of a prayer rug, one step in bedroom slippers, over a gold-domed mosque stitched on a faded background of red.

A clock strikes in the hallway then, one of the German ones; there are five or six of them and the chimes overlap. Another goes, and then another.

"So where are you going?" she says. She thinks he will know the question is a capitulation, an overture: it's now so far outside the conventions of their relationship.

But he shakes his head quietly and picks up his suitcase. He lifts a raincoat from its hook beside the mirror. "I don't know when I'll be back," he says.

"Of course not. And what shall I tell Canada when she asks?"

"I'll say goodbye to her. I'll go in."

"Don't," she says and puts up her hand to stop him. "Don't wake her."

She stands behind the solid door and listens to his steps down the marble stairs, and once or twice the noise of the bulky gray suitcase striking the iron railings, making them ring, and then the sound of the lobby door as it closes behind him.

"IT'S FUNNY," Grace says to Ahmet, "to hear you say what time you will come, or that you need to go to the pharmacy." They are walking along a quiet street near Ahmet's apartment. She has asked him to meet her. "Everything my husband does is veiled in this absurd secrecy."

He says, "It's his work, I suppose, that makes him like this."

"That's what he would say. Don't excuse it. You can't imagine what it's like to live with that manufactured drama all the time—it's as though he's living in a black-and-white movie. Everything is so *fraught*."

Ahmet laughs. She is holding his elbow in broad daylight. The bare trees overhead creak with the wind; the sound is musical, faintly antique. Ahmet wears a yellow scarf wrapped tight around his neck and street clothes.

"What is it you wished to talk about?" he asks.

"About Bahar. I wanted to know what you thought of this adoption business she's involved in."

Ahmet draws a little away and slows his pace. "I don't wish to discuss this matter. It does not concern me."

"It concerns my maid, though."

"Still," says Ahmet. "I have told Bahar that I do not wish to know about it. I will tell you the same thing."

They walk in silence for a time. Ahmet waves to a shopkeeper. The day is cool and clear and the part of the city they are strolling in feels almost European. They pass under striped awnings, by flower vendors, a store selling fancy hats, a bakery with beautiful confectionery stacked architecturally in the window. Beside her, Ahmet has the upright quality of a military officer—which he is, but a different kind than the one she married. Ahmet is stoic and elegant and implacable. He makes her think of foreign legions, of campaigns waged in deserts, of rapiers, crimson sandstorms, silken tents.

"I would advise you not to get involved," he says. "That is my advice."

What more can Grace tell him? She is beholden to Bahar and Bahar sees no reason to release her. She cannot seem to take a step without getting in deeper over her head.

"What do you know about all this? Is it even remotely proper?" By this she means legal, but she cannot quite bring herself to say it.

Ahmet shrugs. "Do not think this is the first time she is making such arrangements. It is a business for her and her husband. I believe it is very lucrative."

"Still, I'm surprised Ali is involved in something like this. He seems so decent."

"Hmm. You are talking of all his charitable work with the poor women of the city."

"You're being facetious."

"Perhaps." Ahmet takes her elbow. "Let's have a coffee."

He steers her deftly through the traffic to a café across the street. When the coffee arrives—very sweet for her, medium for him—he removes his leather gloves and leans forward across the rickety table.

"I am fond of you, as you know. I believe we have become friends."

"That sounds ominous."

He smiles. "Probably. But I want to tell you not to mix yourself up in this. No good will come of it."

Grace sips her sludgy coffee; the tiny cup is enameled in a pretty mosaic pattern. At some point in this country, without noticing it, she's grown accustomed to coffee you could eat with a spoon.

"My friend is overjoyed," she says. "Maybe it isn't so terrible. Unorthodox, but only that. I mean, Firdis wanted to get rid of the baby entirely."

"Perhaps you think this means she does not care about this child. Perhaps it does not occur to you that she sees no other choice." He looks around for a moment. The place is quiet, only a few other tables are occupied. "Look," he says, "it is easy to find Bahar alluring. She is an unusually convincing person." He pauses, twirling the small cup between his palms.

Grace watches him. They have not spoken of his relationship with Bahar, not explicitly. When Grace tries to raise the subject, Ahmet invariably changes it. It's funny how easy it is to put it from her mind, to not think, when his hands are on her, of those same caresses on that familiar woman's skin, of his lips at her slender neck, pressed to the locket of bone at the base of her throat.

"Still," he says, "this is no simple indiscretion. I am speaking of Bahar now. The matter of this baby."

She understands him clearly: what is here between them is temporary. She folds her hands together on the table. "Well, anyway. It's done. And the situation on the other end is more complicated than you might think."

"You are talking like your husband now. All this intrigue and deception. Perhaps you are making too much of it. Maybe all this conspiracy is contagious."

For a moment Grace is certain he is patronizing her. She bristles a little, feeling the need to say something that will absolve her, Edie, even Bahar.

"My friend is really desperate for a child. There's some trouble in their marriage."

Ahmet regards her across the table. "You Americans are too concerned with what happens in the bedrooms of others." He says this in a perfectly level tone, with a faint hint of amusement.

"No doubt. But these things are foolishly complicated when one is with the government. The military. Whoever he works for now. They pay attention to the smallest things."

Ahmet raises an eyebrow, but still covers his hand with hers on the table. She curls her fingers inside his gratefully. Suddenly, she feels as though exposing herself might be the answer, or the antidote, to all the displeasing, secretive, fatiguing aspects of her life.

"Do you have any idea," she says, in a confiding rush, "how they watch us? How they evaluate what we do and what we say, even the parties we give? Rand never much liked this friend of mine. She didn't toe the line, or do what they expected. I think he was afraid it might rub off."

"And do you always do what is expected?" He squeezes her hand; she feels his knee, warm against hers beneath the table.

"We're under a microscope half the time. Honestly, it's lunacy."

"You should kiss me," he says. And he leans forward so she can.

She thinks, I really should remember this. This feeling of being eaten up alive, this wholesale surrender. His face, so close and so amused; that waiter over there, watching, fingering his collar.

She goes on, too hurriedly, "He wanted me to join this club, that one. Knit, sew, organize. Be on the PTA."

"The what?" Ahmet's face is very close. She smells coffee, his cologne—even, she imagines for a moment, his ailing wife.

"Rand never thought Edie was up to being an officer's wife. Can you imagine anything sillier? The list of qualifications is not exactly exhaustive."

He kisses the palm of her hand and lets it go. "It seems very complicated to me. But I am a simple man."

He sighs and drains his coffee cup. "Anyway, I do not know what to tell you. I think you have set on this path and what happens will happen. İnşallah, it will not be a catastrophe." He looks at his watch. "I must go and run some errands for my wife. I have already been too long."

Grace stays at the café nearly a half hour after he's gone: he'd kissed her cheeks formally and strode off, his coat held close around his body. She orders a pastry and looks around the neighborhood. She suspects it was a mistake to come; no more than her childish need to have a man tell her she's doing the right thing. For all that, she does not feel very much better.

How odd, really, the position she finds herself in. Could Ahmet be right? Has she courted as much intrigue as Rand does? And yet, for all the risks, she feels that disaster—real disaster—is not imminent. Maybe she has caught it at last, the ennui of the diplomatic wife: little will not be washed away with time, with mitigating years and intervening miles. Another post, another country; different friends, new rooms, closets, streets, servants. She feels a quick swell of equanimity, the sort of composure she so often envies in Paige Trotter—Paige with her turbans and fortune-telling, her pragmatism and quick mind—a charming, disheveled competence Grace has admired since they first met.

Eventually, Grace rises from the table, nods to the waiter and walks home. She leaves thinking of what Paige has said to her on more than one occasion: Soldier on.

When she returns to the apartment in Gasi Osman Paşa, Firdis is clattering and banging around. In recent days she's become clumsy, and it seems to Grace that she is deliberately making more noise than the chores require, that she is unnecessarily, even purposely, underfoot. She is also, to Grace's eyes if no one else's, quite, quite pregnant.

Grace has recently had a letter from Edie. They are thrilled, it says—she can almost hear Edie's soft, trilling voice—they cannot wait. The letter has a European postmark; Edie had gone to Germany for her ostensible confinement, on Bahar's instruction. It was odd how those two women, strangers to each other, had fallen so quickly into the roles of customer and purveyor. Through Ali, a doctor had been found in Saudi Arabia, and he had produced papers insisting that Edie complete her pregnancy in a climate less harsh than that one. But Edie wrote: *I don't feel at all delicate. To tell you the truth I am having a marvelous time. Were it not for this package you are sending I might never go back to the desert!*

Grace sighs. In the tiny kitchen, smashing pots together, Firdis is waiting to pounce on her, to grab her hands and kiss them punishingly, in her hard-lipped way, to say, "Mersi, madam, mersi. Çok teşakkür." Over and over and over again.

And Grace will say, as she does at least once or twice a day, "Evet, evet, evet," and hurriedly leave the room. Lately she can hardly look at this woman, this shapeless stranger in her house, who would so casually trade her child for American money.

She draws the curtains and stares down through the apartment buildings into the bowl of the city below. Snow has fallen again and it lies across the roofs of the city like an icing she might have made in her kitchen, of sugar and lemon; it frosts the minarets and glazes everything with a sudden prettiness. The day seems to stretch out in a lovely, lazy, Turkish way. She goes out of the room humming "O Little Town of Bethlehem" and thinking of Christmas.

Her romance with Ahmet is happily consuming. She lets herself shiver under his touch, she cultivates the queasiness in her stomach, the electricity coursing along her arms when she catches sight of him—bent over his desk through the grimy window of the trailer, or cleaning out a horse's hoof with deep, sweeping motions, slinging bales of hay. She likes him in her social circle, sitting in the living room during some function, sipping amber liquor from a heavy tumbler, his white hair perfectly groomed, his jacket and tie an odd fit on his small, compact body—he seems to her shorter away from the horses, and altogether more human. And in rooms like these, women and men both surround him, drawn to his gentle charisma, and they coax from him stories of wars and engagements in lands even more distant and exotic to her than this one.

She and Bahar have made an odd peace now, the kind that incorporates their new circumstances and treads more lightly around sensitive topics. They do not mention Ahmet by name; in fact, they do not speak of romance at all, in any form or fashion. Grace is learning, at last, to keep a piece of herself in reserve. She might have taken this lesson to heart years ago, she thinks, and saved herself heartbreak. Grace had noticed long ago that Canada was like this—her friendships were always conditional, more apt to dissipate and fray. They were not the passionate kind Grace remembered having as a girl.

At the table in the living room later, she leafs through travel brochures and thinks of a trip to Istanbul to see the Hagia Sofia, the Blue Mosque and the Topkapi. She wants photographs of the Golden Horn at sunset, when the red light strikes the water in that famous, overdocumented way, building a little bridge of radiance from one shore to another. She wants to fight her way through the Grand Bazaar and haggle for trinkets and treasures, and she wants Ahmet to take her. But it won't be easily arranged, he says. There is not a place for them in that city. He will not risk taking a hotel room.

But Grace wants more than snatched hours in the trailer like a teenager, more than moments in the hayloft, where they might at any moment be discovered by the grooms or the leggy, knowing American girls, who lately give her glances that she shrugs off, telling herself she is imagining things. Flipping the pages of her pamphlets, she dreams of walking through ruins with Ahmet, of crossing the Bosporus in a small rented boat, of fresh fish and wine in a dockside restaurant, of sitting near the water's edge as the sun sets while long, gorgeous minutes slip by.

15

THE SNOWFALL SENT ME TO THE CLOSET. I WAS LOOKING FOR A
scarf I wanted, some hand-knitted disaster sent by a relative, one
that matched the equally terrible hat I was wearing. I was thinking
of going to the sledding hill—hoping I might run into Catherine
there. Early last spring, Catherine and I had swept down the steep
hill together, pressed front to back astride a one-man wooden sled,
afraid to part company even for the swift, blinding seconds that carried us to the foot of the slope. The run ended only inches from the
street, where hurtling cars threw up a dark vomit of muddy snow
and soot and wet, flecked coal. We'd come to a stop with our boots
outstretched, the toes spotlighted a sickening yellow by the headlights. Then, mitten in mitten, we'd struggle back to the top, dragging the sled, our eyes on the ground, chattering. Beside us, all
around us, the Turkish children screamed and shoved and laughed
on the darkening slope. Bundled in coats and balaclavas, with only
their eyes showing, they looked hostile to us (and dangerous).
Catherine had needed me then. There were always skirmishes: boys
pushed us, girls plucked jeeringly at our coats. One evening a tall,
bold boy grabbed our sled away and took it into a circle of his
friends. They stood around it, laughing, kicking at it with their
boots, leaning over in bulky coats to punch it with their fists. Then
three of them clambered aboard and rode it clumsily down the hill;
when they reached the bottom they tumbled shouting to the ground

in a pile, scrambled up and kicked the sled over. Then they stepped off the curb and vanished between the passing lights, their bodies sliding into the darkness like shadows, leaving the sled upturned, its runners in the street. It was the last we saw of that sled, our last time on the hill.

Looking for the scarf, I went pushing around in the front closet, jamming aside the stiff shoulders of coats, cursing in John's Turkish. Suddenly, hands deep inside the closet, I stopped. An absence struck me.

I shoved around among the things on the floor with my foot, accidentally kicking over the straw crèche my mother treasured, the one she assembled in a tableau every Christmas with meticulous, childish care—every figure: each sheep and goat and robed, myrrh-bearing wise man; the baby Jesus, swaddled in blue ceramic, and Mary, with her concerned, peaceful, painted-on countenance. In the fracas, in my hurry, Joseph fell to the floor and was injured, his blue robe chipped and his beard dislodged, revealing a weak, crumbly white chin. Panicked still, I pressed on, pushing my hands deep into the recesses of the closet, fumbling around on the floor, running my hands over every object—every shoe and boot and box and tennis racket. My hands reached the rough walls at the end and I sank back on my knees.

Then I pushed myself upright and stood, brushing my hands on my hips, stopping to check my new breasts as I passed the hall mirror—an obsessive habit I could not break, even in catastrophe. I poked my head into the living room, where the furniture was neatly arranged, the heavy shot-silk curtains hung motionless at the windows and my father's old typewriter sat at the desk in the corner, a fresh piece of paper spooled between the cylinders. The apartment smelled thickly of ammonia and furniture polish, tinged with the tangy, bitter scent of artificial lemon.

In the kitchen I stepped over Firdis, who was bent bulkily on her knees, scrubbing back and forth across the gray-flecked linoleum and humming tunelessly. The door to the balcony was ajar and the curtains drifted inward, admitting the cool, smoky breath of the city.

Of course, it flooded back, then, with Firdis hunched on the floor at my feet: the phone ringing, the sound of my father moving in the house in the darkness, his footsteps, the whispering I'd heard in the hallway. Still, I needed confirmation.

"Where's the suitcase from the front closet? My father's suitcase?" I mimed a square with my hands, holding them in front of her face. "Gray," I said. "Bavul. Gri."

She leaned back on her heels and stared up at me. "Baba go. Evet," she said, nodding. She waved her hand, mirroring mine. "Güle güle Baba." She smiled fiercely, exposing rotten teeth, patches of purply gum.

I flew out of the kitchen and returned to my room, first sitting down on the bed and then getting up and pacing back and forth, from the window to the door, again and again. Outside, the snow deepened, the hill grew soft and white; I heard the distant clamor of children, but I forgot all about it: my scarf, Catherine, sledding.

IN THE weeks after he left, my mother and I sometimes wandered down Tunali to the kebab place by the park, sat at long, communal tables and ate from tin plates, pressed close to loud, happy Turkish families. We ordered lamb smothered in yogurt and tomato sauce, salads of cucumbers and olives and sharp white cheese, and warm Cokes in dusty bottles, which we drank through delicate paper straws. Sometimes Bahar would stroll in, like a minor celebrity, with Ali or one or another of her shiny-faced, eager little boys. My mother brought along her travel books or her stationery, chewed her disintegrating straw, and penned notes in the margins or long letters to her friend Edie.

With my father away, my mother didn't attempt to draw me into conversation, and she virtually ignored my table manners. She abandoned the pretense that I was well brought up and polite, capable of small talk, that I could be trusted not to play with my food. I wonder if she ever noticed that my father cared very little for such things. My mother's concern for decorum was hers alone, and mostly for show. My father never did have a military man's obsession with rules and regulations, with posture and correctness; these were her impositions, though she preferred to attribute them to him. "Try to show your father you weren't raised by wolves," she'd say, before punching me between the shoulders to encourage good posture. But when he was gone, her concentration shifted, her eyes watched doorways instead of other people's cutlery, her hands fidgeted with napkins and linens, and she didn't notice if I stared at unfortunates, if I scraped my fork on my teeth or slouched like a hunchback over my book. She was clearly preoccupied with her own troubles in those days, the outlines of which were clear, though their interiors remained opaque to me.

Paige Trotter came around more often, reading the dregs of coffee or laying out her cards on the coffee table in elaborate designs. Folky music played on the hi-fi. My mother banged out rudimentary carols on the piano. Often, the women—Paige, Bahar, Ben Gul and others—sat around drinking steaming beverages that smelled of liquor, laughing uproariously. By evening the room was always a haze and my mother retired with a crashing headache.

Paige and my mother taught me to play whist and hours passed like this: a fire burning in the grate; raki, giving off its pungent smell of licorice, swirling cloudily in their glasses. We decorated a spindly tree, and when my mother unwrapped the crèche she discovered the tragedy that had befallen Joseph. When she blamed Firdis and swore and wept, I didn't bother—or it didn't occur to me—to correct her.

I didn't miss my father, not so much. I was too accustomed to his absence. It was as familiar to me as smoky rooms and airports and languages I understood only in snatches. In fact, there was very nearly a familiar warmth to it, to the way the rooms shifted and re-configured themselves, the way we ate the things we wanted and never worried if there was nothing for breakfast in the mornings. We subsisted on bread and fruit and pastries, and I was nearly al-ways a little high from the unaccustomed sugar—that, and the thick and heady remains of the women's glasses, which I drained every evening in the kitchen.

Though time had passed, Catherine still wouldn't talk to Kate or me. At school she swung in wide and graceful arcs, ignoring us com-pletely. Not in the studied, careful way girls scorn other girls, but in a quiet way that suggested we did not even exist. She didn't stare through us or turn her head abruptly in another direction when we passed; no, her eyes gave us the same flat, casual attention you would give any insect or inanimate object or stranger. Though it didn't faze Kate at all, it made me queasy. I'd grown to dislike Kate: among other things, she used her position as the headmaster's daughter to extract special favors from the teachers and lord it over the younger children. My mother, too, professed not to care much for her ("a bit sly, isn't she?"), and I found myself defending her, this friend I no longer liked, a compulsion I resented in the extreme.

Ramadan was ending and my mother began to plan for a party. Since my father was gone, it would be a gathering of her friends, the Turkish ladies and their husbands, Paige Trotter, some friends she'd made at the stables. In the days leading up to it she made lists of foods and things she wanted, sending Firdis scurrying all over the city, and at night she sat on the floor in front of the ancient stereo and piled record albums into stacks. She rolled up the big carpet in the living room and polished the more intricate silver herself with a toothbrush. One afternoon, I heard her on the phone trying to bor-row a punch bowl.

The morning of the party, I went to Kate's house to watch the slaughter of the lamb. It was Kurban Bayramı, the Feast of Sacrifice. All over the city, people would be killing animals—sheep, goats, even camels—and giving the meat to the poor. For many Turks, for millions, my father had said, this might be the only meat they would see in the entire year.

The day was chilly and we were out of school for the holiday. The air was clear and the tree was swept of leaves; there were little frost heaves in the earth, and ice palaces, minuscule but intricate, had formed in the depressions made by our tramping feet. Kate's brother and sister had clambered into the limbs above us and they hung there like monkeys, cackling and crinkling cellophane wrappers. We had a clear view over the wall into the neighbor's courtyard. There was a great deal of activity—laughter and shouting, snatches of song. But for a long while nothing important happened. The lamb was standing as it usually was, its face butted into the corner of the wall. We could see the black tip of its tail, its stained bottom, two diminutive hind feet.

Nestled in the tree, we hugged ourselves and stamped our feet against the branches, liking the way they groaned. Kate and I talked and teased, we grabbed at the small ankles and feet that dangled from the upper limbs and pretended to pull at them, to dislodge their owners. When we looked up, the men were already advancing on the lamb with exaggerated steps and gestures. We quickly left off what we were doing—I had Josephine's anklebones pinched between my fingers and when I let go, a little bleat escaped her, a tiny breathless noise of relief.

I smelled fire somewhere nearby; the houses of the neighborhood were spread below us in a patchwork, and smoke rose from chimneys and twisted in the air. Down in the courtyard, men dragged the squealing lamb into the center: the whole family was there, men and women and children. A skinny dog ranged through their legs, barking and whining, taking kicks good-naturedly. The father, large and mustached and jolly with holiday spirit, suddenly caught sight of us, pointed up at our tree and laughed. He waved a hand in a slow, exaggerated fashion, as if he were communicating with the deaf or the infirm, as if he was uncertain whether it was a universal gesture.

Kate's mother came out just once and shook her head in disbelief. "Little savages," she said, and then disappeared again. A few moments later she materialized on an upstairs balcony almost level with the tree and began shaking duvets out over the yard. Feathers flew, crumbs scattered, the down comforters snapped white in the air and then billowed softly down.

The men struggled to hold the lamb quiet; then one produced a piece of cloth and tied it over the animal's eyes. It wriggled desperately under their hands, and for a moment it seemed like they were playing a game at a fair, that the lamb would emerge unharmed, frightened but intact. Then suddenly they stopped, bowed their heads and began to pray. The wind carried the strange words up to us in the tree. The men stood gathered around the animal, their hands disappearing into the wool of its back, their mouths moving and their voices joined in a chant, guttural but somehow lovely, drifting with the smoke and the cold. The rhythm was mesmerizing, singsong and sad; I wanted to close my eyes and listen. But then, just as quickly, the prayer was over and the blade flashed—it seemed to come from nowhere, glinting, curved, massive—and we heard a sharp, strangled cry, a noise like taps left open in a sink and suddenly there was blood: splattering, splashing, pouring.

We hung breathless in the tree, the silence loud as bombs all around us. We were paralyzed by the sudden color, by the actual, astonishing moment of slaughter. Even Kate, so cool, so gaily bloodthirsty, went altogether white in the face.

The men took their hands away and the lamb staggered away from them. In diminishing revolutions it circled the courtyard, tilted awkwardly to one side, just as Kate had said it would. I had not really believed it; I suspect she hadn't either. It was a strange, macabre version of blindman's bluff: the lamb spinning with the rag tied around its head, the hooves beating a frantic little patter on the ground and around its white neck a wide scarf of blood, startlingly red. Little splatters of crimson sprayed the ground and the onlookers—the men, the women and children, the skinny dog. We heard the thud of the animal's last steps before it collapsed, and then cheers went up. One man, the one who had waved, stomped a little dance in the sodden earth, kicking away the too-curious dog, and then, taking a little boy in his arms, he raised him, high, high above his head, circling as he turned—an airplane game I remember my father playing with me, years before, on some distant tree-shaded lawn.

Kate recovered quickly. She scrambled down through the branches. "That was absolutely fantastic," she said. "I could eat a horse. Are you staying?"

I couldn't, I said, and before I had let myself out the side gate, Kate was running the short distance to the house shouting for her mother, demanding lunch.

In the alley behind the house, leading to the shortcut I took to get home, I relinquished breakfast, and then all the contents of my stomach. I brushed my hair back, spit, and looked up to find a pair of eyes regarding me over the edge of the ragged stone wall. Josephine's placid eyes, bright blue beneath her home-cut bangs, her arms in a heathery sweater resting on the uneven stones. She smirked at me. I brushed my arm across my face.

"Bugger off," I said, and she disappeared. I heard her feet hitting the frozen earth as she ran. Walking home, I could only imagine what she would or would not say, sitting across from Kate's piercing gaze, subject to her familiar, tormenting manner, her taunting queries. I saw their huge dining table, the stained oilcloth, the smeary bottles of vinegar and the gritty plastic saltcellar. I saw their mother coming in from the kitchen, smelling of sausage fat and chips, and slumping into a seat beside them, her hands and apron grease-stained: she would press them for all the details in her rough, chiding, affectionate tone.

The day only got worse. At home, Firdis was missing and John was in my mother's kitchen, wiping out crystal punch cups with a soft towel. I recognized him from behind immediately: his back and shoulders, the tapered fit of his white shirt against his body, the way he stood resting his weight on one heel, his toe tapping out a slow, soundless beat. For a moment I thought I must have taken a turn and walked into the wrong apartment.

I opened the door to my parent's bedroom and slid inside. My mother was on the bed, one arm thrown across her eyes, a coverlet up around her ankles. Her mouth was closed, her nostrils distending and closing. She was wearing a slip and one leg was bent, her knee pointed toward the window. She was not asleep but she wasn't quite faking either. Her eyes blinked open.

"Yes?" she said.

"What's he doing here?"

She rubbed at her eyes with her elbow and shifted on the bed. "Party tonight," she said throatily. "I'm lying down."

"I see that. What's he doing here?"

"I have to take a bath." She lifted her body slightly and then fell back heavily against the pillows. "What time is it?"

"Why is John here?" I said again. "You hate him."

Her skin was greasy with night cream; she reeked of orange oil. "Can't be too fussy," she said thickly. "Everything went haywire today. I borrowed him."

I thought about it. "Where's Firdis?" I said. "He's mucking everything up in her kitchen."

My mother sighed; she made that little Turkish harrumph of disgust. "Firdis," she said. "I can't worry about everyone's feelings right now. I need someone presentable." She got creakily up and swung her legs onto the floor. "I feel like hell," she said. "I'm going to need your help tonight. Passing and so forth."

"No one told me about this," I said. "I didn't hear a word."

She patted my back lightly with her hand, a friendly little slap. "Who's a grump-bunny?" she said. And then, in a tone I recognized better: "Sorry you didn't receive the engraved invitation."

She stood and stretched her arms above her head. Her armpits were stippled with black hairs; her pallid upper arms had developed a sag.

"You wouldn't have him here if you knew anything," I said. "You wouldn't let him past the lobby."

"Huh," she said. She was already bending into the mirror above the dressing table, pulling up the skin around her eyes. She smeared something onto her face. A scent rose in the room, medicinal, like the one my father had given off lying there all those weeks.

"Is Firdis having a baby?" I said. "Daddy said she was."

"Did he?" she said, turning slightly, taking me in. "Well, I wouldn't take everything he says as gospel. Though I know it goes against everything you believe in."

I left the room and closed the door behind me, as hard as I dared.

My mother fussed in the living room in that strange, formal period before guests arrived. The house was immaculate, candles lit, the silver gleaming on the table. A bar was set up in hallway outside the kitchen and John stood behind it, his hands clasped behind his back. He wore no discernible expression. In front of him were glasses and bottles, the twisting ribbons of lemon peel he made, olives and onions, toothpicks, a white fan of squared napkins. His eyes did not even flicker—not once—in my direction.

People came. They streamed, milled, chatted and kissed one another near the front door. I took their coats and carried them back to my parents' room, laying them across the bed, where they quickly grew into a disordered mound of material and hides. Just a few months earlier I would have buried myself under that pile, crawling beneath it and breathing in the mingled perfumes and tobaccos, the rich foreign scents of strangers. But such childish activities no longer interested me and I tossed the coats down without a thought and left the room.

Men clustered at the bar and John served them silently. Ice clinked, voices rose, perfumes combined with liquors and smoke. I saw his hands moving efficiently, the robotic turn of his head. The smell of borek baking drifted from the kitchen. I wandered by him in makeup stolen from my mother's drawers, clinking necklaces, a stuffed bra, a floating, twirly skirt; he did not look up.

Bahar didn't seem pleased to see John either: coming in the door later in her fur and heels, with Ali behind her, she paused and spoke quickly over her shoulder. Ali helped her with her coat—she shrugged and it seemed to drop like a great soft animal into his arms—then he put his hand briefly on her shoulder, as if to calm her. My mother was flustered: she wore a long, pleated skirt and a black sweater shot through with silver threads. She greeted people and fussed, at a too-high pitch, full of empty compliments and banter. She had a fall pinned to her new shorter haircut and her bracelets moved musically on her arms. Ahmet arrived alone and he spoke to me briefly in the hallway, his hand against my hair. If you could weave scent, I believe my mother and I would both have wanted a sweater, or a blanket, made entirely of the one that enveloped him.

Soon the apartment was full of Turks and internationals. Music played on the stereo, food piled up on small napkins, drinks glasses became smeary with lipstick and were mislaid by their owners.

Generally my mother's parties were exceptionally boring, composed of the right people doing the right things, working diligently to impress one another. But that night my mother was unusually gay and wound up. In the hallway she took Ahmet from me and swept with him into the living room, in the manner of a woman whose date has just arrived. It was what she meant people to think; it was certainly what she meant me to think. But Ahmet, always gracious, seemed unfazed; he went about on her arm as though it was nothing to him, as if he was accustomed to being co-opted by strange women, to being temporarily owned by them and shown off.

My mother must have been trying to re-create the atmosphere Paige Trotter conjured so effortlessly in her own dirty, whimsical house—the lightness, the bohemian gaiety, the abandonment of diplomacy and politesse. But it would not come off; I could sense it from the start.

The music she played went unnoticed: no one was moved to dance, and when she tried to pull one man and then another from his seat, each politely refused. The guests didn't mix, but instead formed little national cabals in respective corners. You could hear Turkish in the dining room, English near the window, something Scandinavian from the front hall. The room stiffened like meringue and even Paige, with her loud laugh and strange outfit, couldn't alter its disposition.

For hours people drank steadily, though the general mood did not improve. The room slumped. More ambitious guests took the initiative and left, gathering their coats, making their excuses. Paige read cards quietly on the coffee table, and in the unforgiving light of our living room her bare feet looked less exotic than horny, and a little dirty at the edges. Only Bahar formed a small bright spot near the fireplace, where she had gathered a group of admirers and was holding court. Standing in the doorway, a plate half full of meze in my hand, I realized that the party was missing my father. Without him, my mother seemed desperate, half of something that, if not quite a whole, was still an expected convention, and entirely necessary to everyone's comfort.

Edgy and a little frantic—from the atmosphere or the booze, it was unclear—my mother fairly clung to Ahmet. As things declined, as more people made for the door or shifted uneasily in their chairs, trying to catch the eye of their spouses, she goaded them into antiquated parlor games: she suggested charades and forfeits, concentration, blindman's bluff. Over and over again she changed the records, leaping up and pulling them off midsong, sending the needle shrieking across the vinyl. I heard Judy Collins being killed again and again by cats.

Maybe my mother had underestimated the importance of social rules and regulations, of the intricacies of guest lists and suitable pairings, gatherings that hummed quietly around a shared understanding of their purpose. She'd forgotten how such protocols were needed in those circles, how without the boundaries and little rules the whole delicate illusion began to unravel. The people in that room were not truly friends, and they seemed thronged but solitary, like dancers we'd once seen on the Antalya coast: isolated, spinning endlessly in place.

I passed John once on my way to the kitchen. He was behind the bar with his hands folded behind his back. "My mother doesn't even like you," I said. "Our maid is having a baby, that's the only reason you're here." Of course he didn't respond, but turned and took a glass from a uniformed man standing nearby and refilled it.

My mother had had far too much to drink: when I left for bed she was seated too close to Ahmet on the couch. He looked stiff and uncomfortable for once, his hands gripping his knees, his gaze on some spot on the far wall. I stood in the doorway and saw Bahar catch his eye from the across the room, where she lounged against the mantel, rolling an unlit cigarette between long fingers. She was momentarily alone and she stood with supreme ease; her body had the draping posture of a great cat and her eyes were slitted. I saw her flick one eyebrow upward—a minuscule gesture, but laden. Ahmet glanced away and my mother sagged against his shoulder and then pulled herself together. Her face was puffy and her skirt wrinkled: I saw Bahar delicately smooth her own hips, smiling, as some eager man came toward her. I saw her again in the hallway a little later, arguing with John. She put her hand on my head as I passed, and her rings tangled in my hair. "It does not matter what you think," she was saying, and she paused for a moment to extricate her jewelry. "It is not your concern."

He replied in Turkish and I was surprised by his anger, so out of place, so unexpectedly raw and masculine. It was as though he were any man, arguing with a woman of any station. Bahar made that noise Turks are so fond of and gave a contemptuous gesture with her hand, rings flashing. I saw his face as she moved away; whatever it was they were discussing, it was not finished.

As I closed my door my mother was pushing herself off the couch and saying, in a smudgy voice, "Now, who will dance with the hostess?"

For hours I listened to the activity outside, the muted traffic back and forth between the bathroom and the living room. Once, the phone rang. I kicked the covers off and pulled them on again, stared at the window above my head and traced through the room the strange bluish light that entered through the blinds.

It was quiet when I woke, there was no light from the windows, and the hall beyond my door was silent. I got up and slid into the hallway. I wanted to see the remains of her disaster: the smoky living room, the jumble of glasses and ashtrays and discarded records. I wanted to see if she and Ahmet were tangled on the couch, in a heap of limbs and torn-off clothes. I wanted to see all that human and material debris, the smut they had left behind.

My mother and John were standing in the hallway, the light from the living room showed them clearly. She had her hands at her throat and his hands touched her waist. She seemed to bend backward for a moment and then fall against him, laughing at herself. He stepped away, releasing her, and she steadied herself against the wall and stood watching him. She was in her nightgown and he began to gather together the things that were near the door—the bags and boxes and bottles. I saw him pull his loosened tie from his neck and stuff it into the pocket of his slim pants. He slung his jacket over his shoulder, patted his head in that way I knew so well, that old preening, self-conscious gesture. I'd seen him do it a thousand times on Tunali, passing a shop window, half turning to watch himself go by. Vain as a peacock, Catherine had said once, in a proprietary, womanish tone, as we lingered behind him on the pavement.

He turned as he opened the door, placing the garbage and the clinking bottles outside it. He said to my mother, "I think you should see to your daughter. It is far too late for children to be awake."

"Oh," she said uneasily, and put her arms around herself. "Good night then. Thank you for everything. Coming at the last minute like this. You've been a godsend, such a help."

And I heard the door close behind him, her little sigh as she stood there in the deserted hallway.

Sometime before morning I dreamed of her in that same pale nightgown, standing surrounded by dark-faced men in the courtyard outside my school. She was turning in circles, holding her own head by the hair, swinging it in wide and casual arcs. The gown, green as grass, was gorgeous with blood, and John was painting her with the point of a great knife he held in one hand, dipping it into her neck and drawing the blade from her throat to her ankles. He painted her in fine stripes, the sun shone and somewhere, someone was whistling like a bird.

My mother had said once that no one, not even one's lover or mother, is interested in the tedious details of another person's dreams.

16

IT WAS THE SECOND DAY OF THEIR TRIP TO REHOBOTH BEACH
and Edie was napping on the sand, her cotton shirt anchored with
her hands across her face. A breeze lifted it, and from where Grace
stood near the shore Edie was merely a golden torso and splayed
legs, a pink and green madras shroud billowing around her head.
Grace waded out into the water; goose bumps rose on her pale arms
and legs, scraps of seaweed twined around her ankles. She felt the
current at her feet, a sinuous living thing, tendrils of water, coiling
shackles that she shook off with a gentle kick as she waded deeper—
to her knees, her thighs. The water reached her belly and she re-
coiled at the cold, suddenly at the core of her and so unexpectedly
intimate.

Farther out, Greg and Rand were treading water, speaking in little
shouts across the green hills of waves. She had something to say to
Rand, a question about lunch, a warning against sunburn, some trivial thing. She waved her hand; he waved back, absently. Greg's body
was slight and dark beside Rand, who wore a sodden white undershirt
and a hat. Greg smiled, head bobbing with the motion, his fingers
playing on the surface of the water. Grace took one more step and the
current tightened around her legs, a wave loomed, sudden and larger
than she could have expected, and her balance was suddenly gone, her
feet swept from under her. Then she was under water with her eyes
shut tight and her head slamming against the wave-smoothed sand,

little rocks and bits of grit pounding at her eyelids. The moment was a swirl, a froth of panic, and she gulped seawater and flailed with her hands and there was the sensation of dragging, a strange deafening silence and the green solitude of drowning. Then she was upright again, her hands grabbing at the body that had lifted her: her nails raking skin, lips gulping air, the light of the surface weird and blinding.

She was in Greg's arms, not her husband's, and he was carrying her back to the shore and murmuring kind words and patting her back to make her cough, though she didn't need the help, and then he knelt beside her on the sand and watched her, his whole face and the lean of his body a portrait of concern. And when she sat up, Rand was just wading to shore and laughing, and saying something she couldn't hear because water and sand still filled her ears and then he stood over her, blocking the sun, his thick legs, red-kneed, above her, and his face twisting with laughter he was trying to disguise and behind her Edie woke and said, "What's happened?" and Rand shouted out, "Just Grace, doing her ostrich impression."

She heard Edie say, "Oh." Then the noise of Rand fumbling in the cooler for a beer—the sound of ice sloshing—and whispers between the two of them and more laughter, sheepish and delighted from Edie, low and conspiratorial from Rand.

Later she said to him, "I could have drowned," and the words sounded plaintive and dramatic and she bit back tears and he looked at her from across the room where he was toweling off and said, "Not with our hero around. Not with Mr. Fantastic to save the day."

But now just three days after the party, and the birth of Firdis's baby, there is a letter from him, from Mr. Fantastic, and Grace reads it standing on the landing outside the door of the apartment in Ankara, her hand braced on the wall, tumbling shopping bags at her feet.

Edie has left him, Greg writes. Certainly the baby business was the final straw. Grace had surely known about the complications they'd had, the baby they'd lost? The doctors had told them not to try again; the risks to her health were too great, and the results would likely be the same. But then the adoptions that fell through, the false pregnancies and the crazy schemes, and then staying locked up in that dark house on Olson Loop for all those months. The incident in Cairo had been a public scandal—she had snatched a baby, right out in the street. His career would certainly never be the same. It had taken two years to persuade them to send him to Saudi, for him to prove that she was stable enough for another post. Grace must have noticed something? After all, Edie would barely venture past the front stoop. And now he hears she has arranged for a baby on the black market. Has she, by any chance, had word? After all, the two of them are such great friends. *I'm so sorry,* he writes in closing, so sorry to lay all this on you. *It must come as a terrible shock.*

Grace stumbles into the apartment and sinks into a chair in the living room. She rereads the letter several times and lets it flutter to the floor. She hears Firdis on the landing, hears the noise of her gathering up the oranges and the cans that have spilled from the string bag, hears her open the door and stand for a moment in the hallway, staring at the back of Grace's head before she shuffles off to the kitchen.

In the living room, Grace thinks about this letter from Greg. Once, just once, Grace tried to talk Edie out of wanting children; it seemed the least she could do. At the beach that weekend, she had recited, with an accuracy and quickness of thought that surprised even her, all the disadvantages, the negatives, the irretrievable losses. It felt less like a betrayal of her family than a confession, and it helped that she was a bit drunk and had smoked one of Edie's stunted little joints. They sat on the crumbling concrete outside the converted barracks and lifted their shirts when a breeze came in from the water.

They held their tops up around their shoulders, biting the fabric in their teeth, letting the air play on their breasts. Edie wore no bra; Grace could not bring herself to go quite that far.

"And this, for one thing," she said, pointing to her ugly, matronly bra, tugging it down to reveal a puckered white seam in her flesh. "And the noise, and the demands and the dirt."

"I don't mind dirt," said Edie.

"You haven't seen dirt," said Grace.

"I appreciate the thought," said Edie. "Really, I do."

"There are times," said Grace, "I'd happily trade."

"You don't mean that."

"I might. I think I really might."

"Even so," said Edie levelly, "you shouldn't say it."

What Grace heard in her voice was not so much sanction as caution. Against calling up bad luck and ill will. Edie stored superstitions like Grace collected trinkets: she lifted her feet when driving over railroad tracks, held her nose past graveyards, read her horoscope obsessively.

All this was before Grace herself ever thought of such things. But just a week ago now she'd wrapped an evil eye bead in a small envelope and tucked it inside a letter she was sending to the address she'd been given in Frankfurt. She thought Edie would get the joke. She, Grace, so long lapsed from faith, a new convert to cards and tea leaves and kismet.

But what now? In the living room, Grace folds the letter from Greg and places it in the envelope. At this point, it simply seems like more information that she doesn't need to know. And after all, there is nothing, nothing, that she can do.

FIRDIS HAD gone into labor the day of the party she'd given and at the last minute Grace had to ask Simone for John, which galled her.

The messy bits happened here, in the kitchen, and, panicked, Grace called Bahar, who'd come quite calmly and taken Firdis away in a taxi. Later, Bahar appeared at the party and reported that everything was fine: Grace, by then flustered and overwhelmed, had needed several moments to remember the bloody and chaotic events of the afternoon.

Grace and Bahar take a taxi to the orphanage just days after that awful letter comes from Greg. Grace can think of few things she'd less rather do, but when Bahar appears at the door and says she is holding a taxi downstairs, there does not seem to be any graceful way to excuse herself. She picks up her coat and handbag and slips away without a word to Firdis. The taxi ride is quiet: Grace does not intend to share the contents of Greg's letter with Bahar: not yet, not unless she has to.

At the orphanage, Grace sees immediately the power Bahar wields in the grim hallways, the deference she is shown by the frumpy administrators and the weary matrons, who are scurrying in her presence and falling over themselves to please her. Bahar takes the tea they bring her and sets it down politely on a table in the corner of the nursery; she does not even pretend to put her lips to the glass. As they move through the nursery toward the crib that holds Firdis's baby, Grace senses the branching arms of what Bahar called consideration, the oiling of unseen machinery, the backroom transactions and private dealings. She sees how the benefit will be spread around, but it is Bahar and Ali, no doubt, who will take the lion's share. It will be Bahar who will travel and deliver the child to Edie in that distant German city.

Inside its crib, the baby looks like any other baby. Grace cannot quite say why this surprises her as it does. Except that this is the only child in the nursery wearing clothing that is not threadbare; in fact, its tiny footed outfit looks brand new.

Bahar leans into the crib and almost touches the baby's clenched fist. But then, instead, she brushes her hand across the terrycloth fabric of the little blue suit he wears. "This belonged to one of my boys," she says. "I brought it over."

Grace looks down at the baby. The matrons have moved away and a few babies cry softly in their cribs. In their small, whimpering sounds Grace registers a note of resignation, as if these infants do not expect to be comforted or consoled, and are crying only out of habit, and only to themselves. Grace feels something seize inside her chest.

"Perhaps," Grace ventures, "this isn't such a good idea. Firdis seems very down. I think maybe she's changed her mind." Firdis has returned to work, but her activity in the kitchen has taken on a plodding, despondent note.

Bahar steps back from the crib and makes a sharp noise, then she tempers it with a laugh. "Such emotions are common, believe me. When she has this American money she will hum a new song. And anyway, this thing, it is quite done. But it's a shame the baby was a boy. Had it been a girl there would not be this upset, this second thinking."

"What do you mean?"

Bahar looks hard at Grace for a moment. "You should not have had that houseboy that evening. You should not have told Simone about Firdis."

"I had to tell her something," Grace says. "I certainly didn't tell her *everything*."

"It never even occurred to me that you might do such a thing." Bahar shakes her head, wonderingly, in a way that reminds Grace of Rand, when he is trying to impress upon her the stupidity of something she's done. "Simone talks too much. And this is not a nice young man. Trouble. I thought you knew this."

"I was desperate. Anyway, what does it matter?"

"It does not," Bahar says, in a tone that effectively closes the subject. She turns and begins to make her way back across the nursery and Grace follows. Bahar does not even glance into the cribs as she passes them; she simply steps around them with the same blank face she wears on Tunali Hilmi. As though the babies are merely things in her way on the sidewalk, or some street smut that she does not want to get on her shoes.

Later, Grace thinks to address it all with Firdis herself, but she's put off by the complications of language, to say nothing of the embarrassment and dismay that would attend such a wholesale unraveling of hopes and plans. She begins avoiding Firdis's eyes and the sensation—real or imagined—that Firdis is itching to be engaged in conversation. It seems that the most innocuous inquiry or eye contact might provoke some heartfelt confession or plea from Firdis and, accordingly, Grace moves quietly, in the margins of her home, and does not quite light.

Grace cannot begin to imagine how a child of Firdis's might turn out in Edie's care. Firdis's children were thickset, their features hinting of mushrooms. But in a different atmosphere, might one blossom differently? In the dark rooms Edie favored, eating tapioca pudding and pound cake smothered in cream, listening to her accented English, her French records on the turntable, her wizardry with all things fine—needlework and delicate smocking, the musical click of flashing needles—could some transforming miracle occur? Edie had not once said to her, What do the others look like? Are they clever or lovely or imaginative? Tall or short or dull-witted? It had puzzled Grace, and it shamed her, Edie's great, uncomplicated need, utterly without conditions or qualifications.

In her own marriage Canada had been a surprise and Rand

had been displeased, suspecting her, she thought, of deception, some woman's trickery.

He didn't know her well enough to know that this is not a trap she'd have set for either of them.

RAND'S ABSENCE has been pure relief. Without him, everything feels fresher, cleaner, more alive. Even Canada, who has always been a creeper, an unsettlingly quiet child, thuds a bit more down the long hallway and closes the front door with a resonant little bang. Grace does not bother to scold her. She no longer feels the edginess that sharing a space with her daughter always provoked. She even enjoys her presence at the card games they get up in the afternoons, the women coming in flushed with cold and smelling of coal fires and chill.

Canada, her growing hands dealing out cards with her father's precision, or picking at the candied almonds and dried apricots set in crystal dishes along the table's center, is more and more a young lady. Suddenly her daughter's self-sufficiency and autonomy seem like things to be proud of, rather than defiances to be quashed. Grace feels a trace of regret. She's watched with such unease her daughter's lengthening limbs, the peaks that have appeared at the front of her cotton blouses, the smudge of freckles across the bridge of her nose. She'd never really wanted a pretty daughter, not a daughter like Catherine anyway, whose mournful face and bursting mouth are arresting, whose perfection seems unnatural, a little dangerous. Grace suspects Simone does not much like it either; that she will do what she can to hide it, or disguise it, or banish it. She thinks this accounts for Catherine's ridiculous dresses and face lift–tight hairdos, and for more than a little of Simone's own pinched personality. (Envy, her own mother used to say, is bad for the complexion.) She thinks of Simone sharing rooms with her daughter's beauty and wonders if she hopes that the blush on Catherine may only be youth, and fade accordingly.

Does Simone sense, as Grace has in that apartment, the lingering glances her darling houseboy throws at Catherine, and does it make her feel as invisible, as irrelevant and time-ravaged, as it does Grace?

But recently Grace has had fleeting feeling of invincibility, of the kind of power and ease she has long envied in other women. And an entirely new generosity, one that comes of having affection in surplus; she detects a glow to her skin, a new lightness in her limbs. She cannot keep herself from laughing, and she begins to understand Bahar's irresistibility; it is just the beauty of being desired. Now it seems that eyes follow her in the street, and in restaurants waiters hover near her place, anticipating things she hadn't known she wanted.

17

AT CHRISTMAS THE CITY WAS ICY AND COLD AND DARK. A GRAY pall of coal smoke hung so close in the air that it seemed you might thrust out your hand and see it disappear to the elbow. The day itself was long and dull: my mother and I opened our packages and ate a silent meal together at the table. It felt as though we were going through the motions, though we lit the tree for show and my mother made an elaborate holiday feast, using the good china and the Christmas linens. Music tinkled from the stereo and in the afternoon we went to church at the British Embassy. Later, when the dishes were cleared, we sat in the living room reading and adding logs to the fire. Dressed in silky lounging pajamas, my mother took photographs that would later show an entirely different Christmas: none of the dragging hours and edgy little conversations, my mother's attempts at seasonal cheer, my rude rebuffs. It was as though we were waiting for something to happen—the doorbell to ring, the phone to trill in the hallway—and it was a relief when the clock at last struck a reasonable hour for turning in. My mother sighed and rose from the couch, stretching as though she had enjoyed the day and zigzagging off to bed with a wineglass.

A few nights later she dragged me to a party at Simone's. Catherine was locked away in her room—avoiding me, I assumed—and while looking for a place of my own to hide I ran into John in the hallway. We were caught together for a moment, in an awkward dance, trying to pass each other.

"You and my mother," I found myself saying. "I saw you."

He looked at me curiously. "You have bad dreams," he said. "It is common in children." And then he was gone, slipping gracefully around me and disappearing into the kitchen. His hatred for us—all of us—was like an object you could weigh in your hand.

I stood for a time in the bathroom, washing my hands again and again with the lavender guest soap and staring at myself in the mirror. Then I left the bathroom and went uninvited into Catherine's room. It was strange to be there; so much time had passed.

Her face was pitying, her voice stony. After I spoke, repeating what I'd said to John in the hallway, she said, "You. You've been a sick puppy around him forever. I'm not blind. And you're only saying these things because he cares for me." But I think my story must have shaken her a little. How could it not?

"Besides," she said nastily, "he would never have anything to do with your mother."

When she said it, I knew she was right. He wouldn't. You could see that John wanted nothing to do with imperfection. He had no use for the old or the bruised, for anything tired or overtouched. Hadn't I seen him choose fruit?

But that didn't stop me. "He's doing it with your mother too," I said. "They all say so."

"With everyone but you," Catherine said. And she smiled her beautiful smile and returned to her book. Her finger had kept her place the whole time.

But after a moment she looked up and said in a more conversational tone, "That day . . ." The words held an inquiring note, though I knew of course what day she meant. "That day. Well, I got home. I guess you know that. But I saw your mother. Kissing someone in the street, at a café. Not your father of course. She must be very busy, your mother, very popular."

"That's not true," I said. But my face grew hot and I could well imagine it.

"Really?" said Catherine. "Actually it was John who pointed them out. We were walking together that day. You wouldn't know that. But he came to meet me. Strange, that. The way he turned up. I guess he knew something was wrong. He never liked you, of course. Never trusted you."

It seemed I stood there for an eternity, and I do not remember leaving the room.

She said one more thing before we were finished with each other. She said, "You should be careful. You and that mother of yours. I've never seen John so angry. He can't stand either one of you." She tossed her head and her thick hair, and her eyes were no longer tranquil but hard as agate, and just as unforgiving. Oh, I saw it clearly then—though there'd been a million signs that Catherine was outgrowing me. Once, I'd come up behind her in the kitchen and tickled her waist—it was just silliness, giddiness—but she'd whirled on me with a dark, adult, furious face.

"Sorry," I'd said, throwing up my hands and backing away from her. "I'm sorry."

"Yes," she'd said. "Yes, you are."

How did she outpace me so completely, in those few short months? When did her concerns become grown-up ones, and the games we'd manufactured suddenly grow so tiresome and immature?

THE LAST days of the year were smothered in smog and filth: everything I'd looked forward to had slumped by disappointingly. Without my father, without the promise of excursions or his company, the remainder of the school break stretched like an eternity. And then suddenly my mother had plans I wasn't privy to: a little trip that involved museums, shopping and mosques. A train ride, a cheap hotel. She assured me I'd be happier with friends, but she made the arrangements without consulting me.

Ultimately it was not hard to figure out where she was going: she left her paperwork and guidebooks scattered around the apartment. I was sent to stay with Kate and her family. We staged water fights on the rooftop garden of the house despite the cold and played complicated games of truth or dare. We slid back and forth on the icy patches we'd made on the roof and went sledding on the hill down from their house, where Kate and her siblings interacted fearlessly, even belligerently, with the Turkish children. I shared Kate's crumb-littered bed and fought with her for three nights over a share of the grubby duvet.

I was reading a book upstairs one night when Kate came clattering up after supper, breathless. She swung back and forth on the edge of the door and said, "She's bloody gone."

"Who is?"

"Who do you think? The Canadian. Your friend. She's actually buggered off somewhere, run away."

Kate did not know this for a fact, and she had no details, but she'd gleaned bits and pieces. Her parents had been talking loudly, without discretion, over running water and dirty dishes.

"It's supposed to be a secret. Simone's off her rocker. Mum heard the whole thing from someone at church."

Kate tore open a chocolate bar—she had an endless supply of them hidden under her mattress—and licked the brown, sweating inside of the wrapper. "It's bloody marvelous. It's absolutely the most excellent thing I ever heard."

"I have to go home," I said. "My mother's come back early."

"That's a bloody lie," she said. "But I don't care. Do what you want. I'm tired of you anyway."

I told her mother a fib and left Kate's house. I walked all the way home and made the kapıcı let me in. He lived in the basement and I had to bang on the door for a full five minutes before he appeared— heavily mustached, wiping his nose with his sleeve and very irritated by the interruption. For a long moment, as he decided what to do with me, the whole wild impulse hung in jeopardy. Finally he tossed a burning cigarette over my shoulder into the hallway, wrestled his ring of keys from his belt, yelled something to his wife and trudged up the stairs in front of me, speaking incomprehensibly, angrily, under his breath.

I had been alone in the apartment many times, but never once overnight. I opened the windows and the kitchen door that led to the balcony. I ate cold borek from the refrigerator and sat in the living room, playing my mother's records. I did not have quite enough courage to build a fire or pour a glass of brandy, though both those things seemed entirely appropriate to the occasion.

Later, my father telephoned and I picked it up in the hallway. I was thrilled to hear his voice, even the sound of the miles buzzing between us. Had he known somehow that I was alone? I wouldn't have been surprised, he had always seemed that powerful to me. But he said nothing about it, and so when he asked for my mother I didn't bother to make an excuse for her. I made my voice cold and casual, saying I hadn't the faintest idea where she'd gone, that she'd left in a taxi, with her makeup done and a weekend bag. I had no riding lessons scheduled either, I mentioned into the echoing hum of the telephone connection, for coincidentally, Ahmet too had gone away.

We stayed on the line in silence for a few moments. "Where are you?" I said finally. "When are you coming back?"

"I'm not sure," he said, "but I can tell you one thing, it's damn cold here."

He said goodbye then and the line disengaged abruptly.

Afterward, sitting in the quiet alone, I imagined I was Catherine and that it was my hand that John held, leading me down the staircase, my fingers curling inside his. I saw the taxi he called waiting, the hurry in his step because I'd finally agreed but might yet change my mind. As I imagined moving through that morning, I carried Catherine's blue wool coat, her white gloves, a book.

I'd often imagined myself as Catherine: in her skin, her clothes, in the hollows of her bones. Sometimes, I even wore the jewelry she'd given me to hide, the sparkling little pieces from John. Once, Paige spied the bracelet on my wrist and swung me around in her kitchen— where did that come from? She pried back my cuff, bent her powdered face and her blue-caked eyelids, down close to it. That's a lovely one. Where did you find it? Alone in Catherine's room on a thousand occasions I touched her belongings—trailing my fingers along them the way we had done in Simone's bedroom. But I wanted to carry it all away with me—her calm and her undeserved beauty, all her terrible advantages.

In September—it seemed years ago—we'd walked home from school once with a boy who rode our bus. In the center of the construction site near my apartment building was an enormous pile of bricks; every day the men wheeled barrows of these around to various spots. This activity—and eating, and smoking—was the entire extent of any progress we'd seen made there. Passing the site that day, the boy, Marcus, casually lifted a stone from the ground and lobbed it in the direction of the brick pile; it landed squarely, to our amazement, and shattered several. They broke with a surprisingly musical noise, a kind of tinkling: it made you think the bricks were flimsy to begin with and poorly made. A worker was bending over a trough of cement with a shovel and he paused at the noise, lifting his head and turning it slowly, taking in the situation: the boy, the girls, the bricks, and the offending rock, still bouncing across the dirt. Without a word he straightened and lifted the shovel, holding its load of sloppy cement, and flung the contents toward us where we stood, rooted, on the sidewalk. Marcus ducked. But Catherine stood stock-still and the cement hit her full force: it landed on the side of her head and made its way, dripping clingingly, down her cheek, her shoulder, onto her schoolbooks and the tops of her patent shoes. The boy fled; I saw his back, the worn soles of his shoes as he flew the rest of the way down the street and disappeared around the corner.

Upstairs, I put her in the bath like a child, peeling the clothes from her, dropping them on the floor. The cement had hardened in her hair; a tear caught in the gray sludge on her cheek and quivered. There was one bathroom in our apartment, green and ugly; you could in no way compare it to the steamy, scented paradise of Simone's invention. Sometimes, in her absences—stolen minutes, each counting as hours—we had bathed there together, pouring into the steaming water ever less conservative capfuls, heady mixtures of her oils and salts and lotions, until the room was suffocating in steam and competing scents and Catherine and I lounged opposite each other in curving ceramic corners, smiling and drowsy and quite breathless with danger, our lips smeared with lipsticks we had swiped and swiped again in the mirror, sugars and corals and deep-deep darks, applied in thick, vampish smears.

But in my family's bathroom, cheap, too-dark panty hose hung like disembodied legs from the shower rail and the wringer washer squatted in a corner, primitive and unsightly, a heaped basket of neglected ironing to one side. I ran the water scalding hot and put Catherine's head under the faucet. She was suddenly pliable, as easy to move as a doll. She sat with her head flung back, shoulders pearly in the steam, elbows braced on the edges of the tub, the toes of my mother's stockings, with their thick, oversewn seams, trailing over her collarbone and cheeks. From time to time she pushed them from her eyes absently, like bangs grown long. For over an hour I pulled cement from her hair. We didn't speak; my fingers grew puckered and white ridged in the steam. When we heard the front door I slid out of my own wet clothes, quickly, quickly, and eased my body into the water, hands pushing the small globs of cement to the bottom, trapping them under my feet. For a moment we faced each other, knees drawn up to make way in the too-tight green tub—it seemed sudden, that fit; had we grown? I noted for the millionth time her carved features, her smooth skin, the sleek dark curtain of her loosed hair. Then she closed her eyes tight, shutting me out, and it was as if I were suddenly alone in the cooling gray water. The door opened and my mother stood there, surprised but not especially intrigued, then went away.

Sitting alone in the living room that night, having turned on every light in the apartment, I thought of John and Catherine, of my mother and Ahmet, and then suddenly of Angie, the little girl I had played with on Olson Loop. I remembered the hot sticky tar of the driveway and the long yellow curls she twisted around her finger. One night she had slept at my house and then, late and in the dark, when my parents were downstairs with the television going, she had lifted her legs wide in the air and taken my hand and pushed it deep between them. I thought of that, and the vast toy store of her bedroom, the deep shag carpet littered with Barbie clothes and little plastic shoes and cars and furniture, the ovens cooking miniature cakes with lightbulbs, the snap-together train tracks winding through perfect plastic towns and deep green forests. And again, it's that blistering day and across the street my mother is locked away with Edie and there will be nothing for lunch and Angie is standing in front of me in her red playsuit and her white socks and she is running the wheels of her wagon back and forth and somewhere a dog is barking and a bicycle bell is ringing and the sun is hitting her golden hair from behind and I look down at the complex, glistening pattern of tar beneath my dirty sneakers and suddenly I want, I want, I want—I want to see her *there*. And my hands fly forward and strike her shoulders and she falls backward onto her fat bottom and then gets to her feet, her face too stupid with surprise and that isn't good enough at all so I push her again and she falls forward onto her plump knees and then there is bright blood and screaming and then, only then, am I satisfied. Perfectly, perfectly satisfied.

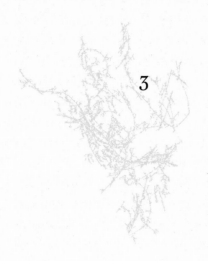

3

JANUARY 1976

18

THE ISTANBUL APARTMENT IN THE SULTANAHMET DISTRICT BE-
longs to the consulate and is kept for important guests and state vis-
itors: Paige, ever influential, has arranged it for the holiday weekend.
She's described it to Grace in detail: the quiet, tree-lined street, the
views of the river from wide windows, and in the distance the six
minarets of the great Blue Mosque. Close to shopping, she said, and
lovely little restaurants.

"If you manage to get outside." This said archly. "If not, don't
tell me." She's given Grace a list of attractions she must visit, shops
they must look in on, using her name. "Lie to me," she says. "The
bartering. The sights, the food. In descriptive detail."

But they do leave it. Early mornings and late at night, when the city
is at its fitful rest, they creep into the streets and buy groceries and
fresh bread and pastries from the bakery and then, roughhousing and
laden with packages, they climb back up the staircase to the light-
filled rooms and sink into their temporary domesticity—their hours
of food and tea and sex and temporary intimacies. At night they walk
the quieted streets of the bazaar and squint into the darkened windows of the shops: here is where she might buy a rug, he tells her, on
another trip. She should remember the address. And at this place, she
will find the kind of puzzle rings that children like; here, the sort of
copper that is beautiful but cannot be used for cooking. But to her
small and unstated dismay, they shun the city's daylight pleasures.

Ahmet does not care for the crowds, the tourists, all the common, well-frequented sights.

And try as she might, Grace cannot draw him into any conversation of a future between them. He will not comfort her in this way. She only wants him to say he wants it, not that he will do it. She's not sure she even wants it herself, only this feeling and to pretend it might not end. But Ahmet is a man who does not like talk of imaginary, impossible things: these are ephemera, frivolous and unsatisfying, and they do not intrigue him.

Lying on the floor, overlooking the river, as the sun sets and that suspension bridge of light she has seen in photographs and books suddenly connects one shore, and one continent, to another, a new feeling creeps up on her. Grace thinks of Bahar, who has left for Europe with Firdis's child: she imagines the meeting between her two friends, in a city once so familiar to her. She can see the wet cobbled streets and the arching lamps overhead and she imagines them in a café or a gasthaus, sitting across a table from each another, while one and then the other jiggles the dark baby on her lap. What will they speak of? She is fleetingly jealous of these women together: she imagines them making little jokes at her expense, speaking of her in light, disparaging terms. It is what she is occupied with when Ahmet presses his hand against her bare stomach and offers a few million lira for her thoughts.

"My friend Edie," she tells him. "This baby business."

Ahmet sighs and rolls away on the carpet. His back is pale and lightly freckled; naked, his age is more apparent.

"Sorry," she says. "I know you don't want to think of it."

"No," he says. "I don't want *you* to think of it. This is why I agreed to come to Istanbul this weekend. To distract you from these arrangements."

Is this true? Grace does not have the courage to press him. She makes a joke of it instead and jollies him until he turns and gathers her up once more in his arms. But it gives her something else to think about, to imagine that she has been capitulated to like a pouting child.

She went to Istanbul seeking peace. But despite her hopes for the trip and all the superficial pleasures it undeniably holds, Grace begins to feel that something intangible has slipped from her fingers.

Ahmet gets up now and moves to the window. He takes his shirt from a chair and buttons it over his chest. Then he lifts his wallet from a table in the corner and tucks it into his pocket. He turns to look at her for a few seconds before leaving the room; Grace watches him go without saying a word.

The room is quiet: just the murmur of water traffic on the Bosporus, the closing of a door in the hallway outside, the gentle whir of the ceiling fan pushing a breeze from the windows. Lying on the floor, Grace is surrounded by the remains of the afternoon—the stained wineglasses and heels of bread, the crumbs of cheese and scattered pillows. She sits up and rests her head on her knees. A sepia-toned photograph on the wall catches her eye: a wedding picture of some old-fashioned strangers, a beaming young bride in white posing with a stiff young man in a dark suit. He is trying so hard, she sees, to look somber and adult but has succeeded only in looking terrified. There is something intensely sweet about the picture, something hopeful and lovely and brave.

It makes Grace think of her own wedding—had she ever felt that way, had it ever shown? She remembers a small stone church in the middle of a once familiar city, her demure ivory suit and tight, borrowed shoes, and the sight of Rand at the end of the aisle, in his dress uniform, surrounded by his army buddies, their faces a childish mixture of alarm and propriety. Later there was cake in someone's drab apartment, and champagne in snap-together flutes, small gifts elaborately wrapped—an enormous lollipop etched with the words "To our favorite sucker," which Rand had mugged with, absurdly, a little grotesquely, for the camera.

Rand had shipped out to Baghdad right after the wedding, with Grace in tow like a new piece of luggage, her packing skills wholly inadequate for the challenge. That would change. A girlfriend had given her a book as a wedding gift, *The Officer's Wife,* and even then it had been a gag. They'd turned the pages together, giggling at the stilted language and the straight-faced suggestions, the rigid politesse of this new life she was embarking on. But it was one she was certain she could triumph over armed with nothing but her modern thinking, her youth, her fine complexion, her handsome husband. It had seemed laughably easy: a lark, a girlish scamp. She hadn't known at the time that she was already pregnant.

But even so it had gone on that way for nearly two years—the pregnancy was easy, and Baghdad was a whirl of exotic scenery and locales, men in uniforms dipping over her hand at parties. Then one morning there was a telephone call from the embassy telling her to pack and pack quickly. One small suitcase, the baby's essentials. Leave the rest, the official on the phone instructed. She was not allowed to speak to Rand, who was reportedly occupied.

Suddenly, bombs were exploding in the city and smoke rose in plumes over the Tigris. They came for her in a convoy, and the truck was filled with other women and their children, women she knew from parties and coffees and the makeshift little church on the American compound. It struck her that she had never seen them without makeup; it was early morning and some still wore housecoats and curlers. Others wore slacks—forbidden in the streets but suddenly those protocols seemed irrelevant. Some, like Grace, carried sleeping babies and fistfuls of diapers, their pockets stuffed with oddities: eyeliners and jewelry, a wooden kitchen spoon, baby booties, wedding photographs folded into squares. A few wept and clung together but for the most part they huddled silently along the hard benches beneath the canvas tarp and turned their faces away from one another, as though they had been caught together in some embarrassing, potentially compromising position. As they drove through the city that morning they saw pitiless young men, wild-eyed and glancing behind them, running aimlessly in the streets, and shouting, looking for a melee or a mob to throw themselves into. Coming across a dog these boys would surely kick it bloody, leave it half dead and broken in the street: such was their great, pointless, uncertain hurry.

But the trucks carrying the women left the city swiftly, turning from the main roads and striking out toward the desert and the border with Iran. Young men with rifles leaned out from the edges of the trucks, clinging to the sides and the frames, their baby faces hardened into soldierly masks. If it hadn't been so terrifying, Grace might have laughed at the thought of them under the protection of these uniformed children. As the trucks met the desert, the women spoke in whispers of their husbands and eventually, as they calmed, of more commonplace valuables, their china and evening gowns and family cookbooks, bedding and cabinetry and photo albums.

Most of them had lost track of their men for the first time. Days passed without word, with only ambiguous briefings from tired officials, who gathered them in dreary rooms and met their questions with statements read from file folders. Later, in a safer country, they would reunite in an airport hangar, the men climbing down from fat-nosed green aircraft and trudging toward them, their clothes smelling of the unknown, their skin gritty and their hands roughened.

Perhaps other men recounted for their wives the events of those six lost days. For his part, Rand was mute and distant, his features remote and his manner terse. Those days seemed to stand between them, and their separate experiences of them: for Grace, the dusty caravan of women and children, the bawdy joking of the soldiers, the cold, fear-filled desert nights, the sick babies and the low, nervous chatter they relied on to pass the hours were insurmountable objects grown up suddenly in the rooms they now shared. The air grew close with their silences and they deliberately spoke of inconsequential things, of their left belongings and goods. They waited nervously for their new orders to arrive. There was no talk of returning to that city, to the little house with the garden and the lemon trees, to the wide streets and boulevards, to the arched doorways and cool tiled floors of their first shared home as a married couple.

"What happened over there?" she had asked in the hours after he first returned. His eyes were squinted up with exhaustion. When he didn't answer she went on in a happy rush; she was overflowing with saved-up stories, with the details and inconveniences she had accumulated for this occasion. She had imagined they would laugh over them together.

"You can't believe how terrible it was. I want to tell you about the soldiers, about what pigs they were, how they watched us go to the bathroom in the sand dunes. They were awful, like naughty little boys."

"That's too bad," he said. "I'm sorry to hear it."

And it did not take a deck of cards to sense he was not interested in these discomforts, that it seemed to him she was mewling, that her stories were plays for sympathy and her troubles feminine and small.

And so she said, "Will you tell me what happened? Tell me about the war. What did you do?"

"The bathrooms were fine," he said. "Nothing to complain about."

Stung, she had left the room. And for inexplicable reasons—reasons that still bewilder her—Grace let that coldness harden between them so that by the time they left those temporary rooms and made for another city, a western one this time, to be reunited with their property, it had become something they packed and carried with them, erecting it again and again in the new quarters they would share.

THE LAST night in Istanbul, near morning, Ahmet lies in the low, tumbled bed while Grace stands at the window, chilled and sleepless. Suddenly her eyes find a figure standing at the curve of the street, in a low doorway. The gulls, everywhere in this city, tremble like broad, ghostly moths above the spired roofs, dipping down into the street, then fluttering up to rest on a lamppost. Still, she can't say for certain. The light is too dim, the figure too shadowed, too still and unmoving. But she feels a prickle on her arms and along her spine; the coat looks like the one, the conformation of the body is right and its stance and the familiar turn of its head in silhouette.

She stands for several minutes, staring. Then quite suddenly the form in the doorway vanishes, and she can't say if she turned her eyes away for a moment, or blinked, or whether it was a phantom, a chimera; that he was never really there at all.

After a moment she leaves the apartment without her coat, slipping down the steps in her bare feet. In the covered doorway outside—colder than mere hours before, a smell coming up from the streets that is fresh only in the absence of other, more immediate, human scents—she stands shivering for a moment and then steps forward into the cobbled Istanbul night.

But everything remains quiet and her voice saying his name is merely a hiss in the dark, empty and echoing, a breath of steam. It's dark overhead and there's no moon at all. She glances up at the window above; it too is dark. No life shows on the street but there are sounds—the scuffle of a rat in an alley, a scrap of paper blowing. She pulls her nightgown up around her neck and runs back up the stairs with the distinct feeling of being pursued. Inside the apartment, nothing has changed: yastiks are scattered on the floor and empty wineglasses, heels of bread and olive pits litter the table. Ahmet sleeps like the dead and clouds drift almost imperceptibly outside the windows. She crawls into the bed beside him, trembling, and tries to sleep.

In the morning, as they are packing their small bags for the train, Paige calls on the telephone, her voice calm and conversational. "I have a favor," she says. "There's a package at the train station. Could you possibly retrieve it?"

At the station, in an overheated office swarming with men and luggage and official business, Grace and Ahmet are surprised to find Simone's daughter, Catherine. She is sitting on a chair calmly reading a book; there is a small suitcase held tightly between her feet. She is, as always, quite impossible to talk to.

"What on earth?" Grace says to her, but receives no satisfactory reply. They leave the office with Catherine in tow—no one there seems particularly interested in what becomes of her—and Ahmet goes off to check the schedule. Waiting for the train to Ankara, the three of them stand on the grimy platform beneath the old arches of the station; Grace holds Catherine's ticket, Ahmet stares off into space. Grace finds that she is annoyed.

"What *is* she doing here?" she says to Ahmet, who simply shrugs and wanders off to buy a newspaper.

Grace looks down at Catherine; not far, for she is very nearly Grace's height. "I'd like an explanation," she says. "Since I'm suddenly your chaperone. If you please."

"I was on a trip with a friend. Our plans changed." The girl watches a train chug into the station on the opposite track. She lifts her suitcase and then puts it down again.

Grace studies her smooth forehead, thinking of Canada. It seems odd that these two girls, so similar in coloring and shape and features, could somehow be so different in terms of beauty, that most abstract of qualities.

They had taken Catherine on trips to the sea more than once, and to see the Sufi dancers during the summer months; she and Canada had once been so close. Grace remembers men's eyes on this charge of hers, in teahouses and cafés and shops that made a certain famous pottery, the way talk would turn to joking and barter—might they not leave this girl, trade her for a lovely plate or bit of ceramic, might she not wish to marry this one's son, another's cousin? And Canada would smile tightly and press herself a little forward, aching for notice, longing for such a magnificent compliment—to be similarly desired and haggled over. Such a valuable friend you've brought along, Rand said to her once, winking. Perhaps we should keep her. Catherine, with her lowered eyes and coy smile, pretending confusion, feigning indignation; and Canada, feet moving in the dirt, a kind of death in her eyes. Grace wanted to slap her: Stop it. Buck up. Show some dignity.

But from time to time the girls were mistaken for sisters and you could see how the comparison pleased one, and how it surprised the other. With Catherine, Grace saw clearly what beauty did for its owner; she noticed how much kinder one felt toward beautiful children, how much more giving, loving and gracious. Still, it was never long before Grace found Catherine difficult. And was the girl perhaps just a little too ethereal? Grace tried to imagine these two, only a few years from now, doing the things girls would do, wearing showy things and setting their mouths in hard lines, smoking stolen cigarettes, wandering away from parties with boys.

"Does Canada know where you are?" Grace says at last.

"Does she know where you are?"

After a moment Ahmet returns. As they board the train to return to Ankara and Catherine goes swaying ahead of them into the carriage, Grace clutches his elbow: she wishes desperately that he will say something to her, something she can hold on to. Standing there, watching Catherine climb into the car, she is suddenly suffused with a terrible feeling of loss, as though this trip has been their final destination. The look Ahmet gives her, as the train wheezes away from the station and gathers speed, as the three of them trip silently toward their compartment, serves only to confirm this feeling.

It is a long ride in close quarters and Grace tries again to engage Catherine. The girl is staring out the window at the passing landscape but finally turns cool greenish eyes on her and says, "John and I were going to Mecca but it didn't work out. They wouldn't let me buy a ticket on my own. So here we are."

"How old are you?" says Grace. Surely this girl, with this unnatural calm, is older than Canada.

Catherine ignores her. "I'd rather not talk about this anymore," she says. "It's going to be bad enough at home."

Grace reflects on this and cannot help agree. Simone will certainly skin her alive. "John?" she says, after a moment. "Why would you go anywhere with the houseboy?"

The girl shrugs and returns to the view.

"Oh my goodness," says Grace, suddenly feeling at least a hundred years old. "Tell me, are you hurt?"

Ahmet is engrossed in his paper; he goes on reading. When they go for lunch in the dining car, leaving Catherine behind, Grace holds him up in the rattling corridor. "I think that child was abducted by the houseboy."

"Or ran off," he says. There has not been, since the moment they encountered Catherine in the station, the slightest betrayal of his feelings on this matter.

"Ahmet," she says, "what on earth are you thinking?"

"That it is odd what you choose to involve yourself in, to become disturbed about."

"You'd think the police would be involved, wouldn't you? You'd think Simone would be simply wild."

"From the looks of it," he says, "your friend simply wants it quiet. No harm done."

Grace stares at him. "What an astonishing thing to say."

He leans down and kisses her head affectionately. It does not escape her that the gesture is utterly without romantic feeling. "You are very naïve," he says. "It seems to me this situation is not so very unlike another I might name. Though I see it seems very different to you."

"The two are hardly comparable," she says. "That's a young girl, a child. I always knew there was something odd going on in that house."

"Well," he says, "if you did, surely this Simone did as well. That seems a reasonable assumption."

"Surely not," she says firmly. Surely, surely not.

Ahmet looks at her in a way that is hard to interpret, and then makes his way ahead of her through the wild, windy platforms between the cars, with the rails racing beneath and the stubborn, sticking doors, and finally into the hazy dining car, where the smoke is a gauze and the smells—of unwashed bodies and scorched coffee and the anisette odor of raki—are almost nauseating.

Outside the train station in Ankara, snow has been falling lightly and the skyline is wreathed in smog. It seems hours later than it is. Ahmet leans in the window of the taxi with his body and tells the driver where to take them, handing a sheaf of garish bills over the seat as if they are just an ordinary family, in some everyday situation. He thumps the taxi's trunk as it pulls away and she sees him through the rear window when she turns, he is hailing his own cab, his bag over his shoulder—suddenly he is just any other stranger on the street.

As the car bounces away, Grace thinks of Canada and what all this—Istanbul, Ahmet, Catherine, Edie—might mean for them later. All at once, she doesn't like the feeling, the idea that she's been so unforgivably absent, and that she's often visited with the thought, without so much as a glimmer of remorse, of perpetrating her own great, romantic escape. On the seat beside her Catherine's profile looks adult and knowing, and when she glances over at Grace, though it may be her imagination, the girl seems more contemptuous than usual.

"I don't suppose," Catherine says as they drive down the hill toward her street, "that you would leave me off here and let me walk?"

Grace doesn't answer. The thought strikes her that in later years, though it seems improbable, she might even mourn the loss of her child as better mothers do. Canada's absence from her household, her disappearance into the distant, labyrinthine territories of adulthood.

And so, unhappily, Grace returns home with an icy clutch around her heart and the feeling that had she only stayed put, had she not tempted fate with her grandiose plans and schemes, things might have continued on indefinitely. But she cannot be sure if she is only borrowing trouble—for hadn't he kissed her as he put her into the taxi, and hadn't he said they'd speak soon?

Stepping inside the doorway of the apartment, the contents of her home feel entirely different—both askew and strangely etched. The items she knows so well—the plates and artifacts, the dervish figurines on the sideboard, the crystal ashtray glinting in deep and thoughtful amber on the coffee table—all of it strikes her as off. Standing there, looking around, smelling the quiet, the layers of tobacco and ammonia and lemon, she catches sight of herself in the hall mirror, trembling and out of sorts. Entirely unlike herself. And then, for some reason, this stirs in her a half moment of uneasy joy. She thinks—hesitates, considers, moves in one direction for a purposeful instant and then stops. She had been thinking she might want to pour a drink, put some old record on. Her mind races—a thousand things jumble through. Skin and words, unkind phrases, clever jokes, words spoken in loving tones but tense with undercurrent, uncomfortable silences suddenly relieved, and unexpected moments of sympathy and tenderness. Does he, did he, mean any of it?

Canada, too, is subdued and the apartment reeks of stale smoke and some small attempts at airing. Grace doesn't really think to tell Canada of her friend's aborted journey, of the purely accidental intervention: she is drained and the prospect seems prohibitively unpleasant. Catherine had slid swiftly from the taxi as it drew up outside her apartment building, and though she'd thanked Grace as if she'd been taken for lunch or an outing, there was disdain in her manner. Grace watched the girl go inside, carrying her suitcase, taking her time. On the ride up the hill, Grace thought her over. What had gone on under Simone's nose, and what, indeed, would become of John?

She remembered the party she'd given, where she'd drunk too much too quickly, and thought briefly of Rand, for she'd had the sensation of trying to drown something quite deep, something infinitely buoyant. She wondered for a moment if he felt that same unpleasant sensation, every minute of every day. Later, when they'd all gone and she was coming from the bathroom with her face shiny and washed and creamed, she found John readying to leave in the front hallway. He was making a pile of packages, things she had told him to take: leftover food, half-empty liquor bottles, the accumulated debris of the evening. It made a ragged, not insignificant little mountain by the front door. Seeing him, she had jumped and pressed her hand to her heart to convey the shock and then stumbled for a split second over the hallway carpet. He caught her and his arms lingered momentarily at her waist. His face was very close; she could make out his pores, the little filings of stubble on his cheeks. He bowed his head, a little apology or admission, but his mouth was immobile and his eyes as insolent as ever. Then he set her upright again.

IT IS less than a week after Grace brings Catherine home from Istanbul that Simone sends her a picture through the mail. In it Rand is sitting on a lounge chair by the Canadian swimming pool, holding a nearly empty glass. Other men stand around in clumsy tableau, hands all at loose ends. Their owlish glasses reflect the light. In the background, Catherine is holding a tray with smeared tumblers and John's disembodied hand hovers at the nape of her neck, like a cat about to grab an errant kitten. In the foreground, the pool glows with underwater lighting; the ripples on the surface look like some opulent material you could pleat with your fingers. In her pinched, precise hand, Simone has written the date on the back of the photograph. As if Grace would need the reminder—it might have been yesterday.

Rand had been trying to catch John's eye for several minutes for a refill. Grace, too, had noticed, but wasn't going out of her way to assist him. In fact, she was on her way to Canada, who stood against the wall, half naked in a bathing suit. Grace was planning to say something sharp to her, something about covering up. Where on earth did she think she was?

Meanwhile, Simone fussed with the camera, taking her time. Rand grew uncomfortable; he could never abide his own drained glass, the sorrowful noise of ice cubes meeting without liquor to buffer them. The men shuffled and adjusted; one held a towel draped around his shoulders as if it were a scarf. The man stood still for so long waiting for Simone to snap the picture that he began to look waxen and absurd. His smile petrified, his glasses fogged. The shutter clicked at last and Rand scrambled to his unsteady feet, tipping the chair, stumbling to get clear of it.

Even now, Grace can see the glass from his hand crashing to the tiles just after that picture was snapped—and then all the rest of it unfolds, rapid-fire, slow motion, it unwinds in her memory with every cinematic trick. Why had Simone finally decided to hand it over, and what had she meant to remind her of? That she and Grace were no different; that they each had things they would rather keep quiet?

Simone's face before the panic erupted: cool and superior, oddly knowing—and strangely, almost immodestly pleased.

Now the situation with Catherine seems to require something of her. At the very least it demands moral outrage and Grace works diligently, with some small success, to dredge it up. Funny that over the next few days, as she waits for the inevitable fallout from this scandal—some official disgrace for John, some phone call from Simone that deftly skirts this indelicacy, some talk among the women in her circle—almost everything goes on quite as usual.

But Firdis does not turn up immediately, which is alarming, for she is nothing if not punctual. Maids and children, Grace thinks more than once, picking up her own overflowing ashtrays. Everywhere when you don't want them, nowhere when you do. Not until the third day does a shrunken Firdis materialize in the kitchen, and they pick up where they had left off.

It is several days later and purely by accident that she discovers what has happened down the hill. She has occasion, simply, to see John on the street. As she drives past in a taxi he is walking quite routinely, even jauntily, down the hill toward Simone's apartment, carrying packages.

And when she rings Paige, thinking to hear some explanation that is reasonable, she hears merely an echo of Ahmet's words on the train. What did you expect? said Paige, everyone's safe and sound. A minor misadventure. And thanks, she added as an afterthought, for your help. I didn't relish going there myself, I'll tell you.

"But why in the world," said Grace, "did Catherine call you to fetch her? Why not Simone?"

"Why not Simone indeed?" said Paige. "In any case, it wasn't Catherine who called me."

Grace hung up the phone entirely puzzled. When she had said, finally, in a tone that felt commensurate with the situation, "Shouldn't that young man be in jail or something?" Paige had only laughed.

"For what? Simone thinks he's a national treasure, in case you hadn't noticed. Anyway, don't you forgive Firdis a great deal?"

WHEN THE call from Germany comes at last Grace snatches the phone from the cradle and stands on her tiptoes in the hallway. Firdis is instantly underfoot; she begins to polish the legs of the small telephone table, muttering apologies, wedging herself beneath Grace's knees. It is Edie on the line, and then Grace can hear Bahar in the background, her lilting syllables, the noise she makes on a cigarette. She is right at Edie's side; they must have the phone between them.

"Oh, Grace," says Edie, and her words spill into Grace's ear. "Oh, it's wonderful. I'm so happy. So grateful."

"So sick of strudel," Grace hears Bahar say, and then the two of them laugh together for an irritating and overlong moment.

But all's well, they tell her. It has gone off just as Bahar promised. (Didn't I say so? she purrs.) Their mingled breath on the line is noisy and Grace cannot catch all of what they are saying. But she intuits that her predictions were not so off the mark: they are getting along beautifully. They talk in shared sentences of museums and sights, of the zoo and the park and a day trip by train to Cologne.

When Grace puts the phone down, she does not feel much relieved, and Firdis, naturally, is still there, hunched at her feet, paying excessive attention to the beveled legs of the telephone table. Grace squeezes out of the tight space and pats Firdis's back gingerly. "Everything's fine," she says to her. "Tamam. All is okay." And Firdis, as she should have expected, bursts immediately into tears and runs away wailing to the kitchen.

19

WE RARELY SPOKE OF MY FATHER, OR WONDERED ABOUT HIS RE-
turn, but we were likely no different from anyone else in those circles: too accustomed to our lives without husbands and fathers, too
used to filling the days, too self-sufficient and devoted to ourselves.
It seemed he left not so much a hole in our lives as a faint impression, no more noticeable than a dent in the couch or a fading bruise.

Some evenings my mother could be found alone at our dinner
table, which she'd set for an intimate meal, with flowers between the
silver candlesticks and a little silver bell to the left of her place setting.
She used the bell to signal the next course, to summon Firdis—an affectation she'd picked up from Simone and from formal dinners at
the American Residence. She would sit with her legs crossed, overdressed for an evening at home, smoking cigarettes and drinking a
sweet Rhine wine from a crystal goblet. Some part of a meal would
remain on the plate in front of her—a few bites of lamb, a brussels
sprout, a forkful of whipped potato. Perhaps she wanted to give the
impression that she always dined in this fashion, alone and surrounded by silver and cut crystal, like an aging stage actress or a night-
club chanteuse. Coming in, I would watch her from the doorway,
listening to the romantic music she was playing, wondering if there
was anything for me to eat. I might walk into the kitchen, looking for
Firdis or leftovers, but I would steer quite clear of my mother. Even

her shoulders had the posture of a person you did not particularly wish to engage.

There were phone calls. She would whisper into the clunky black receiver in the hallway. Then dialogue that included the words, if not the tone, of a disagreement, of a woman trying very hard not to sound dismayed but still in search of an explanation she could swallow. I knew it was Ahmet she was talking to, and I knew that he was throwing her over.

Once, when Firdis's husband came to the house to retrieve her, I saw my mother attempt to engage him in conversation. It went badly. She was complimenting Firdis, moving her hands in a pantomime of gratitude and appreciation. I just couldn't live without her, she was saying, and she brought her clasped hands up to her heart. He stood unsmiling in the stairwell, his thick brows beetled, and when she'd finished he made a motion past her with his hand and then the kind of noise one might make toward an animal or a child, telling it to get cracking. "Well," my mother said shakily, when they had gone, Firdis trailing him obediently down the stairs, "isn't he charming?"

Whatever was between those two women by then crackled in the air of our apartment, clear in the way they stepped wide around each other. Firdis became, if not neglectful, a bit slack in her duties: the things in our apartment lost their burnished gleam and a thin film of dust settled across everything.

My mother even screamed at Firdis once, for misarranging pillows on the sofa. While Firdis stood by with no expression on her face, my mother snatched up the pillows and clutched them to her chest, then plunked them back angrily in the order she preferred. "Like this," she said to Firdis. "Like this! Understand?"

And then just as quickly, Firdis disappeared. A week passed, maybe more. My mother refused to discuss it. She would open the refrigerator door and study, with seeming bewilderment, the empty interior.

When the kapıcı rang the bell, my mother ignored it. I saw her once, drifting furtively away from the door as the bell shrilled, almost on tiptoe.

Suddenly, I missed my father.

I grew bold, wearing the jewelry Catherine gave me to hide, the things that came from John—the Maşallah pendant, the evil eye bracelet—and I didn't bother to conceal them from my mother.

Without Firdis, the apartment fell into melancholy disarray. The dust accumulated, and fruit spoiled, springing tiny flies. Laundry piled up. Everywhere was the thick, unpleasant odor of powdered milk and the unswept ashes, accumulating in a soft, volcanic heap in the fireplace.

ONE MORNING after my mother returned from Istanbul, she insisted on driving to the barn early. She woke me impatiently, hustled me through toothbrushing and dressing, rushed me into the car and drove through traffic with a new and purely Turkish recklessness, her hands gripping the leather cover of the steering wheel, which was unraveling slowly, bits of caramel braiding coming apart one piece at a time. Parking, she checked and reapplied her lipstick in the rearview mirror, patted down her hair, adjusted her bra straps and ran her tongue over her teeth. She seemed just slightly overdressed, one accessory too many; shoes a bit too high of heel, trousers too pale and too tight, a coat you wouldn't think should come in contact with horse slime.

It was very cold and I was annoyed; she'd rushed me and I'd forgotten my gloves. As we came down the hill to the stable entrance we found a car sideways near the gate, where people were discouraged from parking: a big gleaming sedan, silver colored, of German make with dark-tinted windows. It oozed affluence; it was Bahar's car. My mother slowed her steps looking at it and then, in the next moment, quickened them, teetering down the gravel path, touching her hair and nearly breaking a heel on the stones. I slowed down, stuffing my hands into the pockets of my coat and kicking at the ground.

"Hurry up," she said, turning. "Come on."

"Why?" I said. "What's the darn rush?"

The trailer door was closed but you could see there was life inside—a light showed beneath the curtains. My mother seemed unsure what to do next.

Then something came to her. "Go see if you left some gloves in there," she said. "Or borrow a pair."

I shook my head. "I'm fine." I started to walk away, down the path toward the stalls. I meant to leave her there to work it out herself.

"I said," she said then, in a tone that did not brook disobedience, "go see."

I stopped and turned around. She was shifting from one foot to the other, the collar of her coat was pulled up around her neck and her lips, despite the touch-up, were pressed thin, suddenly pale.

"Do it yourself," I said. "You go see."

We looked at each other. In the distance, horses nickered; I heard the grooms arguing over their duties.

She stepped up to the trailer door—it was metal framed, with a torn screen—and raised her fist. She hesitated, then rapped on it lightly. I walked back then, slowly, away from the horses. The door opened after a moment and Bahar stood there, her fur coat taking up most of the small doorway. She looked like a model in a framed picture. She laughed and stepped outside, kissing my mother on both cheeks and exclaiming in both Turkish and English. She came down and I moved forward to let her kiss me as well. I caught her scent of warm flowers, felt her cool powdery cheek. How happy I was to see her.

"Nasılsın?" she said. "What a nice surprise. Hello, Canada!"

It seemed as though we had been the ones absent from the stable, not she. As if she'd been waiting, and we were irresponsibly overdue.

You could not have mistaken her tone. Under the coat, which she shrugged off and tossed back inside the trailer, she was wearing riding clothes: black britches and high boots, an impossibly soft-looking sweater.

Ahmet came out behind her holding a mug of something hot: steam swirled prettily in the air. He didn't look flustered or caught out. He was as composed as always.

He glanced at his watch. "You're early," he said. "But go tack up. Bahar is going to jump and you can join us."

He came forward and kissed my mother in the same manner Bahar had just done—politely, casually. Then he wandered off toward the stalls with his tea and Bahar fell in step beside him. They were built similarly, long-legged and slim, not tall people but exceptionally well made; their hips touched from time to time and they were speaking rapidly in Turkish, laughing in low tones that advertised familiarity.

My mother stood stock-still for what seemed an eternity. Until I socked her in the arm and said, "Pull yourself together."

"You're right," she said, but mostly to herself. "Quite right." She tugged her collar up and headed off after them, her shoes clattering on the cement strip that ran along the stall fronts.

I watched from the gravel courtyard and when my mother reached them, to my surprise it was Bahar's arm she took and held, and it was Bahar she pulled to the side under the corrugated metal awning of the stalls and she with whom my mother began to speak, rapidly, her face shifting between dismay and consternation. Bahar stood with her arms folded and her chin tucked inside the ribbed neck of her sweater. She kicked a little with her riding boots at the stones near her feet. Her face was placid, serene. And then the two women were lost to sight for a moment; a groom led a great gelding past them, he danced in the chill, tossing his head, dappled flanks gleaming, hooves sliding on the ground.

For many days after that Ahmet bey and Bahar took long rides alone across the frostbitten fields; you could hear their hoofbeats coming and going, punching the ground, snapping the frozen scrub. An occasional snowfall would leave the ground strangely patterned, white and wind-marbled. Cold rimed the black mare's nostrils and our breath came out like cartoon bubbles; in her stall I pressed up against her neck for warmth, burying my hands in her mane, stealing extra straw for her bedding. When he was around Ahmet spent more time with me, seeing to my horsemanship, complimenting my riding; he became warmer and kinder, more solicitous than ever. I found I did not begrudge Bahar his company, and even found vicarious pleasure in it, in the attention Ahmet paid her, and what it did to my mother.

A WEEK or so after the Christmas break I was called to the headmaster's office and found my mother waiting there. On the scarred desk were arrayed the little things of Simone's that I had given Kate to hide. Spread on the desk, what they'd taken made a bizarre display. Most of them I'd forgotten, a saltcellar, for instance, a cheap earring, an abstract figurine.

"I'm afraid Kate couldn't keep your secret any longer," said Kate's father. He was hunched behind the desk, smoking. He looked put-upon, grave and dismayed. Kate's father was a big, weary man with a rough beard and a parade of shabby tweed jackets. On Saturday nights, in the basement of the church up the hill, the British transformed the grim room into the Red Lion pub, complete with a ratty embroidered flag. All night Kate's father pulled pints, acting the part of the jolly innkeeper. Sunday mornings he looked as if he'd been dragged by horses.

Now he rubbed his beard vigorously, as if trying to remove it with his hand. "It was wrong of you to involve Kate in this," he said.

My mother sat impassively in a wooden chair with her hands on her lap. She crossed and recrossed her legs.

"Stealing is something we take very seriously. Normally we would expel you as a matter of course, without asking further questions."

The headmaster cleared his throat. Still no reaction from my mother.

"But your mother has asked us to reconsider."

And now my mother looked at me, her eyes sliding over to the doorway where I stood, my knees locked, hands gripping my thighs. The room was bright and cold, a haze of smoke drifted, an undulating white ribbon, over its upper atmosphere.

"She's explained the difficulties with your father having been away, and the recent loss of your grandmother at home. Mrs. Tremblay has agreed not to pursue this—provided you return the remainder of her missing belongings. There is a list here which she has put together." He inhaled deeply on a cigarette and regarded my mother. A piece of paper, folded, passed between them across the desk. "I'm sure you'll understand why my wife and I can no longer allow Canada and Kate to socialize outside of school. You won't be surprised to learn that Mrs. Tremblay feels the same way about Canada's friendship with Catherine."

My mother indicated that she understood this; her expression suggested that she would not much want a child of hers associating with me either. She collected Simone's belongings from the desk and stuffed them inside her handbag. We left the building together and walked up the long hill in silence, accompanied by the puffs of pinkish dust our shoes stirred up on the powdery ground.

When we got into the car she glanced at me, saying, "I don't want to know. I thought I would but it turns out I don't."

"I didn't take those things. I didn't touch them. John did." Why did it matter what she thought of me? She herself took whatever she wanted; she could never see herself, never, not at all.

"I don't care," she said. "Not interested."

"What grandmother?"

She didn't answer, just gripped the wheel with her hands and merged carelessly into the stream of traffic headed up the hill.

"When's Daddy coming home?"

She glanced at me. "I have absolutely no idea. Maybe next week, the one after."

I didn't believe her; she didn't even believe her.

Turkey had changed my mother; it had turned her into a woman who would do the most convenient thing, who would choose expediency over principles. Before we reached the stables, she pulled over on the side of the winding dirt road and dumped those things of Simone's onto the ground, shaking her purse violently free of them. Bits of paper drifted out, tobacco lint, a small pink tablet. She cursed, retrieved her wallet from the ground, her cigarette case, a few papers and a lipstick. Then she snapped the door shut and cut the wheel hard to the left, she gunned the engine and drove on.

20

ONE AFTERNOON IN JANUARY, GRACE DECIDES TO TRY RAISING
Greg on the telephone and braces herself for an ordeal: navigating
the international operators and the military protocols required no
small amount of patience. But when she finally does locate him—
long moments while the call is patched, while desk sergeants hunt
him up, while the line clicks ominously—his voice is cold and his
manner abrupt.

"Listen, Grace," he says, after a few moments of clumsy talk (the
line echoes and she hears their voices layered over each other's, punctuated with static), "I'm afraid all this is going to cause me big trouble
over here. I've spoken to Edie. Why on earth would you get involved
in something like this?"

Grace cannot think of one reasonable thing to say. The silence
lengthens.

"Well, never mind," he says, after a moment. "I'm probably cooked
anyway—with all Edie's goings-on. Past and present. I'll end up in a
basement somewhere Stateside, filing requisitions."

"I'm sure not," she says, though of course he would, there was no
other likely scenario. Perhaps Rand had been right after all.

"I don't know how you managed this, frankly, the two of you.
Didn't you know her history? And don't you know they look very
dimly on baby-selling in this part of the world?"

"Adoption. It's an adoption and I thought you knew. Edie said you were thrilled. I'm so sorry, Greg, I wish there was something I could do.

"Greg," she adds, after a pause, "I wanted to ask you something. Did Rand know about this—about this business with Edie? About whatever happened in Cairo?"

Greg laughs unhappily. "Well, we certainly spoke about it often enough. I bent his ear mercilessly."

Grace shakes her head back and forth. Finally she says, "He never breathed a word of it to me."

The silence on the line seems to indicate his astonishment—not at her words, but at the thought that she might have anticipated anything different.

His voice, when it comes, contains this and more. "Well, Rand's the original sphinx, isn't he? You'd know that better than I."

"It's what you talked about that weekend at the beach," Grace says. "All that walking."

"Mmm," he says. "I thought it would help her, getting out. Rand was concerned about you too—all that time inside, like a couple of mushrooms. Tell me, do you ever swim in the ocean these days?"

Grace laughs neutrally.

Greg continues in a different tone, "You know it was Rand who helped get us reposted. He put in a word with someone. We might still be cooling our heels on Olson Loop if he hadn't stepped in. It was kind of him. Very unexpected." He pauses. "I'll assume he doesn't know anything about this."

They end the conversation soon after, and Grace puts the phone down with a churning stomach and white knuckles. She thinks of Rand extending himself to Greg, the uncharacteristic largesse. Why had he done it? Perhaps he'd only been hoping to get rid of them, to put distance between Edie and his own wife. He'd have been surprised, and not necessarily happily, to find out they'd been posted to Saudi Arabia, a place he himself had often mentioned as desirable.

Sitting in the hallway beside the telephone, Grace recalls so many long and silent evenings with Rand—and her relentlessly bright talk of her day, of the street's doings, of the gossip that had drifted past Edie's screen door. In the living room on Olson Loop, Rand sat in a stupor in front of the television, the news flickering blue on the screen in front of him, the rabbit ears tilted backward and slightly to the left, the only position that ensured reception. Still, Grace had kept up that cheerful, strained patter as long as she could—until Rand rose to change the channel, or push into the kitchen for a beer, his posture telegraphing disinterest, boredom, contempt. At times she had tried to speak of Edie, to recount something Edie had said or done, some charming peculiarity, and Rand would snort dismissively, lift his pipe from the standing ashtray and, with an enraging concentration, begin to fill it, as though tamping Soviet spies into its capacious, burled bowl.

She thought of standing on cool wet sand beside Greg, on the morning they were meant to leave the beach; it was the night before that Edie had broken down in the kitchen. The ocean was still; she studied his profile as he stared out at the water. How handsome he is, she thought.

"Thank you for being such a good friend to Edie," he said. "She's been so unhappy here. You've really cheered her up."

"It isn't me she needs, Greg." But she'd heard the preachy little note in her voice and tried to laugh it away.

"No?" he said. "What is it, do you think?" But there was no sarcasm in his question—rather curiosity, real interest. He was playing with his wristwatch and she heard the repetitive click of the winding mechanism.

She was thinking how to put it when he said, "I don't know what she's said to you. Maybe it was all a mistake, perhaps she did just mean to admire it, to hold it for a moment. But no one took it that way, if you know what I mean. It didn't look like that at all."

"Well," she said, "okay." She didn't know anything about it then and for the life of her she couldn't imagine what he was referring to: she felt as if she'd walked into a conversation at its end, or woken up in the middle. Later, she'd thought of shoplifting, which she'd seen Edie do once or twice, in the commissary or the PX—dropping a toiletry item into her bag, or a box of pudding into her pocket. But Grace had never mentioned it. She'd pretended she didn't see and distracted herself with her purchases, her wallet.

What else had Grace overlooked, in her blinding desire for a friend and a confidante? Might Rand have wondered after her own sanity, those long hours she spent with Edie?

"The tapioca," Greg then said. "The damned tapioca. It's all they fed her in the hospital. She came out craving it."

Hospital?

After hanging up with Greg, Grace sits near the small telephone table, on a sturdy milking stool from Germany, for long minutes. She picks up the phone several times and replaces it; she cannot quite think whom to call.

AFTER THE evacuation from Baghdad, they'd landed in Frankfurt. Their boxes had taken weeks to come, and when they finally did, she unwrapped their scant belongings expectantly. She felt as if she were being reunited with lost family members, old friends. But other hands had packed their things, carelessly, hurriedly, and many were broken or chipped or entirely destroyed. She knelt in the empty, too-bright apartment overlooking the shopping district of that new city and held up one and then another of her lost treasures. She broke down then, over the crèche with its thatched roof, now in tatters, which she remembered from childhood, and the photographs of her sisters and her stern father, scattered and dead, respectively. The pictures were glued together with damp, and tore heartbreakingly when she tried to separate them, leaving rough white patches on the paper, the faces fractured and blotched.

Was it unreasonable that she blamed Rand for this? For the loss of her memories, her precious childhood? And when he had come in waving the papers of his commendation, his award for meritorious service, she'd just held up her dead mother's ring, the diamonds obviously pried from the setting not by hands but by clever little tools. Look what it's gotten me, she said, your wonderful medal, your marvelous commendation.

There had been a flurry of career successes following the war and the evacuation. What for Grace had been trying and frightening and deracinating had for Rand been a boost; whatever he had done in those lost days had made him a kind of minor hero. She saw that afterward, in the commendation ceremonies and the parties that followed, the way men clapped his shoulder and looked at him with admiration, and even women whispered when he entered the room and shoved at one another like schoolgirls. She resented it, being congratulated on her husband's mysterious successes, having no idea what she was approving of, what atrocities he might have committed, what he might have detonated or destroyed or smuggled away. She detected in him a new smugness and self-devotion that irritated her. It made her want to see him brought low. For a time she called him the Big Fish, and joked to the other wives that he was too puffed up to share an apartment with. They'd probably thought her mean-spirited. But really, she was mostly annoyed at being left out, at being excluded so completely and so casually.

Her husband's charm had always had the quality of a bright, warming light, but the radiance was unpredictable and too easily redirected. For all his complaining and reluctance about the pregnancy and the baby's ultimate arrival, he became, for a time, fascinated by his daughter. As an infant she didn't interest him—her needs were too base and unglamorous. Diapers had horrified him, and during feedings he had looked on in rapt disgust. But in Germany, when she began to demonstrate intelligence and curiosity and the most rudimentary signs of personality, Rand had thrown himself assiduously into fatherhood. He taught Canada the German equivalents of all the English words she mastered and liked to parade her into shops and bakeries and show her off. In museums and cathedrals he lectured her—Canada in ruffled knickers and smocked dresses, her fat hands patting his cheeks—on art and ecumenical histories. As Christmas approached, bright packages tumbled concussively from the closets and cabinets.

Nothing Grace said or did, none of her protests or pleas, made any difference. In Canada, Rand found an unquestioning disciple, one who could no longer be counted on to keep the daily secrets of the household. If a critical dinner ingredient fell to the floor and Grace retrieved it and used it anyway, Canada would meet Rand at the door and inform him of the contamination; when Canada got stuck alone in the elevator—Grace had been looking elsewhere, chatting with a neighbor—and the fire brigade had to be called, Canada wasted no time in telling her father the details of her mother's neglect. It wasn't long before Grace felt quite competently ganged up on: she was raising a clever little turncoat. It seemed to her as well that Canada's language skills were far too advanced for her age. Often she felt locked in a battle with her daughter and her husband, no longer a war for affection, because that had been quickly decided, but rather one for survival, for merely keeping her head above water.

Grace complained of it to friends she made through the embassy—older women who'd been at it much longer. She quickly sensed their world-weariness, their inattention to their own children. Not one of them, Grace discovered, wanted to own up to a good marriage. Domestic happiness seemed to them dull and provincial. Instead they preferred to complain, to trade miseries and trespasses: they swarmed like ants at the first sign of marital distress.

But Germany was a coveted post. Many were resting there between wars and less attractive postings, taking a breather from more exotic cities and cultures, from strict dress codes and burdensome religious protocols. In Germany, the life suddenly felt a little glamorous. They could buy the things they needed; they became accustomed to more-sophisticated goods. The women could exchange pleasantries in German and make themselves understood in the grocery store. However simple these skills, they seemed to signal a longed-for polish and worldliness. Sometimes, her heels clicking along the cobbled sidewalks of the city, returning from shopping, Grace felt the way she had meant to feel on her wedding day—stylish and traveled and urbane. And at night there was an atmosphere of abandon. The parties were nonstop, the scandalous antics of the wives winked and whispered about, the men drinking and carousing and a general feeling of ease and self-satisfaction.

But after a time Grace perceived a widespread ennui, an exhausting vacancy, a whiff of corruption. It permeated the air at parties and functions, at endless coffees. She felt a flood of maternal remorse, redoubled her efforts to win Canada's affection: she took an active role in the nursery school and went along as chaperone on trips to the zoo. But her involvement seemed only to spur bad behavior: twice in one week Canada climbed on a desk during lessons and removed her dress as if performing a burlesque. It was gently suggested to Grace that she might find other ways to occupy her time, that Canada's conduct was indicative of her need to separate from her mother. She did that long ago, Grace thought to tell them. In fact, Canada had never been a child who clung to her mother's skirts or wept inconsolably when she left the house. Her father, that was another matter. If Rand was called away on a trip Canada went into an immediate decline: she became impossible to manage and threw world-class tantrums.

Grace began to dread the phone calls in the middle of the night summoning her husband away. The long, uninterrupted days and nights alone with her daughter were a kind of torture, the weekends especially dismal. She did not have the wherewithal, the maternal fortitude, for endless games of Old Maid, for singing a hundred choruses of the "Wheels on the Bus," for dressing up teddy bears in doll clothes. Grace hated this about herself but could not seem to shake it off.

She took German classes several evenings a week and often left Canada with Ava, the maid they had found through a bulletin board at church. Canada had her father's aptitude for languages: each time Grace came home, she was just a little more fluent. It was another barrier between them, another thing that put Canada firmly in her father's camp. When he was home, the two of them spoke together in German, a language Grace could not understand beyond the basics. Her husband and her daughter curled in the tweed chair near the window and read together from the *Little Bear* books, which Canada preferred in German. If Grace picked up the English version, Canada would shake her head violently and open her mouth to howl—and it seemed to Grace that she understood too well her mother's failings, that she had sensed her weaknesses and ferreted out her fears.

Even here in Turkey, Grace senses in Canada a too-acute understanding of things she couldn't possibly know. At the barn, now that Ahmet has grown cool—not unfriendly but aloof, which is somehow worse—Canada snuggles up to him with a new, almost womanish coyness. When Grace approaches them at the stable—they will be grooming a horse, or taking apart some contraption built of leather—they stop talking, or their voices lift from whispers to become bright and smooth. Once, when she finds them together in a stall, Canada is wearing Ahmet's jaunty little cap and when Grace nears she plucks it from her head and returns it to his. There is something deliberately intimate in her gesture, something she wants Grace to appreciate. Now the glances Canada gives Grace over her shoulder telegraph that she is intruding, that she is less than welcome there, among the horses and the grooms and the piled-up hay, the young girls in their riding gear, with their purposeful hands and strong, fluent legs; Grace has no real business in this place.

Canada is always so much more accessible in Grace's imagination than in the living room. Some nights when she and Canada are alone in the apartment, she creeps in and watches her daughter sleep.

Since their return from Istanbul, Ahmet's eyes are apologetic, and once or twice he raises his hands at her in a helpless gesture, one that might encompass any situation, any difficulty at all. When she telephones him, thinking a conversation is in order, his voice is even and polite. She invites him for dinner but he doesn't show up, despite cordial assurances that he will. And now that Bahar has returned—her interest in horses kindled again, for some baffling reason—the two are nearly always together. Sometimes, waiting for Canada, Grace's heart contracts to see their two diminutive figures riding in the fields beyond the flat fenced rings, their horses side by side, their bodies moving in effortless harmony. They return flushed and warm from exertion, the horses foam-flecked from their gallops, their laughter coming up ahead of them, drifting on the wind down the hill, where Grace waits with an all too familiar catch in her throat, hands clasped together inside her sleeves.

Alone with Canada, Grace often thinks she might jump out of her own skin. She is waiting for her daughter to say something cutting or mock sympathetic, to let her know that she intuits Grace's ruin, that it's no secret between them. But Canada says nothing, and sometimes Grace wonders if she is dreaming up these things, all this ill will and evil intent she ascribes to her daughter. She thinks of Catherine, home again with Simone, with John. Grace had delivered the girl right to the front door: she'd been folded back into that household with its inexplicable boundaries and its terrible unspoken consents.

Once after Istanbul, Grace meets Ahmet coming around the corner at the stables; she is holding a travel book near her face, her collar turned up against the wind.

"Don't overdo it," she tells him, "with Canada. Go easy on her."

He looks bewildered. It's such an affectation on his part, that blankness, she suddenly sees it clearly.

"Oh, don't give me that," she says. "You know what I mean."

He doesn't answer, but turns and strikes up a conversation with a groom, the two of them vanishing into a stall. He seems churlish now, this man she had not loved, and she goes away feeling wearied by the whole thing.

She thinks how easy it is in the beginning—friendships, romances, new countries—how easily bewitching they can be. One can feel such affinity with a stranger, or think to throw an entire life over for the promise of some untested ardor.

EVENTUALLY, WORRIED by silence and inaction, cut free of Ahmet and his distracting attentions, Grace decides to confide once more in Paige, who listens to her somberly over coffee in her cluttered living room.

When she finishes, there is a long stretch of silence.

Paige sighs. "Listen, Grace, I like you. I do. You've made some silly mistakes since you've been here, some rather whopping missteps, but on the whole I like you. I've always told people that. But what do you expect me to do with this extraordinary information?"

"I understand," says Grace, and her tone and the movement of her hands are more impatient than she intends. "I understand all that. But what should I do? Shall I just forget the whole thing, hope nothing comes of it? It certainly seems to be working for Simone."

Paige shuffles a deck of cards on her lap; the sound is irksome. "The two situations are quite different."

"I agree. That one seems far more sinister."

"Does it?" says Paige. "I wonder why."

Grace is amazed, as she was on the train that day, hearing Ahmet's similarly offhand reaction.

Paige says, "Perhaps Catherine seems like a different sort of child to you. A bit more valuable."

"No," she says. "That's not remotely the case."

Paige looks at her over folded hands. She says nothing.

Grace says, "I'd like you to tell me you didn't know about this. About John and Catherine. Simone."

Paige returns to her oversize cards, with their ornate renderings of knights and pages and emperors. "I don't pretend to understand everything, Grace. And I don't ask questions about what doesn't concern me. I'd advise you to do the same. It's rarely profitable."

"I find this all utterly outrageous."

"Do you? Perhaps you simply think you should."

"Either way. Take it as you like." Grace feels petty and obstinate; she stares at her hands: the ropy veins, the plain gold band.

"You shouldn't be so heartfelt, Grace, so provincial. So damned American. Tell me, does Rand know about this? Edie? The baby?"

Grace looks up, a little desperately. The American remark pricked. "Yes. No. Paige, look, I know full well I'm living in a glass house, but honestly, isn't this a bit different? Doesn't this violate . . . some . . . some boundaries of decency?"

"You misunderstand me, Grace. I couldn't care less about the horse teacher. That is what it is. You tell me—diversion, exercise, recreation. But, to put it plainly, you seem to forget you've arranged for a baby to be sold on the black market. To a woman you've just come to me and described as a lunatic."

"Hysterical, I think. Troubled. Not crazy. You'd agree there's a difference."

"As you like. But wouldn't you agree your position is precarious? You do know you live in a foreign country? And not the most progressive one in the world either."

This is hard to argue and Grace temporarily abandons the matter; perhaps Paige is right, and what does Catherine have to do with her, really? All this trafficking in children and servants—it's begun to seem almost commonplace. And she remembers Catherine's stubborn expression from the train; it fuses in her mind with the one Canada lately wears.

"I'm probably making something of nothing," she says. "Let's change the subject. Where's Fred these days? Is he off as well, on some mysterious trip?" Fred, Paige's husband, was absent more frequently than Rand. Unassuming and bespectacled, he seemed more interested in antiquities than in his rumored work with the clandestine service. He and Rand had always been chummy; Fred was an eager audience for all Rand's archaeological show-and-tell. They had traveled together into Kurdish territory, into wild places unsafe for women and children, and they had spent hours huddled in the corner of this very room, discussing one arcane object or another.

"He's quite well, I believe, though not at all mysterious," Paige says. "He's at Catal Huyuk as we speak, digging around in the dirt, happy as a clam."

For some reason these words strike Grace, in this moment, as simply too much to be borne. "Oh, come on, Paige," she says. "Do we always have to be so Byzantine? I mean we all know. It's not exactly a secret what he does."

Paige lays out an untidy cross of cards on the sofa in front of her. She is occupied with them for several minutes, turning them up and then down again, clucking a little in her throat.

She looks up at Grace. "What *he* does?" she says finally. "He's an anthropologist. Publishes papers regularly. Lectures at the university. What did you think?"

Grace stares at her. It seems incredible, even outrageous, that at this juncture Paige would keep up these pretenses. After a few moments of stilted silence Grace vacates the couch and lifts her coat from the back of a chair. She brushes the cat hair from it automatically and stands awkwardly before shrugging it on.

"Think," says Paige, without looking up, studying a card with two naked, androgynous figures depicted on its face. "Think hard." The card is one Grace had often hoped for in readings—the lovers—but she'd learned that its meanings were mercurial, and not necessarily benign.

What Paige suggests is not lost on her, but quite suddenly something else occurs to her as well. "All this," she says, still holding the heavy coat, gesturing with it. "Bahar. Firdis. This isn't a surprise to you, is it? I haven't told you anything you didn't know."

"I think," Paige says reflectively, "that Bahar really meant it as a kindness. Helping this friend you'd spoken of so often. Someone else could have been found just as easily. It wouldn't have mattered had you refused. Not in the slightest."

Despite her tone, Grace thinks she sees in Paige's eyes a flash of recognition, of understanding, some sliver of tenderness or pity: she seems to see that on Grace's part, all this had really been no more than a display of feathers, a show of influence.

"But that isn't true," Grace says. "She never expected me to say no, she didn't allow for that, not for a minute. She never does."

"Maybe not. But it really doesn't matter anyway. You didn't say no. And if it eases your mind at all, it is not your maid's baby that is now with your friend. That didn't quite work out. So you can comfortably forget all this. In fact, you can pretend it never happened."

Grace stares at her, bewildered.

"What are you talking about?"

"What I said. Bahar took a different baby to your friend in Germany. Firdis's child is now with relatives in Istanbul."

"And Firdis knows this?"

Paige shrugged. "I don't think so. It's a little complicated. Anyway, Grace, you were never important in this to Bahar, not really."

As Grace stands there, mulling all this, a matted Siamese cat steps daintily across her shoes and makes her jump.

FOR DAYS after that, Grace goes around in a fog. It's brought on obliquely by Paige's revelations and Rand's continuing absence, by Ahmet's withdrawal, by the distant, worrisome matters of Edie and the child, but also by a bottle of pills that Paige had given her that same afternoon, and suggested she use to "take the edge off." Certainly they work—they quiet her racing heart and send little messages of calm through her jangling nerves, they facilitate long afternoon naps and a sense, if not exactly of well-being, then of disaster indefinitely postponed. But there is danger in this, and Grace knows it. She takes the pills sparingly and eventually cuts them with a kitchen knife into tiny chips, with the thought of policing herself.

She cannot help but wonder, in lucid moments, what it is about her, Grace, that creates these impossible situations, these complicated human snarls. The lives of other people seem so straightforward. If she thinks about any of it for too long Grace finds herself reaching for fragments of the little pink pills—one and then another—with their promise of temporary, muzzy-headed peace.

So when Paige appears at the door a week after their conversation carrying a casserole and puts this ridiculous scheme to her—the idea that they will all drive out into the countryside late at night and learn to take the wheels off cars—Grace is less than enthusiastic. A number of women have been invited, some exercise to make them all more self-sufficient, or so goes the advertising. They will drive out beyond the city, Paige says, and take turns changing a tire. Once, Grace might have found this a reasonable entertainment, but now it seems like the absolute height of absurdity. *Fancy Dress,* says the invitation that comes to the apartment later by messenger. *Evening gloves.* Still, Grace does not see how she can possibly decline.

She drops the invitation on the kitchen counter and fumbles in her pocketbook for the pill bottle. Firdis has quit, suddenly and without any coherent explanation. Rand has vanished—he has been gone nearly two months—and Canada is utterly a stranger. From the inside of her head to the unfamiliar, muscular curve of her legs, Grace finds her daughter bewildering. Grace watches her surreptitiously, wondering what ever will become of her, of them. When they talk, or when they are close to each other, Grace will get a whiff of her scent—her girlish, horsey, filched bath-salts odor—and feel an odd catch in her throat. It might be anything, that feeling. Savage and indefinable, it could be love, possibly, or the other.

It seems to Grace these days that Canada's eyes hold too large a question, too vast a worry, and that her hair, so long unnoticed by Grace, is now sleek, tended by hands that are suddenly knowledge-able and adult. She cannot imagine where these skills came from, or the budding breasts she sees beneath childish blouses, or the bracelet around her wrist that Grace did not buy. Canada's Turkish is better than her own now, like her German years earlier. She has her father's dry wit, and, out of nowhere, his sudden, overwhelming shyness.

Later that afternoon, reading a book at the stables, the heat turned up high in the little red car, Grace is surprised to find herself missing Rand. How strange. She thinks of all his charms, lost or long forgot-ten. She remembers the pride she had in him so many years earlier, the way he looked in his uniform, the private jokes they'd shared. And, with the forgiveness of nostalgia, and the renewal of affection that comes on the heels of a close call, her husband begins to seem like not so bad a bargain after all.

Some afternoons Grace and Bahar stand in the cold beside the ring and watch Ahmet circle it astride one of the bigger, more spirited horses. Often Canada trails along behind him, or points her mount toward some obstacle he has indicated with a finger. Bahar leans with her elbows on the splintered railing, her chin propped in her fist. Now Grace sees fresh angles in her old friend, flaws she had quite overlooked. Bahar returned from Germany having gained several pounds—the strudel, no doubt, and the bratwurst, and the beer. Though she is not as perfect as she'd once seemed, she is characteristically breezy—the alarming information Grace had relayed about Edie's history seemed barely to faze her at all.

"She has some talent," Bahar says, watching Canada ride.

"Does she?" says Grace, with blank and honest surprise, for such a thing had not occurred to her.

But overall there is new quiet between the two women, a sense that much has been said or silently agreed to and little remains. Now they speak of the most pedestrian things—Bahar even speaks of her boys, of their behavior at school, their wild ways amid her delicate furnishings, and of Ali and his ever-busier practice. The subject of orphans does not arise between them; the matter of Firdis goes undiscussed.

Once, Bahar says this: "It is only a matter of time before your maid becomes pregnant again. Mark my words."

Grace says nothing of Firdis's absence and replies easily, "If that is the case, I don't wish to know about it."

They laugh for longer than the moment requires, and their mirth seems to sum up all the thoughts they have decided not to voice, all the blame and accusation, the possible disasters, the barely averted calamities.

And there has recently been some news from Edie herself. She has returned to Saudi Arabia and she and Greg have reconciled. The baby—whoever's it is, wherever it came from—has gone with her and Edie writes a few bright, delighted letters about the joys of motherhood. Where Firdis's baby may be, the details of it, its disposition, who knows?

When Grace opens these envelopes, photographs slide out with the stationery. Bahar keeps several of these—"For the scrapbook I am making," she says with what seems to be sincerity, but this may merely be what she thinks is expected of her. The pictures show Greg, Edie, and the child among Edie's old furnishings, or on a busy street with shopping bags, or once, the baby alone, teetering listlessly atop a camel festooned with ribbons. When Grace studies them, she feels both relief and exhaustion—they're an unwelcome reminder of her foolishness, the dire repercussions and possibilities that seem to lie just beyond their plain white margins. Grace wonders, too, if there is something about this baby—in its vacant eyes and strangely clenched hands—that does not seem quite right.

Edie's letters recount the tedium of infancy and child rearing, the discomforts that Grace feels she's just barely recovered from herself, though all that was years ago. Edie has questions Grace can no longer answer: at what age should a baby babble, smile, grab for dangerous objects? Grace skims these with a little shudder, sensing Edie's vague, unspoken worry, then folds them away to reply to at a later date. It is easier to let it slide, to relegate Edie and Greg and those memories to a back corner of her mind, among the clutter and debris of other lost friendships and homes, all those distant, splintered recollections.

ON THE evening of Paige's excursion, Grace dresses hastily. She takes from the back of a drawer a pair of evening gloves that are on their way out anyway—one pearl button missing, some stubborn soiling at an elbow. She chooses a dress she doesn't much care for, one already somewhat overexposed.

She waits at the appointed time just inside the heavy glass door of the lobby, scanning the street for headlights. In her hand she carries a small evening bag—tissues, lipstick, a jeweled compact that had belonged to her mother—and wears on her feet a pair of evening sandals she will not much mourn if they are altogether ruined. In the bag is also a letter from Edie she received that very morning—she intends to discuss the disturbing contents with Paige. But really, Grace does not expect much excitement from the evening: several hours of forced gaiety in the backseat of a car, a bottle passed among the occupants, the eventuality of winding up the evening at the Officers' Club with a story to tell, minimally grease-stained and not much enlightened on matters of automotive repair.

Grace knows most of these women, some better than others. They wind out of the city in a little caravan, driven by their silent, uniformed chauffeurs. Grace shares a car with Paige and several others; their dresses rustle together, they edge their shoes off and curl their stocking feet in the gritty pile of the carpet. Paige has brought champagne, someone else an ornate flask of expensive scotch. They leave the city lights behind them and for a while the conversation is about children and husbands and the absurdity of this particular expedition, which they seem almost to have forgotten they undertook willingly.

Grace wishes to be nearly anywhere else. In fact, for most of the ride, she finds herself thinking of Rand, and of certain quiet evenings before the insanity of diplomatic life overtook them. She thinks, for instance, of the little apartment she had lovingly maintained before they were married, the amateur meals she cooked for him there, pretending to be grown-up. They'd played cards after dinner and he showed her his repertoire: his fancy shuffles, his sleights of hand, his many disappearing tricks.

She remembers the first time he left in the middle of the night: it was in Baghdad, before the war, when everything was still contented and lovely. She can recall the way the cool tile felt on her feet as she slid from the bed they shared in the middle of the night when the baby cried. He didn't have that suitcase yet—not packed, not ready to go at a moment's notice—and when the call came she'd risen from bed with him and gone through the drawers to help. She took out his dark folded socks, his snowy underclothes: she took his second uniform from the depths of the closet and brushed its stiff shoulders free of lint. She remembers his excitement at the prospect of what lay ahead, his thrill at the stealthy, midnight nature of it all. She liked that sudden spark in his eyes, and they shared something like an intoxication as they knelt together in the near dark, whispering so as not to wake the baby. She found an old suitcase in a closet and knelt on the floor beside it while he shaved hurriedly in the bathroom. The light was warm on the bare floors and the sight of the bed—rumpled, still holding their shared heat—made her nearly purr with pleasure. She felt a reluctant, reawakened love for him, the almost-ache of his approaching absence. She imagined the cool of the night air beyond the arched gate of their garden, the swaying palms, the car idling there on the street, waiting to take him away.

Where are you going?

I don't know, he told her. Can't say.

She had thought then of the not too distant desert and the night lights of the city, illuminated somewhere beyond her view, outside her imagination, far from the warm little room with the crumpled counterpane and the sleeping baby, the open suitcase on the floor, its contents lovingly stowed, his toiletries neatly packed in the silky elastic side pockets, socks rolled by her own slim hands.

And since it had all still been between them then—desire, affection, good feeling—she'd pulled him down beside the gray suitcase and made love to him on the floor, her gown riding up around her hips, their bodies sliding and catching against the tiles, while he protested and then succumbed, chuckling, his lemony soap and his smooth skin warm and redolent against her neck.

Then he was gone and the bed felt different—both worse and

better, emptier and more full. His departure left a pretty ache, a small, coin-size hollow at her center, and she thought of him abroad in the world without her, thought of him moving through airfields as dawn broke and climbing onto cold metal transports—huge, whirring, dangerous—that would lift him into the air and carry him away, a suitcase his only anchor to her, their baby, their brand-new, freshly minted life.

IT'S QUITE cold and Grace's evening coat does not properly break the chill: little handfuls of snow beat up against her face, her ankles feel frozen through. The sky is grimy with stars. The women stand on the side of the road and take turns handling the tire iron. They heft it in their gloved hands, remarking, *Oh it's cold!* or *Beastly heavy,* and then pass it along. There are perhaps seven of them there— pretty, snow-blown figures in evening dress, a little tipsy from the ride, laughing, stamping their feet.

They are waiting for someone to call this whole thing off, for Paige to shepherd them back into the cars for cognac and petit fours, to give the order for the Officers' Club. But still they linger, pressing their nearly bare feet to the hard earth, grabbing their coats closer. The drivers stand a safe distance off, deliberately unhelpful, smoking. In the dark their cigarettes glow and fade; a brief, arcing ember flares as a spent butt is tossed to the ground, a cascade of sparks.

And then Paige is leaning down with the heavy iron to undo the lug nuts. They hear her pant in the darkness, the noise of unfamiliar exertion.

Simone says, "You have got to be kidding me. Those tires are perfectly good. They got us here."

Then the sound of the nuts striking the ground, of Paige saying, "Someone get those, we don't want to lose them."

Scrambling, fingernails on gravel, swearing, the clicking of the weighty little objects in someone's hand. Grace has her arms folded at her chest; the wind ruffles her hair, bites down on her neck.

Someone puts an object into her hands. The women have taken off a front tire and Paige is bent over awkwardly, wheeling the spare from the rear of the car.

The tire iron is heavy and cold; the chill penetrates the silky, slippery fabric of her gloves. Grace balances it in her hands like a stick of dynamite.

"Here," says Paige. "Come over here and I'll show you."

Grace approaches. She hears the gritty noise of her heels in the dirt, the swish of her gown against the material of her coat and her sheathed legs. The women stand huddled together around the car; there is the glug of liquid in the flask, laughter, Simone's peevish voice. The drivers in their dark uniforms are little more than a smudge at the edge of her vision.

She bends, feeling the wind between her legs and a gentle fizzing in her veins; she'd swallowed two of the pink pills before leaving the house. She pulls her hands free of the gloves, wraps her bare hands around the icy metal cylinder. Paige holds a flashlight and a cone of light plays over the bare wheel well, the tire discarded on the ground, the spare she has balanced against her knees. Simone's feet, in ridiculously high-heeled shoes, are shifting back and forth; her ankles disappear beneath the velvet folds of her gown.

Through the dark, Simone's voice says, "So, I guess Rand is off traveling again?"

Grace doesn't answer; she is trying to figure out the purpose of the tire iron, which slips and shifts uncooperatively in her cold hands.

Simone laughs. "Oh well, I probably shouldn't ask you. You've so much on your plate these days, and I know how you like to be mysterious."

"I do?"

"So I hear." Her tone is languid, distant, disembodied. "But what do I know? Catherine seems to be the one who knows everything these days—who goes where with whom, who doesn't go anywhere at all. She's such a dreadful, precocious girl."

Grace hefts the tool, she leans forward, aiming it in the direction Paige indicates. Paige is holding the tire where it is meant to go, Simone is fumbling for the lug nuts in the pocket of her coat. Then Simone's long fingers are on her shoulder and Grace reaches back with her hand. But reflexively, it is the hand with the tire iron that she moves, and the cold off-balance weight of it carries her hand back farther and with more force than she intends, and then there is the horrible noise of metal striking Simone's face, which is just there above Grace's shoulder, though she did really not know it. You could never say she knew it for certain.

FEBRUARY 1976

21

I THOUGHT I SAW JOHN FROM TIME TO TIME THAT WINTER. BUT there might have been a thousand young men just like him prowling the Ankara streets: foxy and effete, their humdrum bundles and packages at odds with an aristocratic demeanor that was too studied, perhaps, and too put-on, but credible nonetheless—quite good enough for girls. Maybe they moved in mirrors, in apartments all over that city, places shining with chrome and glass, with jagged art and blond wood, and there bowed and scraped to their own Simones, and took quiet revenge on their daughters.

Sometimes I imagined meeting him in the garden, and played out these fantasies hunched on the stone bench, surrounded by the winter-seared earth, the empty house, the naked trees. If he came through the gate, I thought, he might seem suddenly more ordinary than he had in Simone's home, an average young man, stripped of mystique, and accordingly, of his chancy appeal. With the traffic a rumor in the distance we could speak of new banalities, of my schoolwork, his squabbling aunts and sisters, the predictably terrible weather. Or maybe not: after all, what had ever been between us but Catherine?

In time I learned more about the trip to Istanbul. And I was wrong, she told me. John had not taken her; on the contrary, he had sent her home. She must have followed him: caught up with him at the station, or on the street outside the apartment building as he hailed a taxi. I imagine her begging him to take her along, using all his own words about Simone to make him agree. He was hurried and distracted, and allowing her to come with him may have seemed, in the moment, like the simplest thing.

But above all, John was a practical and even-minded young man. At some point, having accomplished his private errand, he would have been horrified to find himself in Istanbul, with the runaway daughter of a diplomat, and so he'd quickly arranged to return her, unharmed to the naked eye, the way any small stolen thing can be slipped back secretly to where it belongs.

Perhaps they found some solace in each other, my mother and Catherine, watching the miles of brown and jagged country flow by outside the train's grimy windows. I picture them locked in their reveries, beside each other on the vinyl seats, their hopes for a grand finale fading with every passing curiosity of landscape. Ahmet, buried inside his paper, was already back in Ankara, vanished from that compartment in all the important ways, and John, having rid himself of Catherine and made his delivery, toured the fleshpots of the city and returned, after some small time, to Ankara, trusting that anything unpleasant would by then have passed.

And my mother and Catherine, for whom everything had changed, found, of course, that little of importance had.

I think Catherine and my mother had both wanted, above all, only to be asked. But Simone and I were stubborn and silent. Neither of us ever brought up Istanbul; we could not, would not, give them the satisfaction. My mother returned to the apartment with a look of expectation about her. I imagine Catherine's face, opening her own door, wearing the very same expression. Simone and I met them, in those different yet suddenly similar rooms, with blank and disinterested countenances, and not a single question, no trace of shock. We turned our heads away, and our embittered hearts, and would not indulge them.

That long-ago day on the Antalya coast, when they'd argued and my mother had stepped from the car, I'd leaned forward over the seat and whispered into my father's sun-scorched ear, "Let's just leave her here. Let's drive away." Yes, I was that careless with her, willing to abandon her by the side of a bright, stony road. Had she been any less cavalier with me? He'd turned to face me, saying, with only a trace of amusement, "Not today. Perhaps another time."

Often, at the barn, inside the mare's warm stall, or walking the windy streets of my neighborhood, I imagined my father's return. But I no longer really believed in it. When I'd put those letters in his suitcase, when I'd hinted to him about her trip to Istanbul, I'd certainly imagined consequences, but only as they pertained to her—not to me.

More than once that winter, I had the feeling, the suspicion, and the dread, that soon there would be no one left for my mother and me to blame, not a single soul, but each other.

22

SITTING IN THE WAITING ROOM OF THE TURKISH HOSPITAL, while Simone can be heard screaming from an examining room, Grace sits stunned alongside Paige and the other women, all of them still in evening clothes, extravagantly smeared with blood and oil.

They do not speak, only look at one another from time to time with expressions of shock and wonderment. A headache creeps up on Grace, a remnant of the liquor, a little drumbeat behind her eyes, and she folds and refolds her one remaining glove, shaking her head at the floor. The drive back to the city was chaotic, and without the benefit of good lighting it's unclear whether Simone's injuries are minor or traumatic. Somewhere in between, it turns out. When they arrive in the bare-bulb brightness of the hospital, Paige goes immediately to call Ali from a pay phone, so that he can come down and bully the on-duty doctors.

They make quite a picture—Paige points this out as she comes back down the hallway—all of them standing around in their ruined gowns. Like refugees, she says, from a fancy dress ball in a horror film.

In time Ali arrives in his usual manner, sweeping in with his luxurious bag, wearing a cashmere coat over crisp, striped pajamas. He leaves his car running outside and throws his keys to the doctor in charge, who scrambles like a lackey to park it, with no indication of having been insulted.

Ali comes out from behind the curtained partition within a few moments of having gone in, his expression a little wry. Grace has not laid eyes on him in some time, not since she'd visited him with Firdis in tow and Firdis had refused to let him examine her, because she considered it improper. "These women," he'd said to Grace that day in his waiting room, "they are like children. They do not know up from not."

He nods gravely in Grace's direction and addresses himself to Paige. He speaks quietly and uses his hands to touch his face gently, indicating here, and here. The two consult inaudibly, until Grace rises from her seat and walks over, whereupon Ali turns to her and says, "I am saying that your friend is very excitable and will not let the doctors very close to her. But there is some damage, mainly to the teeth, which will have to be dealt with by a specialist. Something else may be fractured as well, but she will not agree to let us use the machinery." His voice is deep and smooth, like the sound of mahogany. "Mrs. Tremblay is very upset. Distraught, I think, is the word I want in English. I've given her a tablet and will drive her home myself."

He bows a little at the waist. "It is quite an evening you ladies have had. I'm very appreciative my own wife was not included in your plans."

Grace takes his arm before he leaves, drawing him aside, suddenly aware of the bright, unflattering light and the disreputable state of her clothes. She hears herself speak urgently: "I feel just awful. It was a dreadful accident. Is she very angry?"

Ali regards her curiously. "I hear Rand is traveling again. I am glad he is feeling better. You must be relieved."

Grace nods absently. "Thank you for everything you've done for us. You've been very kind. She'll be all right, won't she? Simone."

"Fine, I think," he says. "May I give you a piece of advice?"

"Certainly." She folds her arms.

He hesitates before speaking. "Bahar has told me about your friendship with the riding instructor. I know it is not my concern, but . . . in either case, I think you should be careful with this man. Bahar herself feels that perhaps she is responsible for this matter. That she has facilitated this situation by her introductions, by saying to him how fond she is of you, how you have been lonely here and in need of companionship. She has been very distressed about it."

Grace stares at him stupidly. In the hall where they stand, some orderlies are making a racket; they push an empty gurney between them, arguing. The blue sheets catch in the wheels. Grace and Ali step back, automatically, as if synchronized. "There is nothing to be concerned about," she says. "Nothing at all."

Ali inclines his head. "As you say. But I thought I would mention it."

When he turns to go, she puts a hand on his arm. "What has happened to Firdis's baby?" she asks. "Why didn't he go to Germany with Bahar? That was our arrangement."

Ali shakes his head at her and presses his lips together. "Your friend has a baby now, yes?"

"It's very strange, Ali. Is this baby you've given her . . . is it healthy?"

Ali seems to think for a moment. "There are many children. One is very like another. Your friend is pleased, I think?" Then he moves his hands, as if to indicate a shuffling of papers, some bureaucratic necessity. "There was some uproar in the family, I believe. You know this Kemal? The boy Simone calls John? A very angry young man. Very unpleasant. At the last moment there had to be some reorganization. Not to worry."

He turns then and goes, strangely elegant in his nighttime ensemble. Something about his carriage and dress suggests the nineteenth century, some dense and antiquated Russian novel. Grace remains standing where he's left her, her eyes on the door, unseeing and unfocused. Simone comes out a few moments later, her face swathed in bandages up to the eyes, throwing off the arm of a male doctor who is trying to assist her. Paige steps forward and they disappear outside together. Simone does not look once at Grace, and truth be told, Grace is somewhat relieved.

As they drive home together later through the quieted streets, Paige says, "I suppose this was not the best idea I've ever had."

"I don't think this could have been anticipated," Grace says, wearily.

"Oh, I don't know. No intelligent person goes handing out weapons with Simone around."

"Are you making a joke?" says Grace.

"I suppose I am," she replies. "Not in good taste, I know. Still. A little levity never hurts."

"Do you think Bahar handed Ahmet off to me when she was finished with him?"

"The way Simone passes that houseboy around?" Paige says. "That's more it, I think. I would like to know why you hit her, if you don't mind."

Grace, staring out the window, cannot summon the energy to respond. The car begins to chug down into Gasi Osman Paşa; Grace feels the customary lurch in her stomach.

"How did Simone end up with John anyway?"

"I believe I arranged that. If I remember correctly. He's related to your Firdis, you know. I believe she's his mother."

Outside, the darkened windows shops go by, and traffic, in a blur of streaky yellowy light. Grace gathers her single glove and her bag on her lap. She says, "It's a little Alice down the rabbit hole, living with all you people."

"I expect so," says Paige. "I'd think it would be infuriating."

"That's very much the case," says Grace.

They share a wintry silence for a few moments, then Paige looks up and says, "It's not as bad as you think. That Catherine was never really his sort, you know. I really think much of it was her doing, terrible though it is to say. Encouraging him and so forth, making up stories to entertain Canada. I certainly know Simone thinks so."

The car eases to a halt and Grace opens the door and climbs out. She leans her head back inside before the car can pull away. "I'm wondering, is there anything you don't have your hand in? Anything you don't orchestrate? It's funny; I used to think Rand was sneaky."

"Oh, Grace," Paige says, "don't be melodramatic. It doesn't suit you at all." And then with a noise of exasperation she reaches out her gloved hand to pull the door closed. "You're letting in the cold," she says. "And besides, hasn't there been enough upset for one evening? Let's call it a night."

Wholly unsatisfied, reeling a little from the accumulated horrors, Grace makes her way upstairs and lets herself into the apartment. In the living room she takes from her bag and rereads the letter she received from Edie that very morning—the contents have confirmed her nagging suspicions. Doctors have been consulted, Edie writes, and they all agree. Simply: the baby is not healthy, it is not perfect; it is not the child they were promised, or paid for. For this Edie and Greg blame her squarely. And what, they ask her, is she going to do about it?

A WEEK later, purely by chance, Grace runs into John on Tunali Hilmi near a fruit seller. She hasn't seen him since that day she'd passed him on the street walking to Simone's, when she'd been so astonished to find everything going on just as usual.

"I saw you in Istanbul," she says without preamble. "Why?"

He stands without shifting; his hands are empty of packages and he makes his body quite still. Though it's broad daylight, he seems adequately menacing. A moment or two go by like this and then, surprisingly, he shrugs and the threat falls away. "I was watching," he says.

"What is it to you what I do?"

Nearby, a woman dawdles over apricots; she turns them over in a broad, hefting hand. The merchant approaches, dark and suspicious. The honking and blare of traffic form a solid wall behind them; it's difficult to hear and as always he speaks softly.

"You treat my things with such disdain," he says. "My family; coçukllarimiz; the things that belong to my country. This was no longer acceptable to me."

"What did you want?"

"You think American dollars can buy anything—whiskey, cigarettes, our children. My family is not for sale. I would have told you this. Also, perhaps I wanted to frighten you."

"Ne için? You did frighten me. And what about the girl? Catherine. What did you do to her?"

"That girl," he says quietly. "That girl has too much imagination. Too much bad feeling. I do not think it is normal to hate a mother like this."

"Oh, I don't know about that," Grace says. But part of her, she can't deny it, wants to believe him—to ascribe it all to Catherine, as Simone had so easily done: to think her too advanced, too calculating, too manipulative and ripe.

He bends at the waist then, but minimally. "Tamam," he says. "We are finished here, I think."

"Kemal?" she says as he turns. "Why don't you tell your mother where her baby is?"

He stares at her for a moment, as if the suggestion is quite extraordinary.

"O kadın," he says with disgust. "She does not deserve to know this.

She has the money she wanted, your American money. She will have to suffer the consequences of her actions. This was not done for her."

Nearby, the argument over apricots grows heated. Grace steps aside to make room for it.

"Perhaps I shall tell her."

"I do not think so," he says. "It will make no difference to you. What do you people care for children? I have seen the way you treat your own. It is not a thing to admire."

"Would it have been different if the baby had been a girl? Would that have changed anything?"

She has the impression that she's boring him. "I do not wish to talk to you in 'ifs,'" he says. And then, quickly, he is gone, swallowed up in the crowds.

She would not see him again.

OF COURSE, Grace learns, Catherine had never been part of John's plan. No, he'd had other, more important business to attend to in Istanbul. It was John, of course, who'd called Paige about Catherine and she who had mentioned that Grace was in Istanbul. But that is really the least of it.

"He went to the orphanage on the day Bahar was picking up the child," Paige tells her later, reluctantly, when Grace finally has the courage to go over to her house and insist on some answers. Grace has found her in the kitchen, doing some baffling thing with raw chicken and pottery.

"Who knows how he figured it out?" Paige says. She is chopping eggplant ferociously on the counter. "He's a clever boy. Anyway, he made such a scene. He frightened everyone. Not Bahar, of course, but those other women. They operate on such a shoestring anyway and he was making all kinds of threats. He wanted the baby. My brother, he kept saying. Give me my brother. Bahar was very annoyed as you can imagine. Very annoyed indeed. Anyway, from what I understand, it got ugly—lots of shouting and yelling. Talk about the police, the authorities."

"So Bahar gave him the baby?"

Paige looks at Grace over her shoulder. "Of course she did. She doesn't need this kind of trouble. She needed a baby. Firdis's baby or another one. It didn't much matter."

"But why," says Grace, "why . . . ?" she trails off, unable to say the words aloud. Edie's accusations still haunt her. *We were all misled,* Grace has protested in a final, desperate letter, *we were all taken in.* She's received no reply.

"That I don't know," Paige says. She waves a hand; the knife makes big, shining arcs in the air. "Perhaps it seemed to the women at the orphanage an easy way to get rid of one of them. Imperfect babies aren't adoptable in the traditional sense. There was so much upset. She needed a baby, they gave her one. She didn't ask a lot of questions."

"Jesus."

"You can say that again." Paige scrapes a load of vegetables and chicken parts into the clay pot. "Guveç," she says, gesturing toward all this with the knife. "The lid actually bakes right onto the pot. You crack it open with a hammer at the end. It's wonderful. Very dramatic."

"You're having a party?"

"Just a small one. Very small. Listen, Grace, I think Bahar feels terrible about this. I know she does."

"So she'll take the baby back? Give Edie her money?"

Paige laughs. "Not quite that terrible," she says. "It isn't that kind of business, you know. No seven-day-return policy. No store credit. That's why it's so important you trust who you're doing business with. I'd say it's really the most important thing."

Grace looks around the room. The unapologetic film of grease across the lemon-colored counters, which has always struck her as charming and liberated, suddenly seems merely filthy. A creamy cat twines insistently through her ankles, making its terrible Siamese yowl. She gives it a small nudge with her shoe.

"I'm going to go," she says.

"Are you sure?" Paige calls; now her head is deep inside a kitchen closet. "I know I had a hammer somewhere. One of those small ones. Ahmet is coming. Maybe Bahar as well. Just a few people. You're welcome to stay."

"Thank you, no." Grace lets herself out the front door and stands in the tiny courtyard in front of the overgrown house. She turns back just once from the sidewalk to look: the kitchen windows glow with warm light, the ivy on the facade is illuminated with blinking strings of leftover Christmas bulbs, there is smoke from the chimney in the living room, that pretty, cozy room in which she has laughed and dozed and had her fortune told—inaccurately, it seems—far too many times to count.

She turns away and begins walking. It will be three blocks before she can get a taxi. She wishes she'd had Kadir bring her; she wishes she'd worn a heavier coat.

IN THE end, Catherine was sent away to boarding school. Switzerland, I think, though it may have been France. We would hear things in later years, through the usual murky channels: that she'd run off again, sometimes with more success; that longish periods of time would pass without word of her whereabouts. We heard about psychiatric hospitals, drugs and promiscuity, violence, wild behavior. Times had changed by then, and no one, least of all my mother, seemed surprised.

In short order Simone left Ankara—she refused to have her face attended to by barbarians in a backward foreign country. This was commonly known and much repeated among women in my mother's circle.

Simone and Catherine's father would divorce, of course, but that was later. For a time he stayed on after Simone had gone, finishing up his business, living in the bare, evacuated rooms, and sometimes I would walk down the hill in the evening and stand in front of their apartment building: a few lights still glowed inside.

On the street, hearing the dogs in the distance, and the children shrieking on the sledding hill, I stood in the black, tossing shadow of a pine and stared up at the second-story windows. Sometimes I could almost imagine Catherine was still in there, that I might climb those stairs and find that odd interior landscape entirely preserved: John in the kitchen, fussing quietly; Catherine, with her saved-up stories, surrounded by the frilly, outgrown trappings of her room, waiting for my arrival, and even Simone, out of view but still silent and knowing, everywhere and nowhere at once.

Occasionally I stood at the crest of the hill and watched the Turkish children sledding down the rough slope. I lurked, half hidden behind the eroding mound of coal, and studied their masked and bundled faces, thinking I might recognize one or another of them—the boys who stole our sled perhaps, a girl who had once smiled at us, shyly.

But in truth, once Catherine was gone, I found I did not miss her nearly as much as I had when she had lived just a steep block away, when our broken friendship had seemed like an ever-present tragedy. Suddenly, it was almost as if she'd never existed, and I could pretend I'd done nothing wrong. Nothing at all.

It was the beauty of disappearing people—surely my mother knew it—the way you could rewrite things as you preferred, recast yourself in the action; you could make yourself fresh, innocent, blameless. And you would, wouldn't you? Would there be any other choice?

WHEN PAIGE calls at last, Grace goes. She's been half expecting it for some time—since Edie's letter, since the disaster with Simone, since Bahar has suddenly become so completely unavailable. Grace has not been able to reach her, not once, since she spoke with Paige that evening.

She sits with them at a table in the basement of the embassy— the windowless room is stark, crammed with particle-board furniture and stacks of boxes—and reads the paper they hand over. Official-looking, with that all-too-familiar seal.

There's a copy, too, of an interview they've done with Edie. Grace glances up once at Paige. Edie's account is quite detailed and almost entirely accurate, signed and witnessed. It might make Grace laugh, on another occasion, to see how her role has been maximized. How clever she seems in their documents, how important and manipulating. She'd be impressed with herself, really, to have been capable of stage-managing all this. She sees Greg's scrawl at the bottom as well, next to Edie's familiar looping signature.

Grace reads it all slowly, paying no attention to the faces watching her around the room. She looks up finally and meets their eyes.

"Simone?" she says. "Or John?"

"One or the other," Paige says, shrugging. "It's hard to know."

And though Grace doesn't believe her, not at all, it seems unimportant: both of them would certainly have had reasons to betray her.

"What happens to the baby now?"

Paige looks surprised. "I haven't the slightest idea. Does it matter?"

"I'm not sure. So where is Rand? I'm sure he can help straighten this out. I assume you've been in touch with him."

"The thing is, Grace, I can't really say where he is. I thought perhaps you might be able to tell us."

"Oh, you," Grace says. "For God's sake. Spare me." And then she puts the papers down. Though she wants very much to tear them to bits and drop the shreds on the table in front of her. "So what about Bahar and Ali?"

Paige, in her official capacity now, suddenly looks sympathetic;

she reaches a spotted, ringless hand across the table. "The thing is, they insist you leave the country immediately. The Turks. This kind of business smells very bad to them. It isn't at all modern, if you know what I mean." She adjusts her glasses. "Ali, as you know, is a very prominent physician in Ankara. Very well regarded. He's told them this was all a terrible mistake, that he was badly misled."

"Of course he did. So what about my husband? Where is he?"

"Well, frankly," says Paige, sighing, "I'd have expected you to come to us much sooner. I thought perhaps you knew something we didn't. We presumed some marital trouble, something private. Those pills you've been taking, Grace . . . well, maybe you haven't been thinking clearly. And that ugly business with Simone. Everything else. Of course, I haven't wanted to pry. But if there's anything, now would be the time to tell us. Has he left you? It does happen."

"No," she says, uncertainly, "he hasn't. Of course not. He's away."

Paige lifts her hands helplessly. The small movement puts Grace, for a moment, in mind of Ahmet. "You see, Grace, the thing is . . . we didn't send Rand away on assignment. Not any that I know of." She pauses and looks around the room. The men, five or so of them, with their stiff uniforms and practiced expressions, stare off into distances Grace cannot imagine. "When you said he was gone, I assumed, well . . . I assumed you were making it up."

"That's nonsense," Grace says. "The phone rang. The phone rang and he left. You knew. You've known all along."

Paige shrugs, as though Grace has defeated her with some ancient, insoluble riddle.

"Oh, I see," Grace says, looking around at the men. She knows every one of them, but cannot recognize a single face. "I'm crazy? Is that it? Delusional? Hopped up on drugs? How utterly perfect."

For a long moment, Grace hears just the noise of papers moving, of fabric against fabric as someone adjusts his legs beneath the table. A man flicks a silver lighter, over and over and then stops abruptly, leaving a hole, a kind of caesura, in the strange, tuneless music of the room. There's the smell of mildew and the noxious heat from the rattling radiators. Breathing, a subdued cough, a car backfiring in another world, somewhere outside.

"I wouldn't blame myself if I were you, Grace," Paige says at last.

As she stood and efficiently gathered the papers, as the men shuffled and shoved back their chairs, Paige had said, Say whatever makes you comfortable, Grace, but please understand our position, won't you? We can't let this go on indefinitely. Something must be said. There will have to be paperwork. Of course, we'll keep you informed.

As one of the men opened the door for her (as if, she thought, he were ushering out a disease), Paige said quietly. "Consider seeing someone when you get home, will you, Grace? A doctor maybe? Someone to talk to?"

No one says anything more; she couldn't have expected they would. Their eyes were on her, all of them, as she left the room.

Driving away from the embassy, Grace thinks again and again of one small thing: the way Rand had asked her, before he'd gone, if she would be all right, and how it had every quality of a question that didn't want an answer. Of course she'd heard that tone before, and used it herself with Canada from time to time as she hesitated at the door, on her way out for the evening. Anything Grace might have said to him in response that December morning, anything remotely truthful, would have seemed petty and contentious—and he'd always thought her too free with such childish maneuvers.

So, of course she'd said to him, yes, in an indifferent tone of her own, as people did.

I DON'T think Edie would have cooperated with them, had it not turned out the way it did; had the baby not been, in Aynur's strangely apt parlance, broken.

My mother formed one resolution at the embassy, while she was reading their documents and their accusations, conscious of the eyes that were evaluating her, of the net drawing in so neatly around her. It came to her before she'd even looked up from the papers. Now she'd be free to choose an ending that better suited her, one she found more consoling. Who was there to disagree? Not a single soul was left.

So she travels home through the Ankara traffic, and in the backseat weaves the threads that will become, in time, the story as we choose to understand it. An accounting of our family, of my father's disappearance, and of the impossibility of his return. After all, I knew—didn't I?—that tragic things happened every day, in every part of the world, and he might well have been in the middle of any of these, so shrouded was his life, his undertakings, his duties. He becomes just another casualty of our year in Turkey, his death likely, but unconfirmed—in some distant place, under circumstances that could not be explained.

And in some ways I will prefer the explanation she builds for me, and even the way she is implicated within it. That morning she must have contemplated our future and the uncertain path that lay ahead of us: what would she do now, my mother, where would she take us? How would we live outside the close and sheltering world we'd always bucked against, but always known? We would be suddenly, in all ways, unmoored, ill equipped, stark naked.

She tips her head against the icy glass of the car window, thinking. And this fabrication will seem to her—on the streets of a chilled winter morning in Ankara, watching a tired human parade that she is suddenly, unwillingly, a part of—like some tepid consolation. It is a bedtime story to soothe a child, and seems like the very least she can do.

So this is the way my mother comes to rewrite the ending for both of us, and to concoct a fable about our lives, one that is, perversely, more palatable than the truth, more prettily made.

EVEN TODAY I can almost see her as she was that morning: sitting behind Kadir for the last time, upright against the vinyl seat, a clutch purse on her lap, her profile both hopeful and resigned. She is impossible to love, but lovely in her way. And there will be latitude, life being what it is. We will each think we catch sight of him from time to time, in unlikely places, in impossible cities, on certain fantastical days. The edge of a coat vanishing around a building; a dark car slowing past the house, lingering overlong at the corner; a man in the parking garage holding a dated gray suitcase, his back turned as he fumbles for keys.

For a time my mother stands on the sidewalk near the construction site—not much improved in this long, long year—holding her scarf at her neck and looking across the low wall of the vineyard. Snow is falling, coating the dormant arbors and heaping up in painstaking concentration on each gnarled vine; and on the far side, past the whitening rows, the hill drops down to the Tremblays' old street and beyond that to Tunali Hilmi and the bakery and the gold merchants, the shabby little park and the improbably regal swans. She fingers the scripted pendant at her throat, and pulls the scarf down from her neck into her hand. Kadir waits with soldierlike bearing at the car, with his mustache and his fraying cuffs; reliable, ever patient. From the window above, I watch her shoulders whiten, as if she is being slowly covered in ashes; the crimson scarf the single flash of color in this endless gray and alabaster landscape. Suddenly, even Kadir is only an aging statue beside the car and I wonder: is this strange, familiar scene already fading in her mind?

Watch: she is walking toward the door now to face me, rehearsing this new ending, preparing to tell me her story. She disappears under the awning without glancing up. A woman who is suddenly small in this picture, in this city, this world; she is a million miles from home, walking away from one life and toward another, dragging a red scarf.

I hear the lobby door, her little heels on the marble stairs, unhurried but committed, and I know she is coming to tell me what has happened to us.

Wait, I would still call to her if I could . . . wait.

Acknowledgments

Much is owed to the people and animals who tolerantly share their lives with a moody, difficult, psychologically untidy writer: Gary, Lauren, Lindsay and Jessie-Cat, Gulliver, B. and C. I treasure each one of you.

All writers need readers and questioners; mine have been Karen S., Dana K., Michelle Z., Rene U. As well as teachers, touchstones and fellow writers: Diane Seessel, Nance Van Winckel, Francois Camoin, Kate Walbert, Peter Rock, Robin Hemley, Ralph Angel.

I am grateful also to my tribe of walking and riding companions; together we've covered untold miles: Jody, Marty-Ann, Annette, Samantha, Elizabeth S., Heather, LisaClaire, and Surrya. E. M. Traynor was also promised she would find her name here; Peter Griffin wasn't, but he shouldn't be surprised. Thanks also to Tracy Stone-Manning, whose reappearance in my life has been an unforeseen blessing.

My thanks also to Aybars Ortan, for gently reminding me how much Turkish I've forgotten—and correcting it.

Mostly, I am fortunate beyond measure to have had this book land in the care of my editor and friend, Sam Douglas, whose patience, guidance and wit have brought this story into coherence (and for whom I blame everything), and I am indebted to my agent, the always wise and kindly Chris Calhoun, who lies eloquently, consistently, on my behalf. And to the ever-gracious Frances Coady and all the good people at Picador.